AN ELECTION OF
WORDS

Published by Scout Media
Copyright 2021
ISBN: 978-1-7368867-3-1 (Print)
978-1-7368867-4-8 (eBook)

Cover and Story Title Designs by Amy Hunter
Formatted by Kari Holloway

Visit: www.ScoutMediaBooksMusic.com
For more information on all the Of Words anthologies.

Table of Contents

DEVOURED BY THE FAKE
BRIAN PAONE

"Are you ready, Mr. President?" the driver asked as the secret service agent closed the limo door. The driver glanced in the rearview mirror at the leader of the free world and his assigned security sitting next to him on the back row.

The president belched, slid slightly down on the bench seat, and unbuttoned his pants, exhaling a satisfying moan. "Much better. Don't know why the wife keeps making me wear pants so small for me. And, yes, driver, please. Get a move on."

"Right away, Mr. President." The driver shook his head in disgust and averted his gaze to the roadway as he pulled into traffic, the limo flanked by a convoy of black vehicles adorned with the nation's flag, all flapping in the breeze.

The president tapped on the side-window glass next to his head. "You sure these have been reinforced?"

"Yes, Mr. President. With the highest-grade bulletproof material there is," the secret service agent said. "And no one can see inside. It's a one-way mirror."

The president leaned forward and opened the cover to the minibar. He removed an unopened bottle of Serbian plum brandy and raised it to the agent. "Would you like some?"

"No, sir. No drinking on duty." He scanned all the windows for any signs of approaching trouble.

"Well, I'm always on duty, and sometimes I like to drink." The president opened the bottle and, forgoing a glass, put the lip to his mouth and took three long swallows.

The driver grimaced at the thought of the taste.

"You know I can't lose, right?"

The agent took his attention from the empty sidewalks and eyed the president. "My job, sir, is to keep the sitting president alive at all costs. That is all."

The president stuck half his hand into his opened waistband, like Al Bundy from *Married with Children*. "Relax! In a few hours, the people would have spoken, and you will be stuck with me for another term. Cheers!" He tipped the brandy bottle into his mouth again. "All these people"—he waved at the window to an empty street, some brandy sloshing onto his white shirt—"they love me. It'll be a landslide."

The driver stopped at a red light and noticed a horde of people crowding the sidewalks about two blocks ahead. He glanced in the rearview mirror to see if the agent had spotted the possible threat.

The light turned green, and he accelerated through the intersection.

The president's cellphone rang in his blazer pocket. He set the bottle of brandy in the large cupholder. "Hello? Most important person on the planet speaking."

The driver rolled his eyes.

"*Uh-huh.* ... Which channel is running that story? ... Right. ... Well, do we have anyone who can stop the broadcast? ... It'll be fine. The worms are too stupid to believe it anyway. They'll still make that checkmark next to my name. ... If you can, that would be great." The president slipped his cellphone into his pocket and looked out the window at the passing buildings.

The driver noted that the crowd lining the street were all holding something—some had signs; some looked to have chains and bats and other forms of weaponry. The driver inhaled deeply through his nostrils and glanced at the agent through the mirror. He ran his tongue over his teeth and rolled forward, toward the angry mob.

The agent craned his neck to get a glimpse of the roadway ahead. "Driver, is that a mob ahead?"

The president grabbed the bottle of brandy, took a long swig, and placed it between his legs. "Where?"

"Up ahead," the agent said.

"*Ahh*, those are just my supporters. They're rolling out the red carpet for our win tonight!"

"Yes, sir," the driver said loudly to be heard in the rear of the limo. "Looks like people on both sides of the street. They have signs and look angry."

"That's right, driver! They're angry at what this fine country was put through before I became president! They should be angry! God bless them for expressing their feelings, and God bless our country for allowing them to."

The agent touched his earpiece and spoke softly into his shirt collar.

The driver watched the crowd ahead step off the curb but not quite block the street. Then he heard their angry chants.

The president's phone rang again. "Hello? Most important person on the planet speaking. ... We see them too. ... You've already spoken with him?" The president eyed the agent sitting next to him. "Hostile? *Nah*, they're just invigorated! They're passionate about this great country, and so am I! They want to thank us for giving them what they've always needed."

The driver slowed the limo as he approached the first line of the mob.

"Ah, shit!" the president said into his phone as the bottle of brandy slipped from between his knees and tumbled to the floorboard, *ga-lump*-ing a few times as the liquid spilled into the carpet. He snatched the bottle from the floor, spilling some on his hands. "Yeah, I'm still here. Just dropped my coffee."

The driver eyed him in the mirror, one eyebrow raised.

"No, I don't think we should take the alternate route. Let's give the people what they want. Let's show them we work for them, that they voted for the winning team." The president tucked his phone into his pocket and put his hand to his mouth to suck the spilled liquor from his fingers.

The nose of the limo reached the first line of spectators, and the people moved in on the car. The car rocked, swaying its occupants, as the crowd pushed and kicked the sides of it.

The president clicked the window switch, but nothing happened. "Driver! Do you have the child-safety lock on the windows? Roll down my window so I can talk to the people!"

"I don't think that's a good idea, sir," the agent said, pressing his finger against his earpiece again.

The president leaned back to empty half of what remained in the bottle down his throat, then released a long *aaaaahhhhh!* "You don't tell me what is or is not a good idea. All my ideas are fucking *great!*" Spittle flew from his lips and landed on the agent's tactical pants. The president tried the switch again. "Driver! I order you!"

"Mr. President, please calm down and let me handle this," the agent said.

"You tellin' me to calm down, like I'm some fucking stay-at-home housewife who's pissed at her husband? I'm the goddamn *president!*"

The driver kept the limo inching forward as safely as he could, without running over any toes or clipping any torsos with the sideview mirrors. When a loud *thwap!* sounded at the rear of the vehicle, the driver ducked his head.

All three occupants darted their gaze to the back window, finding a burly man with a baseball bat, winding back to take another swing at the glass.

"Now do you think they are friendly, *sir?*" the agent asked through clenched teeth.

Another *thwap!* made them startle. The man was keeping pace with the limo, winding up for another swing. The crowd from the sidewalk filled the street behind the car, like water rushing from a broken dam.

"I don't see the other cars," the president said.

The agent looked out the rear window just as the bat struck the bulletproof glass again and could not see anything past the horde following the limo. He pressed a small button on his shirt collar and whispered into it. After nodding a few times, he faced the president, who had the brandy bottle tipped again into his mouth. "Sir, we are alone on the street. The convoy couldn't follow. The crowd wouldn't let them pass."

The driver's eyes shot to the rearview mirror to spy the two men in the back row. The he refocused on the roadway, getting narrower by the second.

As people shook their fists in anger at the window next to the president's head, he triumphantly and joyfully shook his fist back at them. "Yes!" he yelled at the closed window, even though they couldn't hear or see him. "Yes! I'm excited too! We're taking this county back! You have all made the right choice and are sending your message to the rest of this great land's people!" His voice sounded uncomfortably loud in the otherwise quiet cabin interior.

"Sir, we need to get you out of here," the agent said and pressed his finger to his earpiece. "Driver, don't stop moving but turn right at the next intersection. We can pick up the convoy again there."

The president harrumphed and turned over the empty bottle to watch a single drop of liquor dangle from the lip, then fall to the already saturated floorboard. He hiccupped and belched simultaneously, then placed a hand over his mouth. "Oh, excuse me. Please don't tell the first lady about all"—he wagged a finger at the mess at their feet—"that."

"My only job is to keep you safe, sir. Nothing further."

"Good man, good man." The president slapped the agent's shoulder as his head bobbled slightly. "You comin' to the party tonight? The victory party?"

The agent took his gaze from the side window and looked the president in the eyes. "I have been assigned to you for the next eighteen hours."

"Fantastic! Promise me that you'll share at least one drink with your president tonight at the party, after we squash"—the president drove a fist into an open palm—"that sad excuse for an opposition. Was he just dreadful in those debates or what? Landslide, I tell ya! I killed it up there. It warms my heart to know this country feels it in their bones who is right for them and that they refuse to be devoured by the fake."

A storm of clacking and pounding sounds against the windows filled the limo. Angry faces pressed themselves against the glass; their open mouths as they screamed obscenities left smear marks. Empty fists and weapons-clenched fists beat on all the windows. Wild-eyed citizens kicked and rocked the car as it rolled through the angry mob.

"Yes! I love the passion of my people!" The president flashed an obscured thumbs-up to the mob squished against his window and screamed as if they could hear him. "Your voices have been heard!" He kicked the empty brandy bottle across the floorboard, and it rolled until it struck the back of the driver's seat as the president looked at the agent. "Isn't democracy fantastic?"

The driver noticed a man standing motionless on the left-hand side of the street a few yards ahead, looking like a pillar among chaos.

The nose of the limo inched past the man, and he remained like a statue. As soon as the driver's side window was directly in front of him, he raised his arms and slapped a sign made from a ripped piece of cardboard against the driver's side passenger window. In blue Sharpie, it read *Out To Lunch*.

The driver nodded at the man and glanced in his rearview mirror to check the visibility in the rear. Satisfied that the limo was completely and unequivocally surrounded, with no chance of being seen from any vehicle in the cut-off convoy, he took one last look at the fucking *president*, undid the child-safety door locks, and opened his door. He shifted into Park, leaped from the driver's seat into the sanctity of the mob, and disappeared into their ranks, leaving his door open.

The agent barely got his firearm unholstered before the horde opened the limo's remaining five doors and flooded the interior from all entrances, swarming the president and overpowering the agent.

The sound of the president's garbled and drunken screams faded as the driver manuevered to the outskirts of the mob and vanished from sight.

ALMA MATER
TRAVIS WEST

After making his rounds through the school gymnasium, shaking hands, signing a few books, taking photos, recognizing most of the faces and pretending to recognize ones he didn't, Mike needed a drink. As one of the two famous alumni of his graduating class, he had expected a busy evening, but the amount of attention surprised him; funny how a string of successful novels made those who had never given previous notice suddenly remember their favorite memories of him. He didn't think he would ever get used to it, but he supposed old best friends he'd never had came with the territory.

He contemplated the makeshift bar situated at one end of the gym. His thirst for a gin and tonic bordered on lust, but Dave Everhardt was bartending. In school, Dave was one of those guys, loud and obnoxious, who gave Mike a hard time, altering his last name from Buxton to Butt-Ton. Mike never feared Dave, but he didn't necessarily want to converse with him either. The self-serve punch bowl would do for now.

With a cup of punch in hand, he found a spot against the wall to stand and observe the entire gym—the old schoolmates, aged and changed, bits of conversation drifting in from all directions, and, by God, the Secret Servicemen at every entrance. Mike never would have guessed he'd be searched entering a class reunion.

"Surreal, isn't it?"

He turned toward the direction of the voice, saw no one, then looked down upon a mass of red curls atop a doll's face. "Betsy Hurley? My, you look exactly the same. How've you been, Bite-Size?"

She raised an eyebrow at the old nickname. "You wish you could bite into this, Butt-Ton. Keep dreaming, and it's Ludlow now."

"You got married. Congratulations." Mike raised the punch.

"Save it. I'm going through a divorce."

"Ah, divorce. I had one of those."

"I heard. *60 Minutes*."

He considered her for a moment. "Yes, very surreal. Since you're getting divorced does that mean you might be available for that bite?"

Betsy punched him in the hip, playfully but not so lightly and smiled.

"You're an asshole."

"Just like old times, sister."

"Besides"—she gestured toward the Secret Servicemen—"aren't you waiting for our future vice president?"

"Nadine? Possibly. Probably ... yeah. Who knows if they'll win though? The election is still three months away."

"They'll win. Wow! A bestselling novelist and a United States Vice President from Cortez High School. From the same class no less. I never would have imagined."

"Me neither, to tell the truth. I'm surprised the school isn't swarming with media."

"They don't know she's coming. You did though, huh?"

"Just wishing, I guess." He hoped he didn't blush and give himself away.

"Have you kept in touch with her?"

"No," he lied.

"Is she the only reason you came tonight? You missed our ten- and twenty-year get-togethers."

He almost lied again, then thought better of it. "Yes."

"That's fair. You didn't miss much."

"I missed you, Bets. I missed seeing Richie Meyer before he passed away. I missed Nadine. Even Glenn Cooper."

"Nadine's never made it. Although she's obviously expected tonight. Glenn Cooper, you haven't missed anything. He's wasted himself."

Mike had his own reasons for avoiding Glenn, his high school best friend. "The thing about Glenn is he—"

"He's right there," Betsy interrupted.

Mike searched the gym but didn't see the face he was sure he would recognize.

"Oh no, no!" Betsy began run-walking across the gymnasium.

Mike followed; beyond Betsy, he saw a tall, thin man, balding and gray, almost nose to nose with one of the Secret Service agents. *That's Glenn. God, he's worse than I'd imagined.*

Everyone in their class may have been pushing fifty, but Glenn looked an unhealthy sixty-five, his face terrained with crags and gullies. His eyes revealed his drunkenness.

"I was her boyfriend, pal," Mike heard him declare as he approached. "I loved her. Do you? Huh? You better protect her with your goddamn life, or you'll be answering to Glenn Cooper. That's my name."

"Glenn!" Betsy shouted. "That is enough. Take a seat before you get in trouble."

Glenn faced her. "This is none of yours, Betsy. I've known you since the sixth grade. Don't you cunt up on me now, girl."

Betsy gasped in disbelief, but he had already returned his attention to the agent.

"Nadine Simoneau—*Senator* Nadine Simoneau—is a greater treasure than you'll ever understand, even if her politics don't exactly align with my own. You ever seen her naked, buddy? She ever let you touch her—"

"Glenn Cooper!" Betsy cried out. "Stop this."

Through everything the agent hadn't moved.

Glenn grinned deliriously. "Are you guys like those Royal Guards, not allowed to move or speak? What if I did this?"

To everybody's disbelief, he flicked the man's nose, a *thwack* filling the appalled silence.

The agent reacted faster than Glenn, spinning him against the wall with the offending hand pinned to his back.

Without thinking, Mike stepped forward. "Please stop. Don't arrest him. I'll take him home and ensure he doesn't return. Just let him go, please."

Other Secret Servicemen congregated around them, speaking into walkie-talkies.

"Back up, sir, unless you want to join him," the agent said. He applied more pressure to Glenn's arm, extracting a yelp of pain.

Never one to use his celebrity for gain, Mike decided the circumstances warranted an exception. "Sir, you may not recognize me, but I'm Michael Buxton, author of *Sunny Concern* and *Doomsday Daydream*. Surely, you've seen the film adaptation of *Sunny Concern*. Huge blockbuster, earned Anjuli Russell an Oscar for her portrayal of Sylvia."

The agent paused. "You're Michael Buxton?"

"I am."

"I haven't seen the movie yet, but I loved both of those books. Plus, the one about the rock band."

"*Jimmy Truant*. I'm a personal friend of Senator Simoneau. Let Mister Cooper here go, and through the senator, I'll see that everyone in your—retinue? squad?—gets an autographed copy of all three books. On top of that"—Mike outstretched an arm to address his fellow alumni—"we all put away our phones. Right? That way we keep this incident to ourselves, and off the news. Please delete any video you've taken of this confrontation, alright, people? We're not doing this for Senator Simoneau. We're doing it for *Nadine* Simoneau, class of nineteen ninety. Do we all agree?"

Only a few attendees had their phones in hand, but those who did, assented and clicked their delete buttons.

"Please get him out of here, Mister Buxton." The agent released Glenn, who walked to Mike's side, mumbling under his breath.

Mike put a hand around his skinny bicep and whispered close to his ear, "Goddammit, Glenn. Shut the fuck up if you don't want to go to jail tonight."

Glenn nodded ruefully and staggered toward the door.

"Mister Buxton ..." The agent who had restrained Glenn approached. "Mister Buxton, thank you for your help. By doing so, you've allowed Senator Simoneau to attend as planned. My name is Jeremy Brubaker, by the way, if you'd be so inclined to personalize the autographs."

Mike smiled and shook the agent's hand. "You got it, Jeremy Brubaker."

☑ ☑ ☑

A rare thunderstorm released its deluge onto Phoenix as Mike drove Glenn home down streets which had lost familiarity with time. Leaving the school, the two men didn't speak beyond Glenn giving his address. He lived in Mesa. Given the rain, Mike estimated an hour and a half to drive Glenn home and return to Cortez, which did little for his anxiety. He hoped he would return in time to see Nadine.

"Betsy doesn't like me anymore," Glenn said. "She's hated me since the time we stuffed that snake down her blouse in biology class. Boy, Miss Axelrod was pissed."

"We? The way I remember, it was all you. Betsy doesn't hate you. If she did, she'd have let you keep running your mouth to the Secret Service and watched how that played out for you."

"You thought you were some big hero back there, didn't you? Famous writer guy saves the day. You didn't think twice jumping on this grenade."

"Consider it a favor to Nadine."

"A favor to Nadine." Glenn, Mike came to realize, was drunker than he'd previously thought, little hiccups and involuntary groans escaping between words.

"You always were jealous of me and Nadine, weren't you? I had the girl you couldn't have. Everyone was jealous of the Coop. Although you finally got one over on me, didn't you?"

Mike felt a twinge of panic. "What are you talking about, Glenn?"

"I'm talking about the summer after graduation. After Nadine broke up with me. You two got really tight. So, tell me, how was it, sleeping with her?"

Mike stopped the car at a red light. "Glenn, I did not sleep with Nadine."

Glenn shrugged. "Okay."

Nadine broke up with Glenn within the first week following graduation, but they remained friends, or continued to play the part. Mike, Nadine, and Betsy, as the only ones in their small friend circle to be college bound, became confidants as they planned moves from home, sharing their collective fears, dreams, and grand aspirations with each other. Glenn went straight to work for his father's landscaping business, which also hired Richie Meyer.

Independence Day was on Wednesday that summer. The following Saturday, Betsy would be the first to leave. A July 4th bash was planned at her dad's property in Scottsdale; her dad was infamous for supplying Betsy's get-togethers with alcohol, so, of course, they expected a huge turnout.

Mike and Nadine found themselves alone that Monday. They hung out in his room, smoking pot and listening to *Disintegration* by The Cure. Tentatively, he'd taken her hand, which had led to kissing. Kissing led to … He always remembered the music. *Disintegration*. How fitting, as everything slowly disintegrated from that moment—his life in Arizona, his friendship with Glenn. None of his relationships came to fiery, crashing halts. They were merely set aside for later, then forgotten, collecting dust.

On the Fourth, Nadine drove them all to Scottsdale; she and Glenn sat in the front, Mike and Betsy in the back seat. Everyone groaned when Nadine forced them to listen to The Bangles, her favorite band. She cranked the volume on "In Your Room," locking eyes with Mike in the rearview mirror, sharing information only they knew—the song was a secret. During the guitar solo he broke eye contact to find Glenn staring at him.

☑ ☑ ☑

Glenn had passed out, and Mike gently shook him awake. Getting him from the vehicle to the front door was a chore.

"You all left me behind. I was so popular then. People liked me, but no one's wanted to see me in years."

"No one left you behind, Glenn. People grow up. Sometimes they grow apart."

Glenn grunted and crawled onto the sofa, his back to Mike. "I'm good here. You can go."

Mike stared at the back of his head for a moment, then made to leave.

"I hate you."

Mike paused, hand on the doorknob, then left without looking back.

☑ ☑ ☑

The first thing he noticed was the absence of official-looking vehicles. The reunion appeared to have transformed into an actual party but gone were the Secret Service conducting personal searches at the entrance. Mike ran to the doors, hopeful yet already knowing he had missed Nadine. In a way, it was karmic, as if Glenn had planned his drunken outburst to strategically prevent Mike from seeing the woman who had haunted them both since high school.

He entered the gymnasium. A mirror ball threw tracer beams of light onto middle-aged dancers drunk with alcohol and nostalgia.

"You're a true hero, Michael Buxton."

Mike turned toward the direction of the voice, saw no one, then looked down. "Hey, Bite-Size. I missed her, didn't I?"

Betsy Hurley (Ludlow now, but she was getting divorced) smiled up at him. "Here, yes. Turns out, she only made the trip to see the two of us. The rest of these saps just got lucky. I told her I'd be holding the vice president to a White House tour, VP-style." She laughed, then held out an envelope. "For you. Looks like I'll be taking a rain check on that bite, Butt-Ton."

Shunning discretion, Mike opened the envelope and read.

> *Michael,*
>
> *Betsy told me about your unplanned excursion.*
>
> *I'm sorry you had to clean a mess you didn't make. It sounds like someone hasn't let go of the past. In some ways, Glenn isn't the only one. This weekend is my only true respite for the foreseeable future, and I wanted to spend it here, visiting with you, Betsy, and whoever else I could see. You won't believe what song is playing right now! I'm sitting with Betsy as I write this and The Bangles just came on—that song! So I'm making an official "campaign decision." Long ago, we shared something spe-*

cial "In Your Room." This time, I'll be waiting "In My Room." I'm staying at the Biltmore. My security detail will be expecting you. Have your ID ready. They will put you through the ringer, but I can make it worthwhile. Let's catch up.
    Nadine

Betsy was smiling. She knew. "You'd better go, Michael."

"Betsy, thank you for still being my friend. I'm sorry I never contacted you—ever—during the last thirty years."

"You're forgiven. Just don't let it be another thirty. I made Nadine promise me the same. Now go!"

Mike gave Betsy a long, tight embrace, viewed his old high school gymnasium one last time, then headed for the exit.

BEST INTENTION
GADIEL G. MADRIAGA

The year is 2024 and Gideon has achieved time travel. The need for it seemed to be very appropriate considering the world's current state. He has no interest in making great personal gains. No great love to pursue or desires to become rich and famous. He's tormented by many great regrets in his life but one, in particular, troubles him most. Gideon is regretful with who he had voted for. He intends to go back in time and change it.

Time travel is not as complicated of a task as one might think. After all, Gideon did achieve the feat all by himself. Inspired by popular literature and film, it took him years and years of dedicated research and practice. He studied mathematics and physics, teaching himself all he will need to know. All of which he learned through internet videos, articles, and obscure online forums. All for him to be able to traverse back in time with a single controlled thought.

Gideon focuses on a specific moment in the past and thrusts backward through time. He arrives on Election Day within his body as he was at that time, several years younger. He wastes no time and makes his way to his nearby voting location and casts his ballot for the opposing party. Satisfied with himself, he sticks around to witness the results and embrace the air of a better time.

It came as no surprise- nothing became of his efforts. The results of the election remain unchanged. Gideon feels, at least, like he can have a clear conscience.

Upon returning to his time, Gideon remembers the dystopia he lives in. He begins to fantasize about a better world. He wonders about the possibilities of his new ability. It would be irresponsible of him, he thought, to not make any attempts at bettering the world. He owes it to society. Yet, he is only one man, and the winner of that election was not decided by one vote. He has to give more effort to make real changes. So, he takes his precious time and gives it more thought. He's mastered time travel, after all. He's got all the time in the world.

Gideon returns the next day with a plan. It'll be quite the undertaking, but he believes to have the resolve to take on such endeavors. He set forth many years prior with intentions of convincing others of his reasoning. To have an active role in the community and bring change to as many voters as possible for the cause. He attends rallies and protests. He becomes a figurehead often speaking in front of thousands of potential voters. He becomes a unifying and inspiring force for change. In a short time, he's spearheading many local ballots and offices.

As the general elections approach, Gideon leads a march of thousands of voters to the polls. This time, he thinks, with the support of enough people to make an actual impact. Once again, he votes. Once again, he fails. He loses to his rival for public office. The presidential election result remain unchanged. Neither of which he could understand why. He returns to his time in dejection and without any sense of direction.

Gideon thinks to himself what he might have neglected. He wonders whether he had tried hard enough. Whether he explored all available avenues. Did he not aim high enough? Somewhere higher up the ladder that will afford him more opportunities. He traverses many times more to the past. Each jump redirects his pathway toward his ultimate goal. Using each unique position to do what is right for the people. He treads the floors of the Capitol Building through several attempts. He dabbles with major federal government agencies in a few instances. In others, he enters into judiciary roles within some of the highest courtrooms. Each time leads to the same barren results. Time after time. Position after position. Life after life. Learning more with each role but becoming more callous with each failure.

Back in his time, Gideon grows weary of research. He sits down in his lavish and lofty mansion home in the new successful life he's led. He begins to reminisce of good times and good people. Of all the lives he's lived and all the hard work he's put into his cause. He longs for the bittersweet memories of the many jumps through time. Though the world around him is still in tatters, he realizes now what his efforts have brought him. A distinguished life on the hillsides in a placid gated community. He saunters about his home in fascination with the paintings on his walls. He wonders at the extravagance of the craftsmanship of the architect. Giddy with curiosity and confusion, he studies the many gadgets and gizmos laid about. He stands in the doorway of his extensive garage and stares in awe. A small collection of expensive vehicles- a yacht, an RV, a couple of ATVs, several sports cars, and a top-of-the-line luxury SUV. The latter belonging to his wife.

The memories are flooding into Gideon's mind. He's gotten married since he jumped back from the past. He's in love with this woman but he can't overcome the feeling that she's become unfaithful. She has become distant since the abortion. He thinks about how she was able to take care of that. That she should be thankful for him. Not a single financial worry for once in his life. He cannot complain about his hard-earned, well-deserved wealth.

Gideon stands on his bedroom balcony overlooking the vast city from the hillside. He could see the dark spots where all the lights have shut off and emptiness looms. He feels a slight but sharp pain in his heart. Clutching his chest and shaking his head, he recognizes an omen. "This world deserves better," he reflects. He steps away from the balcony railings. Mentally withdraws himself from the temptations. All for the sake of the world.

Gideon thinks of all that allows for his lifestyle. The products and services he takes advantage of to allow for this luxurious living. All that were enabled by hard-working sweat. By broken backs. By spilled blood. All for the commodities and comforts of strangers. He thinks of what sacrifices it must have taken. The travesties committed. The money involved.

It hits him.

Gideon looks back on his time in various government positions. He recalls certain moments with certain colleagues. Implications to their unwavering devotion for any particular cause. Even in spite of their constituents. Even in spite of morals or ethics.

Gideon jumps back in time and straight to business. His mind dances with thoughts of where he can go if he has more money. What he can accomplish with more money. The many more people who would follow him if he has more money.

The entertainment industry looks most promising to him. Film, musical and athletic stars have not only the money but also the platform to spread a message. To promote a new way of life. He doesn't have those kinds of talents to speak of. He has a different experience from having lived many lives. It allows for his mentality to shift and make the appropriate adjustments.

He takes control as a major corporate executive. From there he sees where the true powers lie. Who and what he can control with such power. He starts focusing on making powerful allies. On gaining trust from wealthy and influential individuals from celebrities to government officials. If they're uncooperative or stubborn, he forces them into compromising situations. He places them into his pockets. Holds them like a retainer with strings attached and paid for with trepidation. When the time comes to move the masses in a certain direction, he places the call and pulls the strings.

Now, all that remains for the world to see is what he wants them to see. If he controls how the people of the world view the world, he controls the narrative. As an omnipresent shadow looming over humanity, he casts himself as a new movie release. A new catchy song. The next festival or convention. The latest tech device or fashion trend. Who won the match? Who lost the bout? Who's terrorizing your countrymen? Who's striking fear in your neighborhood? Inciting anger deep in your psyche and deeper in your hearts. Raising children of hate into a society of violence. While the zealots clutch onto these self-destructive distractions, he slips through undetected.

A bill enters before Congress presenting within it new laws. Many of which benefit him beyond measure. A majority of those representing a seat occupy his influence. All voting to appease him. Whether they're for or against, these people sway in his direction like a moth toward the light. Whether contrary to the public's interests. Whether it enhances the public's livelihoods. Whether it heals, maims, saves, or kills. Whichever direction to progress his cause. To bring him in a position to control the next leader of the "free" world. And so, he does.

The votes no longer matter.

He does it with clever and effortless manipulation. Turning millions of people against each other over trivial pursuits. The majority of the planet quarreling over insignificant concerns. All while he gets behind the wheel and steers society at his whim. He issues the command from atop his castle in the mountains and a new trend appears for everyone to follow. A new scandal emerges to gossip. A new threat to fear. A new crisis to avert.

Many disagree with the direction the country is going. They amass onto the streets wielding homemade signs of defiance. They chant songs of war and revolution. The police intervene, riots ensue, and buildings catch fire. Homes and businesses lay waste to opportunistic looting and wanton destruction. Panic spreading faster than the structure fires could burn and raze. None the wiser to his existence, the world crumbles to its knees before him and into ruins. Leaving only him and his insignificant group of unwitting followers to reign.

All according to plan, he thinks. Nobody will get in the way of achieving his goal of being able to make real change. Nobody will get in his way before all his hard work and determination come to fruition. Even more so as he becomes such a great influence in the global economy that it ebbs and flows with his every movement. Only the sun and moon have more influence on the planet than him.

He sits in his home office with a scenic view now higher up a mountain at the top of the world. Contemplating his victories and recollecting his thoughts, he looks out over his empire and sees the dark spots in a city in tatters. With the image of ruins, he reminds himself of his original timeline. Confused, he travels forth to bear witness the fruits of his labors. Attempts to enable the jump back to where he came from meet him with failure. He realizes where he is. So much time has passed since he last jumped. The future in which he originated has long become past and overwritten. It is no longer a time he can return to. His destiny manifests in an instant.

The votes never mattered.

The thought disturbs him. In dissent with himself and who he has become, he fast forwards into the future. In search of evidence of a thriving world dominated by him, he jumps days at a time. Then by the weeks yet still no signs of a world in wealth. He jumps by the months, then by the years, and still nothing. Though his own prosperity seems to grow, the rest of the world deteriorates further. He jumps decades out into the future from his new timeline and finds himself on his own deathbed and in mental ruins. Having lost his mind in old age, Gideon dies. His consciousness is flung into nothingness. The world now better off without him.

Muttering to himself, Tyler leaned up against a smooth boulder and reached into his bag to find the last of his food. A can of sardines. He read the faded label, the nutrition facts, the barcode, anything and everything to prolong the inevitable, before finally cracking it open. Slick fish oil spilled out over his hands before dripping to the ground. He tasted the oil and immediately gagged.

As he wretched and started to spit out the salty flavor, the heat hit him and it was getting hotter, like someone had opened an oven right behind him. He slowly turned around to see it about fifty yards away. Tyler got his first real good look at the creature. It had six legs and used them to move swiftly like a wolf when chasing down prey. Embers were dripping from its glowing red mouth and its skin was cracked, with flames and smoke rising from it. Something molten was dripping out of each crack, like pus from a wound. The heat from the beast's body was heating the already melted and glassed rock turning it red and causing it to bubble with each step that it took. Hellhounds.

Some of the religious say they came straight from Hell, crawling through fissures during the burning of the world. Hellhound was a fitting name for the beast, and Tyler didn't think it saw him yet, so he slowly knelt behind the boulder, hoping to not be spotted.

"Fuck," he cursed while pulling out his pistol. "A bullet might just piss it off," he thought. He pulled himself up to get another peek over the boulder. The Hellhound was staring at him. It *had* seen him. His chest tightened and he felt lightheaded as terror washed over him. The growl emanating from the creature was as hot as a blast furnace and it sounded like a jet engine. The heat washed over Tyler, and he couldn't breathe or focus. The smell of sulfur wasn't helping. This was it. He started running. All of this, because of that damn election.

One week ago, sweat dripped from Tyler's forehead as he filled in the checkbox. His heart fluttered. The world was at stake as far as he was concerned. "Nothing else matters," he thought. He stared at the check mark for a moment, folded the paper in half, and then folded it one more time. Every vote filled him with guilt. "Sorry, Tom," he whispered to himself. Casey came by with her hat out to collect the ballotsfrom all thirty-five participants.

The air was still. This was a vote Tyler didn't want to make. Someone was going to die today. This is the way it was, how it always has been. Since the world had started to burn. Food was scarce, and this year's crop was a complete failure. Tyler knew that the upcoming winter was going to be harsh. Some of the little ones might not survive. Maybe it would keep the ballots away for an extra year. "Tom's the strongest," he told himself. "He can make it out alive."

Casey took her hat to the village leader Matt and poured the dirty folded papers onto the table in front of him. Matt took a few moments to count. The look on his face as he tallied up the names was a familiar sight for Tyler. The old man sat in silence once he was finished. He let out a sigh and unceremoniously pushed the ballots into a waiting bin. He stood up and said, "Tyler."

Tyler's heart dropped. *Who ... Why do they want me to go?* But the pessimist in him wasn't surprised at all.

"Fuck," he muttered as he trudged towards Matt, his eyes glued to the ground. His fists ache from being clenched so tightly. He managed to pull his gaze up from the ground, only to catch glimpses of those around him looking away when his eyes fell upon them.

"You know the rules, Tyler," Matt said. "You have six hours to gather what you can carry—and to say your goodbyes."

Tyler said nothing as he turned towards his shack. He felt his heart throbbing in his neck; his thoughts were a whirlwind of betrayal. *These were supposed to be my friends.* He was lucky though; he had a much larger backpack than many of the others who had been voted out. He tossed a few old pieces of clothing into the bag and raided his cabinet. Four cans of tuna—likely all that remained in the village—a single can of mixed fruit and another one of sardines. He managed to get some bread, as well as a couple of fresh carrots, and three gallons of water in old milk jugs that could be strapped to the outside of his bags.

He made sure to grab anything and everything sharp he could find. He needed weapons. Maybe there were others out there, but then, *they* were out there too. All the weapons in the world haven't been able to change what had happened.

He was just about done packing when he remembered the Beretta 92 that his uncle had given him when *it* started. He had two magazines with fifteen rounds each. Tyler wasn't confident it would work, but all he needed was a single bullet. He was never comfortable around firearms but knew how this one worked well enough. He tucked it in between his pants and belt and made sure to cover it up with his shirt. He kept it hidden, fearing he could hurt someone with it. He wasn't even supposed to have it in the village. Not after what Steve did four years ago. The village has seventy-five. If Steve hadn't lost it, there would have been around a hundred.

He took a look around. The shack, an old, half rusted tool shed that had been his safe haven was going to be given to someone else, likely one of the orphans. He thought about his chances in the wasteland. He probably wouldn't last long enough to dread eating the sardines. The wasteland would get him first. He took a breath and walked out of the shack.

"You know we have to do this, Tyler."

"I know," Tyler said, rolling his eyes. His mind was still racing as fast as his heart. "It's for them to live through another winter."

"Tammy went north in the last vote, so try south or southwest."

"Like Scott? Or Aaron? This is pointless and there's nothing left out there. There's nobody out there to find."

"Tyler, please. We must keep trying. We need help. They think you're the strongest."

"Fine. South it is."

"Thank you."

"Whatever, Dad."

Matt signaled the gatekeeper to open the large hodgepodge of materials they called a gate. Scorch marks from the last few attacks were still visible on it and on the ground around it. Tyler had been surprised the fire retardant had worked so well, but now the village was low on that too. One, maybe two attacks and it would be over.

The gate lowered, and Tyler stared out over the land. There were fires in the distance, and the smokey haze kept sunlight from getting through. The rocks had melted chunks taken out of them from where *they* brushed against them.

"There's no help for us," he said to himself, as he made his way out of the village.

After a week of wandering south, Tyler's mood shifted a bit. He figured that he had trekked roughly sixty miles south from his village. He now didn't have to take part in any village chores or help anyone with their problems. The charred landscape was cooler, and there were no active fires that he could see. There were even plants beginning to sprout through the blacked earth, like the first plants after a volcanic eruption.

But that was before the creature found Tyler. The flaming hound bounded after him. The searing heat and overwhelming smell of sulfur grew stronger. In a flash of madness, he grabbed his gun, turned and fired a single shot. The bullet hit the creature on its right shoulder, spraying molten innards behind it. But it didn't flinch. The shot was completely ineffective. He raised the barrel up against his head, knowing a bullet is faster than being burned alive. The heat intensified behind him as he hesitated for a split second before pulling the trigger. And that's when he heard the diesel engines, from the same direction that the Hellhound had appeared.

Three water tanker trucks with dripping water cannons came bouncing over the rocks and small ledges. The Hellhound stopped and turned towards the new sound. It let out a roar that instantly turned the ground in front of it into molten lava. The air intensified with the smell of sulfur. Tyler tried to catch his breath, but the toxic air made his lungs burn.

The water cannons started spraying the Hellhound, much of the water turning to steam. But some of it made contact and vaporized on the creature, cooling it. The trucks circled it. The spraying didn't stop. The glow dimmed; the flames disappeared. And the Hellhound slowed, ultimately freezing in place. A fourth vehicle showed up—a simple mobile crane with a simple wrecking ball. The driver pulled up next to the frozen creature, lifted the ball and dropped it. The Hellhound shattered; chunks of its still molten insides splashed out in every direction.

Tyler was speechless. There were survivors. Nomads? Did they have a village of their own? How were they able to effectively fight against a Hellhound?

"That's it! We got him," a woman called from the driver's seat in one of the tankers. She opened the door and climbed out, turning to reach for something next to the driver's seat. Tyler took a few steps toward the small convoy, making sure to put his gun back under his shirt before they could see it. He stopped when the woman turned to face him. Without a word, she tossed a full bottle of water to him. Tyler was startled a bit, but he caught it.

"What the fuck?" Tyler said.

"Is there a problem?" the woman asked, turning towards Tyler.

"How the hell did you get a fresh, sealed bottle of water?"

"Our camp is a bit more fortunate than others. It's an old military base and there are still lots of supplies." She crossed her arms.

"Then you are exactly who I'm looking for." Tyler managed a smile. "My village has about seventy-five people. *Alive.* And we could really use some help. I'm Tyler," he said, approaching her with an outstretched hand.

"How many children?" The woman ignored the gesture.

"Uh, about a dozen or so."

"We'll take them, no adults. The adults can handle themselves. We'll establish some sort of network between our camps so the adults can come by at any time. We just can't support that many people."

"Well, I guess that's something then. Do you want me to show you the way back to my village?" Tyler asked. He couldn't remember the last time he felt optimistic. Maybe Tammy, Scott and Aaron hadn't died out in the wasteland.

"No. We'll head back to our camp first. We need to reload our tankers, and if we encounter a herd, we bug out until we lose them. They can't follow us back. We can barely soak two hounds at once with these trucks."

"There were others from my village. Have you seen any other survivors out here in recent years?" Tyler asked. "My village is about sixty miles or so from here, to the north."

"Sorry, friend. No such luck. It's amazing you went that far without getting killed."

Another member of the convoy came up to the woman, looking impatient. "Hey Allison, are we headed back to reload? We've only got about five hundred gallons left, and I'm not looking for a fight with that."

"Yeah, we're headed out there in a moment." She turned to Tyler and pointed at her friend. "You're in truck two with Alex. He's a good driver, so your lower back will thank you." Alex held out his hand to shake Tyler's. The two climbed into a truck and waited for Allison to take the lead. Something jabbed into his back, and he remembered the gun.

"Hey dude, don't freak out," Tyler said, removing the gun from his belt.

"Why would I?" Alex replied. "We're all packing out here. The bullets are mostly used for ourselves though. They don't do shit against a hound. A bullet beats taking about three minutes to die."

Tyler put the gun on the dashboard and settled back in his seat. Allison's truck revved up and pulled forward, and Alex pulled his tanker behind hers.

"Why are you guys out here like this?" Tyler asked.

"We are trying to save who we can. Allison believes that if we can help, we should. We're alive because of her, so we do things her way." Alex shrugged. "Even if we die, it's dying doing the right thing. And that's fine with me."

"You know what I miss?" Alex said after a few minutes. "Motherfucking tacos. And all of them. Fast food, nice Mexican restaurants, and taco trucks. I mean, we had some old MREs, and I missed out on maybe three or four beef taco recipes. What about you?"

"I miss pizza," Tyler replied, staring out the window.

Alex rummaged around next to his seat and pulled out a brown MRE ration packet. "Here! I was saving it, but you look like you haven't had junk food in years. Good old menu twenty-three."

Tyler stared at it. Pepperoni Pizza Slice. His mouth started to water. Alex handed him a flameless heater and Tyler heated up his treat. After a few minutes it was hot and ready to eat. Tyler took a huge bite.

"This tastes like shit," he said with his mouth full.

"Well enjoy it. It's better than that sardine smell you've had since we picked you up."

Tyler laughed. It had been long since he'd had good company. After swallowing his bite, he turned to Alex. "How long until we reach your camp?"

"Another hour or so. We should have enough fuel. There aren't a whole lot of trips we can make these days. Fuel tanks are almost dry, and we can't produce ethanol either. So, we'll soon be focusing on just sustainability for ourselves and try to live as long as we can. Right now, there are about five hundred of us. On about fifty acres with a couple greenhouses that provide food."

"Sounds nice."

"It works. Home is just on the other side of this mountain."

Tyler finished his likely expired slice of pizza, then settled into his seat and leaned against the window using his arm as a pillow against the shaking of the tanker. His thoughts trailed in a mix of emotions. These were the first outsiders he had seen in about six years. And the first humans he had seen in the week since the vote. He couldn't believe that a village could not only survive, but maybe even thrive.

"Hey, check it out," Alex said. Tyler felt as if he had only just closed his eyes. "We are coming up on it now, home sweet home."

Allison slammed on her brakes, forcing Alex to do the same. "Holy fuck! What is she doing?"

Allison jumped out of her tanker, screaming, clutching the sides of her head. Tyler and Alex scrambled out of their tanker and ran toward her.

Tyler's stomach was all of a sudden in his throat. He couldn't breathe. He saw their camp in flames. But Tyler didn't focus on that. Surrounded by smoke and fire, a large figure stood in the center of the smoldering campsite—about a thousand feet tall, with massive wings, but its body obscured by its own burning.

"I guess they really were demons," Alex said with tears rolling down his face. "That Preacher was right."

"Wha-What preacher?" Tyler stammered as a gunshot rang out to his left. He flipped around only to see that Alex had shot himself. He had put the barrel in his mouth and pulled the trigger. Tyler yelled and ran to Alex's side "Allison! Allison, what the fuck do we do?" He knelt down next to Alex, seeing the blood pool beneath his head.

Allison didn't answer. The towering monster heard the sound of the gunshot and turned their direction with fiery red eyes. Its right arm stretched out to the side as far as it would go, and it swung forward in a sweeping motion, sending a shockwave that set everything ablaze.

"Allison, we have to get out of here!" Tyler yelled as he turned toward her. He heard the second gunshot. Allison's body crumpled to the ground, followed by a half dozen more gunshots. The convoy was gone, and Tyler was left alone.

The shockwave bore down on Tyler. The land ahead of him seemed to explode as the blast spread across it. He reached behind his back to pull his own gun, only to grab the fabric of his pants. He had left it inside the truck. Tyler dove for Allison's gun, but it was too late. The shockwave was faster. The searing heat made Tyler scream as his flesh began to blister and boil. He inhaled. *Of fucking course this would happen to me. That damn election.* The heat scorched his lungs. His screams stopped. The last thing his eyes saw before they melted was the shockwave peeling the molten surface off the earth, as if to bury humanity.

CHOCOLATE OR CRANBERRY
DAMSEL NAPIER

"Thank you for choosing to eat breakfast at The Busy Bean. Please vote for next week's speciality muffin before leaving. Happy eating and remember! Your vote matters."

A crack of thunder rattles the windows. It distracts me and I grab for my cup a second too late. Hot coffee sloshes onto my hand. The 'bot ignores my yelp of pain. There was a time I'd demand an apology. Nowadays, 'bots never respond to complaints, and silence wears a girl down. Better to talk to no-one.

I use the end of my scarf to mop up the mess. Despite my hand, I am grateful to be here. To have this time. Outside is death, ashes and whatever thrives when the State quarantines a city. In here, there's electric light, clean water, coffee. From 0500 to 1000, this place operates as old-normal. When I am here, I am living in before. I'm someone who likes my latte hot and my bagel toasted. After 10.15, forget it. You are required to leave and no matter how many times you swipe your loyalty card, you aren't getting back in.

A gust of wind splatters raindrops against the window. I scald my mouth with coffee. Even though the timing of this storm is strange, there's a deep satisfaction in being warm and snug inside. Since the State walled the city, storms have swept in on the evening wind. Fierce, but they never last. I like to imagine the city makes the rain, sends water weeping through its streets. That these empty buildings are crying for their people.

The truth is, out there, what is left of the dead is melting away. On the other side of the glass, three million or so bodies are dissolving. After feeding the rats, the last of the remains are being slowly washed into the soil and the sewers. I want to see the rain as tears, but it's the State who makes these storms, who laces the rain with cleaning chemicals. Keeps us safe. So, I tell myself that in spring, my friends will return as flowers. I will recognise them by the scent of roses and kindness. It is the nature of friendships, to meet, part and meet again. This soft dissolving means that Adam is here when he's gone. We're woven into each other, like the tendrils of dreams, or laughter. Or love.

Only I don't dissolve. I am here, annoyingly alive. Not a rat. Spilling coffee and eating bagels. Voting for my muffin. I'm the last rebel, the sole reason why they haven't declared the city empty. If the State hopes to wash me out, the joke is on them. They can do what they like with their quarantine and their wall. They can make all the weather they want. Drive us through these murdered neighbourhoods. If they dropped the restrictions tomorrow, where would I go?

Thunder mutters again. The tarmac is a shimming with rats. Rains force them out of the sewers. Some nights, water comes boiling out of the manholes and turns roads into rivers. Writhing masses of rodents get swept along in the current and sucked into whirlpools. I've come across the aftermath of storms before. Huge piles of fur, pathetic in death, melting in the sun.

My hands shake at the memory, and I put my cup down.

I don't want to be the only living thing inside the wall.

We used to meet here, in this very shop, on Sundays. It was Adam who convinced the owner—Fiona, a skinny girl with tattooed arms—to set up the vote for a favourite muffin. Such an innocent start to a rebellion. It wasn't even voting then, Fiona called it 'stating a preference.' It wasn't going to be compulsory. Adam talked her into making it the only way to get the exit door to work. If all of us were guilty, no-one was. It was a wonderful, terrifying time. We were too many, too few. Trapped but free. Too full of hope to be allowed to live.

My coffee's getting cold. The running rats keep scratching at my mind. It's hard to relax. To remember. To close my eyes and float a little, adrift in memory.

Another rattle of rain and I give up trying to meld into the past. This isn't normal weather. Surely, though, it is better to be inside. Storms don't last. Not once have I left before closing. And, I haven't chosen how to cast my vote yet. Adam. He was so sure that if we voted, we would change. People would wonder, why can't they have a say? Why can't I state a prefer-ence, for the school, or work? Why can't I choose my leaders or move to a new house?

This café was the start of the end for Adam and me. Feeding on the devotions of the masses, Adam bloated into someone confident. Important. I brought him down. I asked all the wrong questions. Questions like, if he was an authority, who was I equal to? Or whether something compulsory truly set you free. Or if voting for everything becomes a vote for nothing. Or how to choose when, you didn't want either op-tion. Or if he loved me.

All I really know is that, here, you need to swipe your loyalty card and vote, or you can't get out.

Even so, my choice of muffin is redundant. What-ever it was that the place needs to bake them has gone. Perhaps, Fiona and the rest of the crowd covered each other with icing and danced as they died. Perhaps there were orgies and cookies. It would be nice to think the dead died happy. I wouldn't know. I was hospitalised with anorexia when the State poisoned us. By the time I got out, the 'bot had cleared the café. The irony of my sickness keeping me well is not lost on me.

Wind flings yet another handful of raindrops at the windowpane. It is early morning, but the whole sky is black. More rain pelting down. I should heed the rats. Only leaving means running with them, on them. I did that before. And when I fell, they would not let me get up. They ran over me, took a bite or two, and kept going. I was lucky. They were not so hungry then. Now the rains are ruining their food supply. The animals are more alert. Only, if I wait too long before I run, I'll be at the mercy of the floodwaters. Swept along like a rat myself. When you look at it like that, going out seems like a terrible idea. There's still time.

Besides, I have my work cut out, deciding what button to press. What flavour to vote for. I pretend that I like to mix it up, but the truth is, it feels like every vote matters. One day I am going to get it wrong. If I press the wrong button, perhaps my loyalty card will stop working. Or the drinking water will dry up, or the food runs out. If I choose wrong, the State might come. What if I choose right? Will Adam finally answer my questions? Will I know what the point was of all this? Even when as water rises, this decision can't be rushed.

A scratching noise turns my head. A lone rat is outside, balanced on the window ledge. Against all probability, it is hugging the glass. Beyond the rat, the water is moving. More rain is coming down hard, little bullets of wet. The animal is leaking threads of blood. I blink, distracted. My hand tightens on my cup. Beyond the rat, a car is floating. That never happened before. None of it. A tree branch bangs against the window, long fingers screeching down the length of the glass. As I watch, the tree and the rat and even the car are gone. The window whines a little, protesting.

Running for the bathroom, I throw up. Then I use the tap water to wash my mouth and face.

This storm isn't like the others. It's happening at the wrong time. It's harder. Stronger. There is no sign of it stopping. Poor rats. I could be the sole survivor of a city murdered by muffins. Even I let out a wild hoot of laughter and clap my free hand over my mouth. Crazy. That's how I sound. Completely crazy. If I don't get it together, then this postscript to events will be all I ever amounted to. I survived before by being sick. I am not that person anymore. Adam isn't here anymore. If I survive today, it will be by being strong. I sniff the coffee cup. That's who I am. Coffee. Bagels. Adam.

Water gurgles in the toilet. My sick starts to come back up, out of the sink. A little puddle of water trickles under the bathroom door. Not much, but there is enough bleach in it to start melting my shoes. I grab my cup and pull myself upright. This is a café. There must be something that floats here. Out of the bathroom, the 'bot is busy mopping around my table. They are made of wood, but it would be hard to get them free. Almost impossible with a 'bot right there in front of me.

Me. The 'bot. Which one of us will the floods dissolve first?

My mind ponders this while my eyes skate over plastic bottles, stainless steel worktops, plastic chairs. The coffeemaker. The till. Water up to my ankles and my heart is running too fast. It won't be long before the water is licking the 'bot tom of my jeans. You don't want the water to touch you. I twirl around, careful not to splash. There. In the kitchen. Some sacks of sealed plastic are bobbing in the current. I make my way over to them and touch one. The water does not seem to affect the plastic. Even better, whatever was that was inside the bags has run out, or mostly run out. It turns out that what I thought was several sacks is one huge single sack, big as a beanbag. If it can squash this through the door, I can float. Maybe even find a way to protect myself from the rain. I balance the cup on the sack and start to tug the plastic towards the door.

When I step back into the dining area the 'bot comes whirring towards me. He wants me gone. My eyes dart to the clock. I must have spent longer in the bathroom than I realised. The 'bot reaches for me, and I bend down and scoop some filthy water into my cup. The 'bot halts at the sight of it.

That's right. I'm a registered customer. There's liquid in my cup. You can't throw me out. Not quite yet. I haven't voted. I get an extra ten minutes.

The 'bot revs backwards, returns to mopping. No matter that the mop is melting too.

I hold onto the cup while tying one end of my scarf around the corner of the sack. The water has eaten most of my shoes. My jeans are getting wet. Getting this sack out of the door is going to be hard. Maybe, if we are tied together, the 'bot will evict us both.

Adam was the one who wanted to have the 'bot. Safer than staff, he had said. He'd programmed it himself, spending whole nights at Fiona's to do so. I never asked why, or where he slept. If he slept. I had seen what asking why did to Adam. I had moved on. I was too busy making war on my own body by the time he was with Fiona. I never tried to steal from the café before. How good a programmer was Adam? On such small matters, such huge consequences lie.

The size of the sack makes progress almost impossible. The current is against me, and the size of the bag means pushing the tables back. Moving the tables upsets the 'bot. So, I must move a table, pull the bag, tether the bag to the table, keep the tether to me, go back, and put the table right before the 'bot arrives. It isn't long before the rising water is licking higher up my jeans, and I am crying, because it's exhausting. The tables, my scarf, the 'bot, my coffee cup with its inch at the bottom. I must have been doing this for longer than ten minutes already. It feels like forever. Damn Adam and his dreams. Did he ever once stop to think of the damage he would do? Did he hang his head in shame at the idea of killing a city? Or did he blame everyone but himself, like he always did?

There's a flash of orange outside but I can't pay attention to it. I've got enough to do. My cup is floating. My time over.

"Hit the button!"

What?

My head whips up. There is a real, live, person outside. On a boat. A boat that isn't melting. It's a man, like Adam was a man, and he's got some sort of uniform on. Since when did the State enter a walled city when there were people alive inside? Wasn't that the whole point of quarantine? There's a springing hope inside of me that I squash down. Adam is dead. Fiona too. And Jack, Marsha, Jessie, and Zen. They're dead. I'm alive. For now. Ignore them outside. I need to focus.

"Vote, damn it!"

I lose it entirely and start laughing, doubled over laughing. My legs are on fire. I might be crying. Adam always did want the State to tell us to vote.

If only Adam was here. Real Adam, not this imposter. Real-Adam would record this on his stupid phone and put it on all channels. Behold, he would say, the State admits that voting matters.

But it is me here. Me, who watched the end of the city from my hospital bed. The State met with the rebels, said they would treat us democratically and to prove it they killed everyone. Now this stranger who looks awfully like Adam wants me to vote. Is screaming at me to vote. Hasn't he seen the bodies? Does he think I don't know what voting in front of a representative of the State leads to? I can't vote. No vote. So, no exit.

I turn away from the front door and grab the scarf. It falls apart in my hands. Of course. Fine. I can tow the boat with my hands. There must be another exit. Surely. This sack could not have fitted through the front door. Not when it was full. I need to go back and find the other exit. Because whoever is out there, in front of me, he's crazier than I am.

The 'bot is still working. He trundles towards me. What is it now? I am trying to leave. Can he evict me, this once? Then I don't have to vote. Only no-one ever did do what I wanted them to. Even now, the 'bot simply wants to take my survival sack, my boat, away from me. The 'bot wants the bag back in the kitchen cupboard, where it is supposed to be. He pulls at it. I pull back, holding on my side of the plastic. I could climb on it now, even. paddle it back towards the kitchen. The 'bot pulls harder, and the plastic tears open. Flour stains the water. I sag into the burning wet. The 'bot takes his half of the bag and trundles away. Waves spread from his wake.

Not-Adam has left the boat. He's outside the door, plastered against the glass. Yelling and banging on the door with the butt of his gun. Just another rat, a State rat, trying to get in. If I wait long enough, the rain will wash him away. It washes everyone away. The water's pushing me in a circle. It isn't that bad. The rain was cold at first, then hot, but it's warm now. Comforting. All the best people are dead. All the worst people too. It wasn't like I knew what I was do-ing.

I'm wrapping myself in plastic when a vice seizes me from behind, opens the door, and throws me out. The 'bot. Finally, Eviction is so sudden there is no time for fear. I don't fight when the current takes me, but become outraged when Not-Adam, picks me up and dumps me in a boat. He cuts off my clothes and pours sweet water over me. As though something so simple could wash away my sins.

Not-Adam tries to talk to me. Mouth moving and bad breath and words. I can't take it. I can't under-stand. He's too big. Too loud. Faces. More people.

They have emotion on them. Their skin smells strange, and their eyes keep staring. Focus on me. Each other. Back to me. It's too much. All of it. I curl up under the plastic, coughing out my screams.

The boat takes me out of the city and docks by the river. The wall is being taken down. An ambulance carries me away. The man is still here, holding my hand. He tells me he's Adam, real-Adam, that the rebellion worked. That he loves me. That Fiona loves me. I can go and live with them, he says, once I get well.

The State was always an excellent liar. Old-Adam told me that. The past is always dissolving, and the people you love return and retreat like the tide. He is excited, jubilant, his face alight as he tells me that I can vote now, for whatever I want.

I close my eyes against the tide of words. This echo-of-Adam talks on, not realising that, like the muffins, everything I want has already gone.

"What do we want?" The chant was barely audible through the small crack in the door, but the emotion in the speaker's voice was clear. "Freedom!" The crowd roared their approval, and Winston Blake, chief of police, winced.

"Nice of you to join us, Chief."

Winston looked down the hall of the theater and smiled at the speaker. "Apologies, General. I got caught up in the crowd." Winston winced again when his hands touched his rain-slicked coat. He ignored the pain and made his way toward the group, letting the door close behind him. He leaped onto the stage and took his seat in between the head blacksmith, Gabriel Stubb, and the Logistics Head, Rachael May. "What did I miss?"

"We're just about to vote." The General gestured to the thick stack of papers in front of her. "The other members voted earlier, it's just you three left."

"All right." Winston clapped and rubbed his hands. "Let's get to it."

"Before we start," The General stopped Winston as he was reaching for a pen, "we have to discuss our views."

"Why?"

"Because we're at an impasse." The General gestured to Rachael and Gabriel. "You're the tie breaker, and if I remember correctly, you said—"

"I vote, we stand and fight."

Rachael sighed, and Gabriel grunted. The General kept her face impassive. "I'll let you discuss, and I will moderate."

Gabriel looked sideways at Winston and sneered at Rachael before he started. "Siding with Virginia would give us security and assure that we'd be able to live our lives peacefully."

"They gave us an ultimatum, Gabriel," Rachael picked up a slip of paper with Virginia's state seal on the upper right-hand corner, "not an offer. Plus, we can't meet their expectations and survive on our own. They're asking for too much."

"I agree," Winston chimed in. "We can't afford to give them supplies. We have them stockpiled for this coming winter."

Rachael nodded. "Winston is right, but despite what you two think, we need to agree to the Northern Alliance's offer."

Gabriel scoffed and leveled his finger at Rachael. "You're delusional"—he turned his finger onto Winston—"and you're just insane. There is no way that we'll survive an attack from Virginia. They have three, four states backing them up, and if the rumors are true, they've dug up old tech and—"

"Don't we have old tech ourselves?"

Gabriel waved his hand dismissively toward Winston. "Yeah, we do, but it doesn't function properly.

So, compared to them, I have impressive looking junk sitting in my storage."

Rachael pinched the bridge of her nose. "Isn't the Professor helping you decipher it?"

"Barely," Gabriel replied, "but he's so damn busy with you, and you, and everyone else that we haven't gotten into this thing's guts! Not to mention, we don't have anything that can directly deal with their old tech, and if we did, we don't have the resources to—"

"We could get some of the citizens to man the walls, learn the weaponry, et cetera," Winston beamed.

Gabriel counted off the issues on one hand. "We don't have the time to train this force, Virginia and the Northern Alliance are at our southern and northern borders respectively. We don't have the resources to upkeep the weapons required to deal with old tech, and more importantly, if the rumors are true, we have no way of dealing with any old tech Virginia throws at us. They have the numbers, the experience, everything! We're better off siding with them."

Rachael shifted in her seat. "Winston." Her voice was soft, and she sighed. "If more people joined the state's army, there'd be a steep decrease in supplies. The state's military requires more per individual than the average citizen, and as it stands now, we have a precarious balance with our supplies and who, or which organization gets what and how much of it." She turned to Gabriel. "That's why we'll be killing ourselves, if we bow to Virginia."

"A few months of hardship would—"

"Thousands would die. We'd lose the ability to farm as effectively leading to a loss of crops. There will be less people working in silos which will increase criminal activity. Siding with Virginia is suicide," Rachael said.

"You're being overdramatic. You forget how strong, how prideful, we are."

"Gabriel, you're right." Winston wagged his finger at him. "And Rachael, you're right as well, but we don't need to bow to one state or to join an alliance that could lead to nowhere." He stared at the two. "We can fight them off with no problem."

"What makes you think we—"

"Because you said it yourself, Gabe. We're a strong, prideful people, and believe me, I've heard both of your arguments. But you two are already giving up without a fight—"

"If we fight and lose, that's the end of us. There'll be no treaty, no one to protect us. We'll be at the mercy of whoever claims the land and holds it," Gabriel said coldly.

"I rather die on my feet than live on my knees."

"But it's not living on your knees!" Rachael shouted. "We'll be a part of an alliance. We'll have protection and—"

"Last time I checked, the Northern Alliance doesn't have old tech. Hell, they barely have any tanks." Gabriel slapped the report on his desk. "The only advantage they have is numbers. Everything else they don't have is what we have. Don't you see the danger in this?"

"All the more reason to join them," Rachael retorted, "rather than live under a tyrannical state blinded by delusions of grandeur."

"If anyone's blinded by their delusions"—Gabriel jerked his thumb toward Winston—"it's him."

Winston raised his eyebrows at Gabriel. "I'm delusional because I believe in the people of this state?"

"No, that makes you stubborn," Rachael said dryly.

"Look here, my position has me cross paths with the common folk daily, more so than you two. I listen to their plights, their dreams, and everything in between. I know that they don't want to join Virginia, and the same can be said regarding the Northern Alliance."

"What's the point of you saying this?"

"The point," Winston said, voice thick with irritation, "is if either of you cared about these people, you'd help me convince the rest that it's in our best interests to rip apart Virginia's ultimatum in their faces and respectfully deny the Northern Alliance's offer."

Rachael dropped her head into her hands. When she looked up, she looked centuries older. "I'm sorry, Winston, but ..." She sighed, picked up the pen in front of her and scribbled her vote on paper before handing it to the General. "I care for the people here just as much as you, and I feel this is the best choice."

"Winston, you are one stubborn man." Gabriel scowled as he scribbled his vote and threw the pen away from him. "I respect that, but I can't let you ruin this because of your 'good intentions.'"

"I'll stand with the people of Maryland." Without another word, Winston pushed himself from the table and started to rise.

"I take it that your votes are in."

Winston stopped midway in his seat and faced the General, offering a nod.

"Yes, General," Rachael started, "hopefully we can convene again under a better mindset to get through this impa—" Rachael's body flew out of her chair, the bullet hole through her chest still smoking.

Winston's face fell as he watched Rachael's body hit the floor. He fumbled for the gun at his waist, cursing the General through tears. Just as he placed his hand on the grip, another shot rang out, punching him through the heart. He was dead before he hit the table, gun still in hand.

Gabriel stared at the bodies, fear keeping him still.

"I'm surprised that Rachael didn't side with Winston."

Gabriel tore his eyes from his friends, not hearing a word she, said, he gazed at her with tears in his eyes. He tried to form words, but all that came out was a sob.

The General wiped her gun with a cloth, her face impassive as it was earlier speaking as if discussing the weather, "Seeing their relationship, but ..." She let out a breath. "Oh well." She gave Gabriel a predatory smile. "You chose well. Siding with Virginia, just like the others." She finished wiping her gun down and discarded the cloth.

Gabriel followed its slow descent, his eyes widening when it landed next to Winston's face. His friend's eyes were opened in shock, and his mouth hung slack, a curse trapped on his lips.

"Hey, hey." The General lightly slapped his face. "Don't stare too long or else you'll get si—" She barely leaped out of the way as Gabriel threw up his stomach's contents. After he finished, the General was at his side. "Get yourself together. I need you performing at your best for—"

"Why?" Gabriel managed through sobs, his throat raw.

The General raised an eyebrow, her lips curling into a cruel smirk. "Because I envision a country that isn't divided like it is now, and Virginia promised me, and a few others, positions in the new government they plan on making. It's a win-win situation." She waited a few moments longer. Confident that he had no more questions, she walked off stage and started up the aisle to the exit. "Don't worry about the mess," she called back. "I'll have one of my soldiers clean up. Just leave whenever."

Moments later, the door opened, followed by a crack of thunder. Gabriel heard the crowd faintly as the ringing in his ears subsided, seconds passed, and he regained his full hearing. Upon hearing their next chant, he groaned, remembering Winston's words. He turned moments before the door closed, noticed that the crowd had thinned, only the most devoted stayed behind protesting, despite the acid rain that was falling heavily now. Gabriel turned back to Winston's hand, to the gun. With shaky hands he reached out and grasped it by the barrel. He tugged softly, releasing a small groan when it slipped out and Winston's hand fell to the side. For a moment, he examined it, felt its weight, and ran his hands over the smooth surface before pointing the gun at himself. He placed his other hand on the grip and fingered the trigger. He opened his mouth and slid the barrel inside. He let it sit there for a few seconds. After a dozen deep breaths, he cocked the pistol and pulled the trigger.

Click.

Empty.

He blinked tears out of his eyes and tried again.

Click.

Empty.

He couldn't stop the tears from falling. His hands shook, so he took another breath to steady them and pressed again.

Click.

Empty.

He dropped the gun, and through quiet sobs, he watched the door, wishing for the General to return. The door opened, and he almost smiled. He wiped his face and opened his arms. Instead of a gunshot, he heard heavy footfalls and a loud thud, then a soft voice whispering to him.

"It'll be okay, sir. We'll get revenge for your friends."

"What?" He opened his eyes as a female soldier leaned over him.

"The General told me everything," She checked him for wounds.

The soldier's name tag read Sanders, and from her rank Gabriel saw that she was a Staff Sergeant. "What did she say, Staff Sergeant?"

She brought her head up to face his, there were tears in her eyes. "The Northern Alliance," she spat, "during your vote, they attempted to assassinate all of you." She sniffed. "They killed a few of the others, even the Major but." She wiped her face, mumbling sorry. "But we got them. And The General swears on her life that she'll get revenge for you, for them."

CULT OF THE OCCULT
A DAVID BARRETT & W SCHENCK

"Hello spirits and demons, and welcome to the 2020 election for The Office of Possession. I am your host, Marcus Tullius Cicero, and we are gathered here tonight for the first of many debates between the two front runners of each side: The Demons and The Spirits!"

A montage of fanfare music, accompanied by spotlights, aligned themselves onto the center stage.

"To the left is the leading choice for demonic superiority, Abraxas!" hollered Cicero, a loud cheer exploding from the left side of the auditorium following his grand announcement.

"Alright, alright. Save some love for the spirit of choice, Edward the Martyr!" More cheering tailed his speech. "Settle down, settle down, please. Now let's go to our experts on the matter, the Panel of Possession!"

To the left of the stage in a skybox sat the Panel of Possession.

"First off, we have the infamous creator of s'mores, Vlad the Impaler! Vlad, can I call you Vlad? Anyway, do you have any first impressions on the subject?"

A spotlight swung in the skybox's direction, briefly blinding those inside. Some grunts, and a few choice words, escaped Vlad's lips.

"Futu-ți gâtu' măti!" he yelled, covering his eyes.

"Really? Is that all you have to say there, Vlad?"

"Du te Dracu."

A few seconds inched by before Cicero spoke again. "Oookay. Thank you for that great insight, Vlad. On to the next person in the Panel of Possession."

The spotlight moved over one more seat, resting on a man clad in armor with long, unkempt hair.

"William Wallace, everyone! William, what do you have to say about all of this?"

"We're a' Jock Tamson's bairns!"

"Alright, what an intuitive perspective, thank you, William. And last, but certainly not least, we have the one, the only, Billy Shakespeare!"

A middle-aged man with a receding hairline and a terrible haircut, wearing a shirt that looked like he had a lace doily around his neck, stood up and cleared his throat. The congression of demons and spirits leaned forward in anticipation. "O, what such folly is this? What such host hath bearing on the lives of men, the host of hell gathered en masse determining the fate of thy reckoning! A reception, nay, a prison, cast upon the poor souls of ..."

"Fantastic! What a remarkably long-winded explanation that was hard to follow and explained nothing! Thank you, one and all: this is sure to be quite the quintessential debate! And now a word from our sponsors while we take a quick break. We'll be right back, folks!"

Cicero spun around in his seat, his white toga getting tangled up as he waved his arms in irritation. "What the hell, guys? I thought we talked about this! Either stick to the topic we give you or you can get the fu—"

The microphone was abruptly cut off as the operator frantically switched the screen from Cicero's red face to an advertisement for Paranormal Vitality, unequivocally sure to make your bedroom performance undeniably supernatural. Immediately afterward, another bulletin aired on the viewers' screens.

"Has your afterlife been restless lately? Have you been cranky and irritable? Have you been turning over in your grave? Well, do we have the product for you! Introducing the new Vitamin Boo supplement! Paranormally proven to help you rest in peace."

Following the last advertisement, the viewers' screens switched back to the debate once again. The cameras panned wide, zooming in on each candidate. On the right stood the ever-stoic Edward the Martyr, nodding soberly to the camera. Moving on to the left, steadfast and confident, Abraxas smirked as he pointed to a few separate succubi in the screaming crowd who swooned as the conglomerate chanted his name.

"Welcome back, everyone, to the 1,467th quadrennial debate for The Office of Possession!" Cicero announced, his immaculate smile back in place. "We have a full debate to get to tonight so let's dive right back into it!"

The cheers of the crowd thundered over the voice of the announcer as he tried to re-introduce the candidates. The cameraman panned over all of the spectral and monstrous forms of the viewers, slowly making his way back to the stars of the show.

"Alright, everyone excited to get started?" gleamed Cicero.

The crowd roared its acquiescence as Abraxas took his place at the center podium. Spotlights focused on Cicero and Abraxas as the drum roll queued the first question.

"Abraxas, Are you ready for the first topic?"

He nodded gently, a slight smile dancing across his thin reptilian lips, "Yes, of course."

Cicero cleared his throat. "What would be your first act if sworn into The Office of Possession?"

He cleared his throat. "Well, I would make sure the transition into my residency of the office would be smooth and not cause any unwanted complications."

"We all know what happens when you have displeased subjects," he added slyly, giving Edward a sideways glance.

"Could you be a little more specific on the long-term plans?"

The crowd chattered with laughter, and Abraxas gave a toothy grin. "I'm so glad you asked, Cicero. Too long have my predecessors let this noble title be squandered, neglectful of their role, treating it as more of a B-rated Hollywood film rather than the illustrious position that it is meant to be. I would fulfill this role and treat it as is warranted, with respect and deference! I would bring prosperity back to the office, putting my duties above my own wants and desires!"

He raised his arms above his head to accentuate his point, letting his fans chant his name like a rock star.

"Well put. But we have a lot more to hear from our other candidate," Cicero said, turning to face Edward. "So, Eddy. How would you start off your glorious induction if you were lucky enough to be selected?"

Edward leaned forward and tapped on the mic, causing feedback that screeched over the speakers. "Um, is this thing working? Yes? Okay, well I think I would start off by really keeping things the same. I know I don't like change, so why try to fix something that isn't broken? Change is only needed if what we already have becomes irrelevant. What we have in place has worked for quite a few millennia, so why rock the boat, so to speak?"

He rubbed his hands together nervously, waiting for the next prompt. After glancing around for a moment, he then realized there wasn't going to be one. "Um, that's about all I have to say about that."

Cicero tugged at his collar, "Wonderful! I feel truly enlightened! Abraxas, anything you want to add?"

The demon let out a rolling chuckle. "What makes you think this lonely soul is right for office? An evil stepmother setting up his assassination using a huntsman? His story might as well have been written by Walt Disney himself!"

"Alright, alright. Save that moxie for the open debate at the end of the questions. Let's move on to the next. Edward, we will start with you."

Cicero turned to Edward, who in turn smiled nervously at the camera, host, and crowd. "Eddy, the next topic is the one related very closely to the position you two are battling for. What will you do about possession in pop culture? Nowadays it's seen as a novelty, something that's sought after as a form of entertainment."

He leaned into the mic once more, lips scraping against the coarse metal framework. "So, what is your question?"

Cicero chuckled. "How are you going to strike fear back into the masses? What will you do to make this department less of a joke?"

"Ah, yes. I would bring back the regularly scheduled possessions of people on a weekly basis. Put the haunt back into haunted houses." He gave a weak smile in hopes to bring the crowd over to his side. "I would spook so many people they would need to bring back exorcisms; maybe even have them bring some chiropractors to the spiritual events. Give the church something more to do than collect tithes from their parishioners."

"Braxy? What do you think? What would you do?"

Abraxas stretched languishly, a lithe smile dancing across his lips. "Well, as candid as my opponent is, he has missed the most important aspect of the position that he is fighting for ... What possession is truly used for. Anarchy! Time and time again, haven't we seen the effects of those possessed during their time in office? I mean, just take one of our very own recent examples, for instance, the President of the United States. Since possessing him, we have achieved global pandemic, riots, and division of state within the span of only a few months. I would say the results speak for themselves, wouldn't you?"

"Well said. I'm not quite sure who won that round though if I am being completely honest. Eddy over here had some excellent points. Let's consult with our Panel of Possession to see what they think."

The camera moved smoothly over to the Panel's box above the crowd. Happy and hopeful entities tried waving to loved ones as the lens flashed over them.

"Wallace, have any more insightful Scottish gibberish for us?"

"Whit's fur ye'll no go by ye!" William guffawed.

"Uh, right! That was as inspiring as always. Billy Spears? Are you related to Brittney by chance? Never mind, that doesn't matter. What do you think of the debate so far?"

"O, fate, twas such that laid low the youth in their prime, eating the soul away afore it hath done growing! By God, by man, by that holy affliction which doth possess us all, I declare the Spirit forth-coming by that as we declare it as such!"

"Bill, is that all? Is that the only great... advice that we are going to get out of you tonight?"

"Doth doves mate for life?"

"Yup. That's what I thought. Vlad, come on. Tell me you have something useful."

"Du-te in pizda ma-tii!," Vlad huffed.

Cicero pressed his finger to his earpiece, listening intently to the translation coming through. His face contorted in a sour expression, quickly morphing back to a professional smile.

"That's not very nice," he said through gritted teeth. Looking off to the left, he whispered, "Can we get him outta here? No? Okay, Vlad... Please behave."

"Pizda."

"Still, not very nice there Vlad. Anyway, let's hear from another sponsor before we get back into the nitty-gritty details. I'll have a quick chat with the wonderful Panel of Possession about the appropriate conduct to have during these kinds of professional de-bates."

The live stream ended on a smiling face of Cicero before changing to an extremely generous sponsored ad.

"Have you been having difficulty possessing hu-man bodies for lengthy periods of time? Is the entry not what it used to be? Has the act of possession been hard on you with old age? Dry? Chapped and worn? Demon-ease is the all-new occupancy lubricant spe-cially formulated for the older demons with a healthy tenureship. The proprietary blend ensures that "exit only" is no longer the only option."

The stream switched from the regulated ads back to the current live event. On the screens of millions of viewers, Cicero could be seen talking to the panel briefly before noticing the cameras aimed in his direction. He quickly gave his trademarked bright, but fake, smile toward the crowd in the wide-angle frame before retaking his seat near the podiums.

"Welcome back ghouls and succubi. Let's get right into it," said Cicero, picking up his neat pile of notecards off the desk in front of him. He shuffled through them to find one at random. He quickly pulled one out and read it briefly. His eyes darted from the card to the candidates, then back to the card. "I'm not sure how this one got into the pile but I kind of like it. Let's roll with it and see what happens. What would you do to help with the wait times at the Department of Human Possession? We have had countless complaints filed that it takes too long to get processed through the possession portals. Abraxas, you're up first for this question, how would you rectify this situation?"

"I am glad you asked that, Cicero. I have worked hard on a solution to that very troublesome issue. First off, we would quadruple the number of portals we currently employ. Then we would implement specific location-based portals, dividing everyone up for the right country of their destination, followed by more intricate parameters surrounding the exact needs of each possession."

The crowd cheered in agreement, giving their deafening approval of these much-needed improvements. Cicero turned to calm the vocal supporters, arms raised high.

"Alright, alright. Let's settle down. I, like everyone else, agree with everything he has said. But to have a fair debate we need to see what Eddy has to say."

He turned back to the candidates, focusing on Edward in particular, "Eddy, what's your take?"

He cleared his throat. "Well, Cicero, instead of cluttering up our already cluttered department with hundreds of more possession portals, I would propose that we branch out and build more housing developments that are equally dispersed throughout the region to relocate the current number of portals, thus reducing the strain on the centrally located portal housing. This would mean that those of us who are unable to travel the longer distances to the Departments' headquarters would have access that is more localized, giving everyone the chance for possession that we all deserve; coincidentally, also solving the issue related to the congestion of the portals!"

"All wonderful points," exclaimed Cicero, cocking his head to the side, "just listen to that crowd roar! Alright, normally I would take this moment to have an insightful commentarial by our Panel of Possession, but, as I understand it, they have been banned from speaking for the remainder of this event, leaving us with no other option but to leave on a high note like that. We have one more commercial break to get to then we will be back to the program and the stunning conclusion for the night's event. Stay tuned everyone, we will be right back!"

DARLING INDIGO, LET THERE BE LIGHT

SORIA DAVIS

The alarm sounds at four a.m., startling Sol Elio. Since midnight, Sol wavered between wake, worry, and disconnected sleep. In the middle of the night, weary, he had placated Evangeline.

Past two a.m., Sol was wide-eyed, anticipating Indigo. In the midst, the Senator pondered Proposition 19. And just when he succumbed to exhaustion, it was time to heed the clock.

After quickly shaving and showering, Sol dresses quietly to not disturb Evangeline. He selects his patriotic best: a white shirt and red tie, and his finest navy suit; the jacket adorned with an American flag pin.

Awake but silent, Evangeline glimpses Sol dabbing cologne on his long, muscular neck. She arranges for the custom clothing that complements Sol's lean, athletic build; and she purchases the pleasant scents that enhance his persona.

Married twenty years, Evangeline has molded Sol. She bore him two sons; and she takes impeccable care of her husband, children, and household. She helped propel Sol to his current stature.

"I'm so proud of you, darling," purrs Evangeline.

His back to his wife, Sol winces. He had hoped their vigorous, late-night lovemaking would have kept

Evangeline asleep until after he left home this morning. Her tone, however, indicates her wrath has dissipated.

Sol faces Evangeline and smiles. "Good morning. I didn't mean to wake you."

Evangeline sits up in bed, pulling their cozy, bright yellow comforter over her bare breasts. "Trying to disappear in the morning darkness?" she asks, laughing.

Sol walks to Evangeline's side of their bed and sits down. "Wouldn't that be something?"

"Yes, I can see the news now: 'Senator who authored coveted legislation to bring evening light disappears in morning darkness.'"

Evangeline continues, "Then they cut to a clip of a Mystic Province mom: 'Fall and winter mornings are already dark! Year-round daylight saving time will force our kids to walk to the bus stop and school in even darker and colder conditions!'

"Then cut back to the reporter: 'Senator Sol, at the pinnacle of his political career, seems to have suffered the same ominous fate people feared for their children with passage of Proposition 19!'"

Genuinely humored by Evangeline's theatrics, Sol gazes into Evangeline's light green eyes and smiles generously. "I love you, Lina."

Pleased, Evangeline reaches her hand to Sol's cheek. She fondly caresses his dimple with her thumb before Sol gently rests his face in her palm.

In this very moment, Evangeline is confident in the significance of her care; and in the bond she and Sol share. She is emboldened.

"I meant what I said last night, Sol. I can walk in your shadow, but I can no longer withstand your dalliance with your Darling Indigo."

At the mention of his longtime lover's name, Sol begins to rise. Evangeline grabs both his wrists and proceeds with her tirade.

"Proposition 19 to adopt daylight saving time year-round is finally on the verge of voter approval. Two annual clock shifts will be no more. And no more to your two shifts, one in my bed and one in hers!

"Your constituents have always been a priority and that is right. But when the darkness falls later each day, permanently, I should benefit. I should be the one with you to bask in the light."

Silence ensues and Sol is compelled to speak. Softly, he pleads, "Lina, darling, I have a long drive. If I don't leave now, I will be late for final meetings with retailers, restaurant owners, and at the golf clubs. I need their support. I need your support."

Sol takes Evangeline's hands into his own. He raises her right hand to his lips for an endearing kiss.

Sol says softly, "When Proposition 19 passes, there will be more light for shopping, for recreation, for us." He then exits the bedroom and heads out of their storybook home, into the darkness of morning.

Sol's easy exit leaves Evangeline questioning her hysteria. She rationalizes; she equates Indigo to the spring forward clock change in which there is one twenty-three-hour day in late winter/early spring where 2:30 a.m. does not exist. In her mind, Evangeline places Indigo right there at 2:30; where she cannot exist or affect Evangeline's future with Sol.

At the wheel of his car, Sol simultaneously contemplates the "fall back" clock shift which allows one twenty-five-hour day: more time to delve into darkness and illicit affairs.

Following the fall election, and specifically the vote on Proposition 19, Sol knows, either way, the sun will continue to be a star, exuding light. The Earth will continue orbiting the sun, while rotating around its axis. The amount of sunshine will remain the same.

THE DAY OF THE BLAME

RUEL R CARO JR

Alinna hated when this thing happens. She felt forced, but she didn't had any choice. She can't let her mother and her young brother does this for the family; it was her responsibility. She walked to the town hall and found a growing lane of people. It broke her heart seeing numerous old folks in their torn-out working clothes. She stood at the end of the line, tried not to empathize too much, and waited for her turn.

"Good morning young lady," a mid-aged, badged woman behind the table told Alinna; a cue that it was her turn.

She sat at the wooden stool in front of the woman's table—still warm from the previous commoner.

"Is this your first time, young lady?" the woman asked as she hand her a familiar textured parchment.

"Actually, it's my fourth." She smiled and started writing.

Alinna, of the Stewel Family

"Young lady! Momus must've given you luck to survive three draws," the woman said, slightly stunned.

Alinna gave back the signed parchment with a bitter smile. "I'll need that luck again."

Before going to her work, Alinna needed to meet Felix on the Acacia tree, just on the town's outskirts where the farmland starts. Just by the thought of his name, the harsh feeling from the town hall fades to nothing. As she arrived near the tree, she could clearly see his shadows on the ground—tall and long enough hair to be blown by the wind. "Thinking something?" She approached as she noticed the great worry in his face. "It's your turn this time, right?" She sat beside him.

He nodded. "My two brothers are done. So yes, it's my turn this time," he said as he threw a pebble on the barren farmland. "But I'm worried about you," he added.

"Don't worry about me. I've done this three times before. In fact, I'm afraid for you. This will be your first time," she said honestly.

He radiated a strange kind of happiness from his eyes. He has this look every time he knew Alinna was okay.

Alinna knew exactly this look and was always assured by it.

"I just wish you had someone on your family who can take turns with you," Felix said sincerely, eyes fixed on her. He had brothers to take turns, but Alinna hadn't. "I can't wait for us to be married. You know, so every time this happen, I can assure your safety ... I want us to be a family already," he added with no windows for her to cut him off.

"We will be a family," she affirmed with strong emphasis on 'be.' "We'll build a house, out of here," she added, calmly panning her gaze out into the scorching sky. "Here. My mom used to give me a duck feather as a reminder not to get lost with the thoughts of the future," she said with a pleasant face and presented an old, ragged cyan feather.

That's all the time they had; they needed to get to work. Felix had gone off to the dried irrigation canal of the barren wheat field. All the farmlands are now devoid of life and the crops had been infested by pests; same as to where Alinna was working—Tomato and Aubergine farm. The greenery now was merely brown. Alinna had just arrived to her workplace, and a bad news welcomed her. "All workers are suspended until further notice due to the crisis." This hasn't happened before.

As she walked home to her mother and her little brother, she was thinking how she will be able to provide for them. Drought like this can last as short as a week or unpredictable numbers of months. When she told her mother, it wasn't a big deal. According to her, she had collected a dozen of eggs from her two ducks.

"We will get through this," her mother said before they slept. Alinna wanted to believe it. "If you'll be picked tomorrow, know that—"

"Don't think that," Alinna cut her. But she knew it was possible. "Take a rest, Mum." She smiled at her. Tomorrow was the day she hated.

The Day of the Blame came. At exactly 6 a.m., groups of badged people will roam streets after street. They are carrying a box with the parchments on which had a name of representatives per family. Each and every one will have to draw one name. The three most drawn names will be sacrifice, a human offering to Momus, the spirit of blame and unfair criticism.

"Good morning, folks!" a man announced with a voice trained to be loud enough.

Some walked out into the pavement, some opened their creaky windows. Everyone was unsettled.

"The Day of the Blame has come. We need to agree for someone to take all the blame for why this crisis happened to us," the man explained; Alinna hated how loud and clear it was. The crowd murmured. "Please, those sixteen years old and above, form a line. We know the process. Draw one paper, read the name, and put it back."

The line of people slowly shortened. Alinna didn't draw her name or Felix's, that's a good sign. After the drawing, tears and sobbing were everywhere, some neighbor even hugged her apologizing. She understood that it was inevitable.

"The result will be announced before the sunset," the man said and left.

Just an hour left before the sunset. The crowd in front of the town hall grew bigger and bigger. Alinna and Felix were standing side by side, holding hands.

"Don't think about it," Alinna told him. She felt him really nervous, but she couldn't blame him, this was his first time.

"What?" he asked innocently.

"Don't think about the result," she said, forcing a smile.

He seemed to be calmed.

With him by her side, and a beautiful sun set, it would've been perfect, if not for the fact that she might loss him.

Her mother was on her side too watching everyone. She handed Alinna a beautiful blue-ish green feather that reflects an orange tint. "This is the only gift I can give," she said.

Before Alinna could protest, a voice echoed over the crowd. "We have the results," a new man announced. "The three names are here. The ones we can blame for this crisis," he added, showing a folded parchment on his hands. "These names are not in order. If you are called, please come forward." His smile was unusual.

Alinna didn't know why, but her bones were trembling. She was trying to keep herself together with ropes and resins.

"Lash, of the McPear family!" The first name was called.

A loud cry boomed from the other side of the crowd.

Alinna's trembling multiplied.

"Tyrant, of the Bow family!"

Another episode of sobs was heard.

Only one left. Alinna's heart calmed a bit. Maybe she was really lucky.

Felix gripped her hand tighter.

She could hear his heartbeat through his hand.

"Alinna, of the Stewel family!"

Alinna, of the Stewel family.

Her world crumpled how a helpless parchment does; ropes and resins didn't help. She felt her bones turned to rubbles. The feather on her hand weighted a lot heavier now than ever.

Felix hugged her so tight, but she couldn't feel it.

"Please, come forward," the man said.

It snapped her back to the reality.

Felix tried to beam the familiar happiness; it felt like the last sunlight before the sun explodes.

"It's okay," she told her mother and hugged her. She turned to Felix and kissed him. "I'll be all right." She handed him the feather her mother gave her. "We'll be a family. We were a family."

She smiled one last time and faded into the crowd.

EARL AND THE TERRIBLE, HORRIBLE, VERY BAD DAY

TRACY ODEN

It is two weeks before the 2020 presidential election when I enter the clinic for an early morning session with Earl. He is slumped on the waiting room couch—hair standing on end, his shirt bloodstained and an eggplant-purple bruise blooming around his left eye. He looks awful but smells worse. He exudes the noxious odor of alcohol, puke and dried blood.

He came to my office straight from jail. Too bad he didn't go home and shower first. I may need to fumigate the waiting room.

"It's not as bad as it looks, Doc," Earl says flashing a tight, self-conscious smile that reveals a missing tooth.

I sigh and motion him into the office. We both sit and I face him, raise my pen to my notepad and say, "How are you, Earl?" It's ridiculous, given his appearance, but it's how I begin every session.

"Fine," he mutters like a surly sixth grader. He doesn't want to be here, he never does. Earl is my patient only because he was given an ultimatum by his agent, Max.

According to Max, I'm the 'therapist to the stars.' His clients are successful people – but I'm not sure they're as famous as Max likes to believe. However, I play along, and he sends me clients regularly. Earl is a young, successful comedy writer whose depression is starting to affect his work. You'd be surprised how morose comedy writers are.

Today at 4:00 a.m., Earl called Max begging to be bailed out of jail. Max agreed on the condition that Earl come see me immediately upon release and "figure out what the hell is wrong with you!" So here we are, both of us submitting to Max's demands at the crack of dawn.

I lean over making eye contact.

"I'm fine, Doc, really!" he snaps.

"You don't look fine," I snap back. I don't like being summoned before normal business hours to counsel an ungrateful, uncooperative man-child.

He looks at me through his one good eye, the one with the purple bruise is swollen shut. "Well, I'm great Doc. It's the world that's fucked up."

Wow. Earl never shows emotion. In our previous sessions he was cocky and talked incessantly about his achievements. He's written for Colbert, Seth Meyers, *SNL* ... lots of big names, but he was most proud of his screenplay. It became a hit movie (He *actually* is famous!).

He talked about the movie ad nauseum, although, if Tom Hanks was in my movie, I'd talk about it too. I'd seen it when it came out. The story was about a political candidate (played brilliantly, of course, by Mr. Hanks) who injures his head making him say exactly what is on his mind - no sound bites, no political correctness, or slogans. The protagonist brought honesty and integrity back to government. Cliché, I know—but I loved it and it was critically acclaimed. So, I may have been slightly star-struck as I listened to Earl's self-congratulatory orations. I knew he was avoiding talking about his problems, but I hoped he would eventually open up to me. However, after five sessions he has yet to offer access to his inner demons. So today, I'm going to push him.

"Why don't you tell me about last night?" I prod.

"There's nothing to tell." He slouches lower—the brilliant, witty writer reduced to pouting.

"Earl ..." I coax, modulating my tone, working to get my own irritation under control. "Look at you. There's a story here."

He is unable to avoid indulging in every writer's greatest joy, the opportunity to spin a tale. He begins, "I was working on a monologue for Colbert. It wasn't going well. The audience is tired of hearing about our 'Very Stable Genius' or 'Fake News.' I think they're tired of it all."

"You could be right," I sympathize.

He continues, "It all used to be funny: cronyism, racism, nepotism, lying, gross incompetence ..."

"Hmmm ..." I say, "'Funny' is not the first word that comes to mind."

"Look, it used to be funny because it didn't happen every damn day and when writers called a politician out, the politician paid for it. It gave writers power. We held public figures accountable. It's like when the bully in a movie finally gets taken down; everyone applauds. We were heroes in a way"

Earl rises from the couch. "But now the bully is winning!" he begins, gesturing and pacing. "It's like Cobra Kai won the match in *Karate Kid*!" Spittle flies as his voice crescendos.

"The country is being run by incompetent billionaires with no experience; and the highest office in the land is occupied by a bully who lies, slings schoolyard taunts, sends out irresponsible tweets and generally abuses his power. That's not the way the movie is supposed to end!"

Finally, some honest emotion from my patient, but he needs to be calmer to explore his feelings. "Earl, let's do a soothing exercise ... think of a place where you feel happy."

He breathes deeply and sits. His face relaxes and melts into a peaceful, contented expression; he looks up—visualizing. All he needs is a beam of light shining on his face and the hallelujah chorus in the background to complete his transformation. He sighs, "The writers' room at the *Daily Show*, 2014. I was part of something important. We cared about the truth. Back then lying could end a political career."

He pauses. "Now, all we can do is keep a running total of the number of lies! There are no consequences, no pay-off for digging out the truth. It's all futile!" He clenches his fist, his nostrils flare. "My life is meaningless!"

Earl is having a full-blown existential crisis! The growing fear that his life's work has had no impact has him hyperventilating. His emotions, usually channeled into cynicism and acerbic comedy, are out of control.

"Breathe Earl. Relax your body. Think of a happy place that's not political. Maybe time with your family?"

Earl stiffens like he's been hit with a taser. "God, no! Going home is like one of those news shows where partisan positions all get equal time. My father hates AOC; my mother thinks she's brilliant. My brother is a Trumper, and I am blue-no-matter-who. My grandmother is still wearing a pink pussy-hat and working needlepoint that says, *A woman's place is in the White House*; Grandpa thinks women should be barefoot and pregnant." Earl's good eye twitches compulsively.

"Okay, Earl, let's try something else, picture a beautiful sandy beach with the sun rising over the ocean. Can you see it?" I soothe.

The tic increases. "The ocean is rising, global warming is destroying the planet, and people think science is a menu and they can choose what they want to believe!" Earl is twitching uncontrollably now, almost bouncing off the couch.

"Earl! Try counting backward from a hundred. Come on, work with me."

Earl counts backward all the way to thirty-nine before his body stops trembling and his eye loses the glisten of mania. His breathing finally returns to normal.

"Okay," I say, "forget the exercises. Let's talk about what landed you in jail. You were writing, and it wasn't going well ..."

Earl's tongue probes the gap where his tooth used to be, and he drags his hand over his face. "About 5:30, I realized I hadn't eaten all day, so I went to the tavern to grab a burger. I also ordered a rum and coke. It hit me quickly since I hadn't eaten all day. Sometimes a buzz helps me write, so, I grabbed a napkin, started writing and ordered another drink. A cute blonde sat down at the bar and started flirting with me. I was flattered, but I really needed to get some good material cranked out and the buzz was helping. So, I just nodded, smiled, and got back to work.

"Since I wasn't responding, she asked the bartender to change the channel on the TV to FOX news. Shit! I tried to ignore it. I didn't want to interrupt the flow. Then she asked him to turn up the volume! I started shouting at the TV and fact-checking Hannity. A little voice inside me told me I was being irrational, but by now I was on my third drink, and I wasn't listening.

"The bartender tried to calm me down. He was doing a good job until he said, 'Relax, the election will fix everything.' That did it. I started educating him, rather loudly, about gerrymandering, voter suppression, Russian interference, Facebook bots, big money and THE ELECTORAL COLLEGE!" Earl is rising to his feet again, his good eye gleaming with panic. The twitch is returning.

"Earl," I command, "count backward again."

He is calm by sixty this time. He takes a deep breath and continues, "Sorry, Doc. Anyway, while educating the bartender I mentioned the lying Orange

Cheeto in the Oval Office. The blonde cleared her throat loudly, glared at me and then stood up and pulled open her jacket, all dramatic, like she's Clark Kent, transforming into superman. And there, emblazoned across her boobs is a giant MAGA—'make America great again.' Seriously? I snickered, and she proceeded to march up to me and stood way too close. I looked down at her, wondering what the hell she was doing. Then, she poked her finger in my chest and snapped, 'Do not disrespect my president!' Good grief, I was ready to laugh out loud, but before I could she said, in all seriousness, '*He is real and honest; an anti-politician who is a breath of fresh air in the stale confines of our political system.*'"

To my surprise, Earl looks like he's going to cry. I'm speechless. I've never seen him look this vulnerable. He sniffs and murmurs, "Her words were an exact quote from my movie."

I thought for a moment, and then I remembered the pivotal scene in Earl's crowning achievement. "Oh, that was an amazing speech," I say, "It gave me goosebumps."

"Well, hearing her repeat it made me sick. She was defending the damned antithesis of everything I believe in, with *my* words! Just because Trump is politically incorrect and shocking doesn't mean he's honest or good for the country." Earl crosses his arms, drawing into himself.

His body language tells me everything, but I need him to keep talking, "Earl, how are you feeling?"

He glares at me. "Like a fucking punch-line in a very bad joke."

I feel his pain but push on. "What happened next?"

"I threw a fifty on the bar and left. Unfortunately, MAGA-boobs followed me trying to force a debate. I ignored her and headed for Starbucks two blocks away. I thought coffee would help sober me up, but there was a crowd in front of Starbucks. Can you believe it was a protest, AND a counter-protest, over the holiday coffee cup?!"

Earl's eyes are getting that look again. Poor guy, he can't escape politics even when he tries. I attempt to get him back on track. "So, how did you end up in jail?"

He looks indignant as he resumes his story. "This gigantic guy was shouting about the 'war on Christmas.' That little voice inside me told me to keep walking, and I did, but as I walked past ..." Earl looks down and speaks quietly, "I kinda voiced my concern about his inability to deal with the design of a fucking cup."

I hide a smile behind my notepad.

"He didn't appreciate my candor. He called me a snowflake and I called him a pussy." Earl looks up with that purple bruise and says, "I thought we were fighting a war of words, but apparently, he preferred fists. Just as I was about to give him a verbal lashing, he threw a punch that slammed me to the ground and knocked out my front tooth. Then he hauled me up by the front of my shirt, to knock me down again, I assume, but the pain of the first blow was so intense that I puked all over him." One side of Earl's mouth curls up in a self-depreciating smile. "I guess I showed him."

I chuckle.

"He was kicking my ass when some counter protesters in Bernie t-shirts came to my rescue. They jumped the giant, and then his friends jumped them, and ... someone broke a window, sirens went off. And, um ... well ... we may have started a riot."

"Oh my god! Earl! I heard about that on the news. That was you?"

"Hey, *he* threw the first punch!" He's pouting again. "I don't remember it very well. At some point I saw MAGA-Boobs dive into the fray. She was yelling about Trump and Christmas and ... the rest is a blur. Eventually the police came, and everyone scattered. They caught a few of us: me, the Bernie bros, MAGA-boobs, the giant-who-hates-coffee-cups, and a buttoned-up executive type who just came in for a cup of coffee; poor guy. We all ended up in the tank."

He finally seems calm. I need to ask the required questions. "Do you want to hurt anyone? Or yourself?"

"No. I just want a damn shower." He looks defeated.

"Is there anything else you need to talk about?" It's a standard question, but sometimes it's amazing what comes out after you think a client has told you everything.

He begins slowly, "It was really weird in lockup. The Bernie Bros and MAGA Boobs were arguing about the election." He pauses. "But I didn't say one single thing. I was completely incapable of joining the conversation because I was having a nervous break-down."

Wow, I can't believe Earl just admitted this.

"After a while, the giant-who-hates-coffee-cups, who had been staring at me for hours says, 'Dude, you look like shit.'"

Earl snorts. "Gee thanks, right? But I didn't have the energy for anything else, so, I just told him the truth, 'I drank too much last night, and I'm probably going to lose my job.' Everyone got really quiet, and then the giant invited me to his AA group, 'because it saved his life.' I'm sure I looked like a fish out of wa-ter, with my mouth hanging open. I started to ask him if his higher power told him to hate coffee cups, but I didn't want another ass kicking. Then that little voice said, 'You're being a jerk,' and I decided to lis-ten to it."

"Good for you," I said.

Earl huffs, "So, I said, 'Maybe I'll come.' That made the giant grin, and the Bernie Bros smiled like they approved.

"Then, I'll be damned if buttoned-up-business-guy, who had been silent all night, didn't speak up. He said, 'You all should come to my P.E.T.S. group.' I wasn't sure what he was talking about, but one of the Bernie bros immediately started talking about his

Corgi and MAGA-boobs went all gooey about her Pitbull named Princess. They were both totally wrong.

"It turned out P.E.T.S. stands for Post-Election Trauma Support group. Buttoned-up-business-guy had been going since the 2016 election. He explained how you are required to pair up with a person whose beliefs are different than yours and sponsor each other. His sponsor voted for Jill Stein, and he voted for Hillary."

Earl smiles, a genuine smile. "My god, I'd loved to have been in the room the first time they talked." Earl rolls his eye with glee. After a moment, the smile slides into a frown, and he says, "Then MAGA-boobs suggested we sponsor each other."

I can't hide my surprise. "Wow! What did you say?"

"I told her to fuck off."

"Oh, Earl!" I exclaim, unable to cover my disappointment.

He grumbles, "She was pissed! If the men and women hadn't been separated by bars, I'd be missing more than a tooth." Then Earl exhales and groans, "But then that stupid little voice started talking again. It told me I was being a douche."

"Good word choice," I whisper and Earl glares at me. *Ooops, did I say that out loud?*

He snaps, "I told her I'd do it. Are you happy?"

"I am, but how do *you* feel?" I say in all seriousness.

Earl glares at me. "Aaaawwwfffuulll!" he stretches out the word, the sullen preteen again. "I've already heard everything she could possibly say."

I suppress a smile and say, "Maybe if you talk *to* each other instead of *at* each other, you can find some middle ground."

He dismisses my comment. "Maybe I'll get some good material. Or … maybe I'll get my mojo back and change the world with my award-winning writing." His swollen mouth curls into a crooked, cynical smile.

"As your therapist, let me remind you that the only one you can change is you. You are not responsible for the whole world. And take a break from politics sometimes! Maybe you can talk to 'MAGA-boobs' about Princess." I make air quotes as I say MAGA-boobs, feeling a little guilty for using the name.

He snorts, then looks at me skeptically. "You're not worried that I'm hearing voices?"

His puffy face, disheveled clothes and wild hair make him look crazy, but I'm confident he's not. "That little voice is doing a good job. You should keep listening to it."

I could see the gears working. He wants to say something cynical or ironic. Instead, he just sucks at the empty space where his tooth had been and says, "We'll see, Doc."

We finish up, and Earl eagerly heads home for a shower. I am pleased with the session, he finally opened up to me and made progress.

I open his chart and write a new diagnosis: *Existential crisis precipitated by post-election trauma and pre-election political overload.*

I file it away and sigh. It's been a long year; that's not the first time I've written that diagnosis. I wonder if it will get any easier after the election.

Today's the day. You've been working hard, traveling, making new friends and enemies. You get dressed in the new outfit the campaign manager selected and look in the mirror. You say what crosses your mind. "Am I a winner or a loser?" The answer will come in seventeen hours, give or take.

You eat a light private breakfast and go to your designated station. One of two car rides planned for today. It goes agonizingly slow as the world seems to have slowed down just for you. Finally, after spending what seemed like several lifetimes in the car, you arrive. The light from the sun and cameras are warming up the brisk morning as you walk into the election center. The election staff checks ID and voter registration. After they're satisfied, they hand you your ballot.

That simple paper ballot feels like liquid lightning in your hands. You look at it again to see if it's glowing like St. Elmo's Fire from static. Is it all in your head? You move into the voting booth. You mark the appropriate boxes using the provided marker. Each mark supporting candidates and possibly dooming others. Once finished, the ballot is sucked into a scanning machine and scanned for the votes marked, then stored in case of recounts.

Time to go to the party and wait for results. Back into the car for a fifteen-minute drive that once again drags on for days. The minutes were, once again, going by like lifetimes. Eventually, you arrive at your headquarters and start watching the news, getting the numbers that will make or break your campaign. Numbers that slowly climb.

As you eat a light lunch to keep the hunger pangs away yet not too much that the butterflies acting like Stuka dive bombers would make you nauseous. Too close to call, no one pulling ahead, everyone staying neck and neck as the numbers climb higher and higher. You start sweating bullets as the time left starts to dwindle.

Sixty percent in, still tied up, your energy running high, you're feeling wired after the full carafe of coffee you've drunk. Is it dinnertime already? The lunch you had is long gone. You begin to snack on some cold cuts someone brought in as appetizers to sate the hunger of the volunteers and staff congregating in your offices with their eyes on the TV as well.

Seventy percent in, polls are closing, more coffee, still neck and neck. A news crew has arrived and begins to take background footage and interview you and a few others. Their questions are almost pedantic but, you still attempt to engage and sway their perceived neutrality.

Seventy-five percent, the news is going crazy on the race, more coffee, the two speeches have been written and await the final count. The count is still within a two percent error. The morning shows are calling for interviews while the night shows are writing jokes about this race.

Eighty percent, all polls are closed, the nation is now watching. Keep smiling. Your stress is water off a duck's back. Drink more coffee. Keep cool. The poll stations are coming in faster than fireworks at an Independence Day show finale. The error settings are from two to four percent. The count is still edging upward, with no candidate taking a real lead.

Eighty-five percent, you started to pull away, but suddenly your opponent caught up and took a slight lead. The remaining areas have evenly split between the parties, with the error is down to three percent. Exit polls are making it a 50/50 battle with an error of five percent make them worthless but encouraging as you haven't lost. More coffee follows.

Ninety percent, the numbers are now slowed as the remaining stations are few in numbers. The error has gone back to two percent, with most areas have a final tally that is screamingly close to a victory dance with a 51/49 split. Your Chief of Staff is smiling as they grab the bottles of sparkling cider.

Ninety-five percent, the split is gone, ate up in some neighborhoods that went the other way. The numbers are within automatic recount territory, which means that it's looking like it'll be an overnight process. You look at the clock on the wall. It's eleven o'clock. You've been going for eighteen hours, fed by hors d'oeuvres, coffee, and willpower. Your mind is telling you a caffeine crash is imminent. Your will to stay positive is ebbing. The numbers are looking like spots on the TV. Your heart is hammering in your chest like it's trying to escape.

With all the polling stations in the winner can be declared. After such an incredible race, the end had come. The two challengers were such competitors that the close race seemed predestined but, there can be only one victor while the other must go home. The talking heads start, "And the winner is …"

ELECTION, SET, MATCH ☑

CALLIE RAE SUTTON

Muffled murmuring quickly hushed in the school auditorium when Principal Carson approached the podium.

"Good afternoon, students. You all have been working hard over the past three years for this moment. So, it brings me great pride to welcome to the stage, your nominees for senior class office.

Mara rolled her eyes at her friend when she noticed "Miss Perfect" Kaitlin stand and move to the side aisle before Principal Carson could even begin introducing the candidates.

Lacey giggled and patted Mara on the shoulder. "I don't know why you let her bug you so much."

"Your nominees for Secretary are Abby Green and Ashley Wilson." Principal Carson encouraged applause after each announcement. He always says that every student is worth an applause.

The effort of Mara's and Lacey's support was haphazard at best, resembling a sloth sauntering to the ground for its weekly whiz.

"How could I not *let* her get under my skin? That she-devil has been after me since middle school. It's senior year and just last week she welcomed me back to school by putting a bag of poop in my locker from that cotton ball she calls a dog."

"*Ew*, gross."

"Duh."

"Still, it is senior year. Anything could happen."

"*Pfft*. Sure."

They clapped again for the announcement of the forever unopposed Kelsey Betters, the other half of the plastic-doll duo, for vice president. "And finally, for class president, Kaitlin Waters ..."

Mara raised her hands to clap, as did many fellow students, when Principal Carson continued, "... And for the first time for the class of 2020, Ms. Waters will have some company. Please come to the stage, Mara Philips."

For a split second, you could hear the crickets.

Lacey stood up. "Yeah!"

All heads turned to them.

"Mara, stand up. He called your name."

"But, how?"

Lacey nudged her friend to standing. "You can thank me later." She then shooed Mara to the center aisle. "Yea," she shouted again.

Surprisingly, the whole auditorium roared.

Straightening out her awkwardness, Mara rushed up to the stage, and claimed a place next to Kaitlin, whose fake smile wasn't fooling anyone.

"What are you doing?" The tension in Kaitlin's jaw was slightly amusing to Mara.

"Kicking your sorry ass out of office." Mara waived at her classmates.

"You will regret this, Fatty Philips."

Blood drained from Mara's face at her haunted memories just as Kaitlin's smile became more confident: a truer version to her sinister self.

☑   ☑   ☑

"What were you thinking nominating me to go against 'The Plastic Pageants'?"

"Oh, you'll be fine. Just think about what it could do for your college applications."

"I'm already set for college. My grades are great, and I have enough extra curriculars."

"*Um*, reading books under the bleachers during games and creating a 'Friends Forever Club' to excuse us from attending extra curriculars doesn't necessarily qualify."

"Whatever. The point is, now I must spend my senior year digging more poop from my locker. Or worse ..."

"What do you mean 'or worse'?"

"Up on stage, Kaitlin called me 'Fatty Philips.'"

"Okay, and?"

"And? That's not part of my life anymore. Wasn't really my shining moment."

"No. I suppose not. But that was years ago. It fizzled out. No one remembers that. Plus, then you went to fat camp, lost a ton of weight, your pants haven't ripped on you, and, I'm assuming, you know how to use tampons now?"

"Damn, bitch. You took it all the way home."

Lacey giggled which caused Mara to laugh at herself.

"Maybe you're right. I mean, you heard them in there, right? I think the people have spoken. They want a new leader."

Dropping her book bag, Mara jumped up onto the closest bench and belted out, "Seniors of 2020, I am Mara Philips, your class prez."

Lacey keeled over in laughter, tripped over Mara's book bag, and lunged right into Mara. The two girls finally caught their breath lying on the grass.

"Here I come bitches."

☑ ☑ ☑

"Hey, Mrs. Philips. Is Mara ready?"

Mrs. Philips ushered Lacey inside and shut the door. "She said she isn't feeling well."

"Do you mind if I talk to her?"

"Of course. You know where to go."

"Thanks, Mrs. Philips."

Lacey ran up the stairs two at a time.

"Mara. It isn't as bad as it looks."

"Really. Easy for you to say. You don't have a picture of you eating a hotdog, oh wait, of a dick in a bun, floating around the internet. You also have all of your hair. I can't even sit in class without worrying if one of Kaitlin's secret minions is stalking me with scissors. The pile of poop baggies seems so micro at this point."

"But you can't give in. You can't let her win."

"Lacey, you can't tell me what to do in this situation. I didn't even sign up for this. You did that wonderful thing without my consent. I don't want this for my life. I just want to get out of high school and go to college where the airheads just stick to themselves and leave the education for the actual intellectuals."

Lacey backed up from her friend and plopped on the bed. "I'm sorry I caused all this for you. It wasn't my intention."

"I know. It isn't you. But what if today's prank is…I don't know, throwing bleach on the hair that I have left. I did smell some yesterday.

"I think that means that they cleaned the bathrooms…finally."

"I hear girls laughing up there. Does that mean school is a go?" Mrs. Philip's yelled from the bottom of the steps.

Mara sighed then let her head drop to a very reluctant nod.

"We'll be right down, Mrs. Philips."

"What's one more day anyway. Tomorrow is Election Day."

"That's the spirit."

☑   ☑   ☑

"See, that wasn't so bad."

Both Lacey and Mara walked home from school. The jocks clique followed them and the "most adorable" couple who has been together since kindergarten walked ahead.

"I have a feeling that their silence today simply marked the calm before the storm."

"Oh, relax. You have this election in the bag. I took secret votes from everyone except *them* today and trust me when I say, you're a shoo-in. You have nothing to fear."

Lacey's phone chimed. The couple's phones sang out in the same ringtone, and then the jocks' phones behind them also sounded.

"I guess I'm not invited to the party." Even though she attempted a snicker, Mara knew she couldn't ignore her gut. *Here entereth the storm.*

"Yup, no partying for you." Lacey went to jam her phone back into her pocket.

"Tell me, Lacey."

But just then her phone beeped. Keeping her eyes on Lacey, Mara pulled her phone out from her back pocket.

It was a text message from an unknown number. Mara clicked it open to find a GIF of a fat cartoon girl twerking. Each time the booty came toward the screen, the cartoon ripped its pants, revealing a bleeding cat.

Mara threw her phone down onto the sidewalk and ran. Tears rushed down her cheeks and neck. At every street she approached, her peers were snickering, and Mara knew they were laughing at her.

☑ ☑ ☑

The stage was ready for the nominees to make their final remarks before the winners were announced.

Principal Carson peeked from the stage's curtain and locked eyes with Lacey as if questioning where Mara was.

Lacey upturned her palms and shrugged.

Applause began when the curtain parted and revealed Principal Carson at the podium.

"The winner of the class 2020 president is...Mara Philips."

From the shadows of the stage's wings, Mara stepped onto the stage. Principal Carson sighed in relief then began the wave of applause.

After shaking the principal's hand, Mara took her place at the podium for her acceptance speech.

"Thank you. With our great leader's permission, I'd like to add a slide show for my speech."

The rosy-cheeked man nodded.

A projector screen lowered as the lights dimmed.

Grainy numbers counted down: three, two, one. The screen blackened as Mara began her speech.

"I want to take a moment to talk about my honorable and worthy opponent. You all know Kaitlin Waters."

Pictures of Mara's nemesis flashed on the big screen. "She came to your school as a freshman and quickly rose to the top of the cheer pyramid, was the easy choice for class president, and, like, totally throws the best parties!"

Some of the student body *whooed* as Kaitlin took a not so humble yet forced curtsy from her place on stage.

"But what you don't know, is that your beloved Kaitlin was once known as Nancy."

A photo of her appeared from her elementary days. She was shoving chocolate bars in her mouth and looked to be about five times heavier.

Kaitlin lost all composure, mouth agape.

Mara simply winked at her, then continued.

"Nancy was a fat girl. Yup, just like me. You may be asking how she managed to climb to the top of your school looking like that, right?"

The next photo that flashed was a very recent photo of her throwing up into the porcelain throne.

"That's right. Instead of going to fat camp, as she had promised me, her once best friend, she got rid of all that lard by vomiting it all up. *Mmmm*, doesn't that sound delicious?"

A video started playing.

Mortified, Kaitlin ran off stage. Vice Principal Hudson followed her while the principal went down the stage stairs, making his way to the projector room.

"I know how much you all enjoyed the pictures of me in my heyday, and really, who wouldn't love that GIF."

Mara stayed strong and held back the tears even though she knew that the GIF was playing right above her. Before the principal made it to the back of the room, Mara turned to the projector, struck a match, and lit a string that dangled from the bottom of the screen.

Screaming students started stumbling over each other, racing to get to the exit. Lacey went in the opposite direction when she noticed Mara simply watching the screen go up in flames.

"Mara, let's go," her friend shouted.

Closing her eyes, Mara could feel the warmth on her skin. Her tears began to fall.

She was jolted from her thoughts, and she saw Kaitlin run past her, down the stairs following everyone else.

Mara flailed trying to escape the grips of whomever had picked her up like a sack of potatoes. "Let me go. I don't want to be here anymore."

Finally reaching outside, Mara was plopped onto the ground, a short distance from the rest of the students. Lacey stayed with her while the vice principal went to meet up with Principal Carson.

"Are you okay?" Lacey asked.

Mara curled into a ball on the grass. "I was a fool to think that this year would be any different than any other year. I just want it to be over."

"I don't think that setting the school on fire was the best way to speed up the school year."

Mara stood up. Backing away from her friend, she shouted, "No. You don't get it. I don't want to be here anymore. I hate my past. I hate my life. I hate Kaitlin or Nancy, or whatever you want to call her. I hate the adults. They never see what's going on. No one pays attention. Even now...what do you think will happen now? I'll be the one in trouble because I had the guts to show the truth. Kaitlin will take her place as class president. And I...if they can find me, I'll probably end up sitting in front of doctors asking me, 'How does that make you feel?'"

"Mr. Hudson!" Lacey, growing more concerned now for her friend's mental state, called for some adult backup. "Mr. Carson!"

Continuing to add distance between her and her friend, Mara took in a deep breath of fresh air. "Save your breath, Lace. I'm tired of fighting the world and their expectations. They are more worried about their precious school burning down anyway." She turned and walked away.

Sirens and lights whistled and flashed as rescue teams arrived on site.

"Mara!"

☑   ☑   ☑

Mara sat under her willow tree by the lake. She watched as blood flowed from her wrists into the calm waters she soaked in. She closed her heavy eyelids. A slight wrestling of leaves caught her attention, but she no longer had the curiosity nor the energy to look.

"Mara, can you hear me? Wake up. Don't leave me."

"Step back, Lacey. We'll take it from here. Mara, I'm a paramedic. I'm here to help. Stay with us, okay?"

EXPERIMENTAL 

SARI MATTILA

I was sitting in a big, green armchair in Oliphant house, where she kept her office.

"Boss lady." I wondered why she kept that sign on her desk? To keep her patients in check? To up her status?

It amused me, that's what it did. I laughed inside and put up half a smile, which she probably noticed.

"So, Ciara. Have you collected all your belongings?" the lady doctor said.

"What? My belongings?"

"No? Well, that's okay, we can send for them later. I assume you can give up the key to your apartment?"

"Why?" I asked, blinking like an idiot.

"Well, your first day of voluntary treatment is about to begin. We discussed this before, miss Young."

I tried to think hard but had no idea what she was talking about.

"This is a hospital for voluntary closed ward treatment, including the one you applied for. You remember? The form said: 'I'd like to apply for an experimental course of treatment.' 'Those elected will be informed later.' Miss Young, you were lucky enough to be elected." She continued, "Your movements will be somewhat restricted; this is a closed ward after all—but we will take good care of you and monitor your health frequently. You've made the right choice," she said with a smile and showed me out.

At first, I was numb. Then waves of anxiety took over me.

What had I done?

Well, I had tried to kill myself a few months back, but that wasn't news. A few friends knew about it, since they had escorted me back home from the hospital.

As much as it'd been a nice gesture of friendship to reminisce on, it'd rather been a feeling of complete shame and humiliation of my own creation.

And once again I was suffering from my own stupid actions.

'*You were elected.*' For what exactly?

I looked at the pills the nurses offered me and gulped them down with the sour taste of contempt, then put my head gently against my pillow. I let the situation sink in and the salty tears run free.

An acute ward meant closed windows and doors, no exit without permission. And I had signed myself in for the next three months. I couldn't believe it.

The room spinning, I closed my eyes and drifted off.

I woke up two in the afternoon the next day. I jumped straight out of the bed in a cold sweat and headed to the office.

"We believe in swift execution. To treat your symptoms, we've made an excellent plan and there's nothing more effective than starting early," an older male in a long, white jacket said to me right after I was shown to his room.

"Oh, I am Doctor Joseph Carlyle. The specialist treating you while your stay with us," he said in a well-learned, friendly manner and shook my flaccid hand, still sweaty and cold.

A bit lightheaded, I replied with a soft 'mmm.'

"The idea is you can explore the other participants reactions and motivation. Perhaps you can learn something – what you don't want to become, for example."

Learn what I don't want to become? What the hell did he mean by that?

"So, it's a type of group therapy?" I asked.

"No, not at all. You'll be paired with one patient only for your sessions. We believe we've made the right choice in your case," he said with a smirk that was surely meant to be assuring but only left me confused.

"With your disorder, Miss Young, you have a slight risk of psychosis. Sometimes preventive work is giving a moral shock to your system. So, today you'll meet someone with a very violent past and numerous psychotic breaks. Perhaps that'll motivate you to keep taking your meds. Mr. Badgley has refused to take his and ... Well, you may see the results yourself today."

A sweat surfaced on my skin.

"We'll begin soon," the doctor said and showed me out of the room.

I felt waves of trepidation move through my body. I kept walking along the hall, just to get the uneasiness off my chest.

What was to come? I hadn't expected anything like this. Then again, I hadn't had expectations at all.

I was led into something that looked like a small conference room. There was a man not much older than me, already sitting and waiting in a chair. He kept his dark brown eyes pinned on me from the moment I entered.

I'd barely sat down when he already started talking.

"I'm Ricky B, as in"—he flew his hand across the air in a wavelike motion and made a buzzing sound—"you know, bees. The creative, hardworking little champs you step on every summer, and they sting like hell." He smirked and let out an extremely off-putting, shrill laugh.

I kept silent. This was what they'd thought would cure me? Seeing a lunatic at work?

"I bet you have some pretty name like Cindy or Bella. No, don't tell me. You are ... It's—" he kept muttering and breathing heavily at me. I found it unnerving, so I opened my mouth.

"My name is Ciara," I said.

"I knew that! Why'd you tell me?" he said, standing up from the chair, hand fisted. Two nurses in the corner of the room moved a few steps closer, ready to take over.

His eyes burned for a moment, before he suddenly sat down again, gave a hard sigh, and flailed the nurses off with his hand.

"I'm fine, I'm fine. Take a pill, Agnes," he said to one of the nurses and smiled in amusement.

"So, where were we doctor? Can you properly introduce my new partner in crime?" he exclaimed and laughed hard at his own joke.

Really, I thought again, this was supposed to help me?

The sessions continued, as weeks rolled on. I didn't learn much, except how angry Ricky could become when questioned for his antics.

Before one session I asked Doctor Carlyle how many more he was planning for.

"Truth be told, Ciara, we're calling this off. The board and I have made an evaluation of the situation and it seems ... Uhm ... It seems we've made a mistake," he said looking down and swallowed.

"Really?" I said, my eyes widening.

"Yes. All we have to do is tell Ricky this'll be the final session," he said quietly.

I entered the room with him and saw Ricky already sitting there. The doctor explained the situation as calmly as he could.

"So, this will be the last session between you two," he said with a steady voice.

Only seconds later Ricky grimaced with contempt and rage, and shot from his chair over to mine, and took a hold of my neck with his left arm. In his right hand he had what looked like a sharpened butter knife.

"One step closer, and I'll stab her!" he yelled.

The doctor and nurses left speechless, couldn't do anything when Ricky took off with me in the side of his arm, then rampaged his way through the cafeteria and found his way to the biggest window facing the garden outside.

He looked at the window with enthusiasm and then me.

"No—you won't, won't you?" I said and right after he pulled me through with him.

I felt the glass cut my skin but that was nothing compared to the pain in my knees after falling five feet.

Ricky stood up and dragged me with him. I didn't protest; I was too scared for my life.

We ran, until he saw an old man standing by his car, pushed him aside and told me to get in.

I did as he said, even though a voice in the back of my head told me not to.

Then, driving off recklessly, he opened the glove-box and smirked.

"We can definitely use this," he said holding a gun. "Have you ever fired one?"

"No," I said shaking with fear.

"The beer in there isn't bad either," he said, took the gun to his side and pushed the pedal violently.

After a few miles into the highway, we saw a cop speeding our way.

"Take the gun."

"What? Why?" I said.

"That cop is following us. Take him out," Ricky said with a blank expression, keeping his eyes on the road.

"What? No, no I won't!" I cried and shook my head.

"Do it now," he said tightening his voice.

"Stop it!" I yelled. My heart raced in panic.

"Do I need to do everything myself? You're not being too helpful, Ciara. Mark my words, you're not," he said and steered while reaching for the gun.

I gasped as if it was going to be my last breath and closed my eyes.

I heard a shot and next saw the police car fishtail off the road.

"Oh my god!" I screamed and pulled back in my seat, looking back one more time at the crashed car, before Ricky pushed the pedal to the floor again.

"Hand me the beer," he ordered.

"You're driving!"

"I just killed a man. Does it look like I care?" he said with a piercing stare.

Silently I handed over the beer.

We landed a small motel room in the middle of god-knows-where. No phones, nothing. Not even a fridge.

Ricky jumped on the bed with the gun and gave me a firm stare.

"Come on. Relax. We're good now."

"Far from it," I said standing at a distance, still nervous from what had happened.

Here I was, sharing a motel room with an insane killer—a room with 70's brightly colored flower tapestry, which didn't make it any better.

"Sit with me," he ordered.

I didn't reply. I kept looking around for a way to escape.

"Baby cheeks, you should lighten up. Life's a party, not a funeral. Well, for us it isn't. Sit down."

I couldn't believe this.

"What did you call me?" I said.

"You have cute, chubby cheeks, just like a baby. That's what," he said with an undisrupted stare.

"You're saying I'm fat?"

"Sit or I'll shoot you and then you'll definitely sit - to the sound of my bullets," he said raising his voice just enough, so that I followed his orders.

"So, how'd you try to off yourself?" he asked with a straight face.

"Excuse me?"

"I read the file they gave me, don't pretend you didn't. So, tell me," he said and popped another beer open.

"Pills. Just pills," I said, trying to cover my nervousness with a small sigh.

"Ha. That's the coward's way out. I prefer a shot in the head. There's something poetic about it, I guess, maybe," he said and gulped down half a can all at once.

"You're ... you're cray–" I stammered.

"What—crazy? Just try me," he said flashing his teeth in a grimace.

My chin trembled as tears came out, then my whole body followed. I felt like I was trapped in a bad dream.

Ricky sat up and stared at me.

"The society has made you think that we need to be whatever they want us to be. You think you know who I am because of some ink on a piece of paper? Don't you go calling people names when you don't know shit about them. Understood?"

"Y-yes," I replied eyes closed, still shaking.

"Good," he said and lay back on the bed. "You're my ticket to freedom. I thought I'd reward you by letting you go, but you've become too much of a risk and an asset at this point. Sorry for that, I guess."

I heard a lighter snap and smelled a strong aroma of tobacco.

I opened my eyes and confronted his.

"Are you going to kill me?" I asked quietly.

"Don't pretend like you know my next move," he said and blew smoke out of his mouth.

"It was an honest question," I said toughening my voice a bit.

"Well, I'm sort of fond of your chubby cheeks. But then again, you might deceive me. Our friendship is the most uncommon one."

"Friendship? There isn't one! You kidnapped me," I said with my eyes wide. This man!

He took to his left side and moved closer.

"Like I said: it's the most uncommon one. Peculiar. Created by circumstance only; you need me, I need you," he said and smirked at me followed by a devilish laugh.

"Has anyone ever told you you're delusional?" I said sparked with irritation.

"You like gambling, do you? Little girl, I'd advise you not to. You've seen my rage."

In a flash, he came even closer, sending his eyes across my face and body in what seemed excitement. Waves of trepidation rushed right through me.

"You said you need me, so I should be fine. And I'm not a girl, I'm 28," I replied as confident as I could.

"And she's got attitude. Shut the lights. I want to sleep. And don't even think about running. The motel owner is my friend."

With that command I shut the lights and started a night of crippling anxiety, in a bed I could never truly sleep in, with only one thought in my head: I wished I'd never been elected.

A few days went by, and I couldn't get a moment to myself without Ricky constantly monitoring my every move. Escaping seemed impossible, until I figured it out.

Another morning came and he woke up to the sight of me kissing his belly.

He startled and reached for the gun.

"Just relax," I said and instantly felt like I had sold my soul to the devil.

The moment passed and I felt like I had him in his weakest state.

"I could lay here forever, baby cheeks," he said smiling at me.

"You're the most confusing person I've ever met. And I've met a few contradicting assholes in my time," I replied still in his arms.

"You've met the wrong assholes. I'm a new brand of bad; you can never have enough of me, and I can never have enough of you," he said breathing down my neck.

"God, the confidence. You're pure evil," I sneered.

"But don't you like the taste of it?" he said flashing his crazy eyes.

As defenseless as he seemed laying there, butt naked on the dirty sheets, I couldn't trust my luck enough to grab the keys and run. I scolded myself in my thoughts.

Then suddenly he said: "Let's hit the road. I'm tired of this place." And so, we did.

We drove down the highway and stopped by some lakeside hills. It was a pretty scene, to be honest.

We sat down on a lonely piece of rock facing the lake.

"I killed some people, you know," he said.

I froze up.

"Why'd you do it?" I said trying to look chill.

"You really want to know? You want to hear all the gory details?" he said his eyes lit up.

"No. I just want to ... maybe, understand you."

"I killed them because I wanted to see if it'd make me feel something," he replied, his eyes lost somewhere in the distance.

"Well, did it?" I said genuinely waiting for the answer.

"No."

I gulped and just stared, while he kept pondering.

Before I got the chance to choke on the unnerving silence, he kicked a can of beer down the rock.

I startled.

"I fuckin' hate people, man," he murmured.

Then he shook himself to perk up.

In that moment, I noticed the car keys drop out of his pocket, just behind him.

I tried to control myself. I had to be clever with this.

"By the way, did they give you the full description?" Ricky said with a slight, quickly disappearing sneer.

"Of what?" I said, frowning.

"Of me, babe. Did you read the part where it says we have the same disorder?" he proclaimed smiling wider and wider as the thought sank into my head.

"No."

"Yes, babe. You and I are the same crazy."

The words sank even deeper, and I shut off.

"Really? They left that out. How inconsiderate," Ricky snickered.

"Shut up, shitface! You're playing me!" I yelled, cheeks flushed, unable to control myself anymore.

"No fuckin' way. I'm telling the truth," Ricky said and burst into an uncontrollable laughter.

He kept shaking his head in amusement.

The keys were finally in my grasp. I took them while he was still distracted by his own laugh.

Then, after a moment he said: "Really. After all this … You don't know? I am the absolute truth, even when it fuckin' hurts. I am the judge. The one who keeps balancing the death score. Saints and sinners, everyone's the SAME. I don't separate."

The look on his face was as serious as it could get.

"What the hell are you talking about?" I said anxiety pounding in my chest.

"I don't lie. I just take what's mine."

That was the moment I knew I had to do it.

I stood up, kicked him to the water and ran as fast as I could.

He fired at me, and the bullet hit the side of my leg.

I kept running even thought my knees felt weak, and finally managed to reach the car, put the keys in and speed off.

A few hours later the car ran out of gas and finally gave in half a mile before I reached the asylum.

I dragged myself across the blooming garden and reached the door right before my knees went weak again.

I opened the door with my left hand while the other one was holding my still bleeding right leg.

Blood kept dripping on the floor as I dragged myself to the information desk.

I think I'm ready now," I said out of breath.

"Ready for what?" the lady behind the desk asked.

"Therapy," I said, fell to the ground and lost consciousness.

THE FOREIGNER
ADAM D SIPPERLY 

Jax sat in the back of a high-speed cruiser with his face plastered against the rear window. He paid little attention to his driver's ramblings and watched as his former kingdom faded in the distance. It was near impossible for Jax to accept how quickly things had fallen apart. In a single election, everything had changed. The Exiled now ruled and chaos spread throughout the lands unchecked.

The Fifths, Jax's people and rightful rulers of the kingdom were now on the run. Most had fled to the Burnt Oasis while others had retreated through the Southern Passage. Several battles were now underway as the fight for a place to call home spread like wildfire.

Things were never meant to be this way. Jax had been a fair and just king. He had worked hard to bring peace to the land and deserved admiration, respect, and loyalty. Yet still, his followers had turned on him in favor of empty promises. The Exiled had wormed their way back in and undone everything. Jax felt a chill race up his spine and he pulled his cloak tight. He cast one final glance toward his kingdom and made a silent promise to one day return and restore order.

Twelve Days Earlier

King Jax stood in his throne room admiring the grand kingdom spread out before him. This room, at the top of his Tower, was one of his favorites. He could see all. From his neighboring clan in the Burnt Oasis to the furthest clan of the Dunes. This land was his to command.

"The Fourths have made steady progress," a quiet voice chirped from the king's left. A portly man with bucked teeth peered around the king to admire the Burnt Oasis. "Several new plateaus in the last week alone. From what I have heard they've done it all with only one casualty." Jeremiah slid his spectacles up the bridge of his nose. "Impressive."

"We need to keep a close eye on them." Victoria stood at the Tower's edge, her cloak whipping freely in the winds. "I fear they will make a pass for the crown soon."

Victoria was the antithesis of Jeremiah. While he was a quiet strategist, she was a fiery warrior. She kept her hair short and wore a freshly pressed uniform each day. Jax had never seen without a spear across her back and daggers by her side.

"Bah!" Jeremiah called out. "They would lose the election and you know it!"

The king grinned. Jeremiah was his most loyal supporter.

"Perhaps, but still." Victoria leaned over the Tower's edge.

"Would you mind stepping back from that ledge?"

Victoria took great effort to roll her eyes at Jeremiah. The two were always butting heads like this but the king needed them. One to help decide where force was needed and the other to apply it.

"Be a shame if I, oh!" Victoria spun suddenly so that one leg was dangling over the Tower's edge.

"Stop it!" Jeremiah crept backward, visibly shaken. "You know I hate that!"

Victoria hung over the edge with just one foot and three fingers keeping her safe. Her smile was devious.

"Come on, V." Jax waved her in. "You've tortured the poor man enough."

"Fine." Victoria pursed her lips and vaulted back to safety. "But you know I was okay." She casually strolled to Jax's side and took a seat, feet draped over the side of his throne. "Have you heard about the new guy?"

"New guy?" Jax's left eyebrow rose.

"Came over the wall a few days back like it was nothing. Been in the Dunes since."

"One of theirs then?"

"Foreigner." Victoria had pulled one of her daggers free and was balancing it on her outstretched palm. "No clan has claimed him."

"Jeremiah ..." Jax's brow had furrowed. "Send a runner through the Southern Passage. I'd like to meet this newcomer."

"Yes sir!"

Jeremiah saluted and shimmed across the back wall. Victoria laughed as he scuttled down the stairs.

Ten Days Earlier

"Ready for the election?" Victoria had her back to the king, both feet dangling over the Tower's edge.

"Of course." Jax sat in his throne with a drink in hand. "Nobody even bothers running against me anymore. It's almost too easy."

"Mmm." She nodded and continued to stare out at the Burnt Oasis. "I suppose so."

"King!" Jeremiah came storming into the room, red-faced and breathing hard. "The runners have returned." He doubled over and tried to catch his breath.

"Deep breaths." Jax held his drink out to Jeremiah. "Is the newcomer with them?"

"No." Jeremiah took a swig of the drink. A few droplets dribbled down his chin. "He's on his way still. Told the runners he was visiting the Great Forest first."

"To what end?" Jax's brow furrowed.

"Sightseeing?" Victoria shrugged her shoulders but did not turn to face the men.

"I wish she wouldn't sit out there." Jeremiah handed the cup back to his king and retreated into the stairwell. "May I go?"

Jax waved his hand and Jeremiah hurried down the stairs. The king settled back into his chair with arms folded across his chest. He stared out to the Great Forest, wondering what this newcomer was up to.

Seven Days Earlier

The air rang with echoes of wood against wood and the grunts of soldiers. There was a thick cloud of dust hanging in the air between Jax and Victoria as they sparred with training spears. Victoria currently had the upper hand with Jax pinned against the arena wall. She pressed her body into his, her breath hot on the nape of his neck.

"Yield!" She shouted the words though they were mere inches apart.

"No!" he grunted back.

Victoria was a great fighter but at times she relied too heavily on brute force. Jax knew how to use this against her. With one fluid motion he stopped struggling, allowed her to slip into him, and twisted free of her hold. Victoria fell into the wall and Jax pounced. There was a trickle of blood at the corner of her mouth.

"Yield." He almost laughed at the look on her face as he pushed her into the wall.

At that very moment, Jeremiah came stumbling onto the practice field. Jax, momentarily distracted, released his pressure on Victoria. She slipped from his hold, swung her spear, and cracked him across the ribs. Jax let out a groan and crumpled to the ground. Victoria placed the blunted tip of her spear into his back.

"Dead."

"Cheat." He pushed the word through gritted teeth.

"A good fighter uses what they're given. You taught me that." She removed the spear from his back and retreated.

"My lord ..." Jeremiah helped the king stand. "Apologies for the interruption but I bring news on our visitor."

"Again, with this blasted man! What now? Why is he not standing before me yet?" Jax stood and dusted off his shirt.

"He now travels to the Burnt Oasis. Word is he meets with their clan leader."

"I'm done waiting!" Jax tossed his spear to Victoria who caught it without flinching. "Tomorrow we ride! I will face this newcomer on my own!"

Six Days Earlier

"Rise for your king!" Victoria's voice echoed throughout the tunnels.

The king and his troop of soldiers had come upon the clans of the Southern Passage amid a mid-day meal. Upon Victoria's proclamation, all had dropped their plates and hastened to their feet. Or at least to their knees. The ceiling was low in this section of the tunnel and many could not stand to their full height.

"King Jax." A woman covered in dirt and sweat crawled forward. "We had not expected you on this day. What brings you to our lands?"

"We travel in search of a foreigner. He has been using your tunnels to travel freely between our brother clans. I seek his intent."

"Yes." The woman cast a nervous glance back to her clansmen. "He thought you may visit."

"He did?" Jeremiah added from behind.

"He is gathering support from the clans."

"Support?" Victoria's jaw clenched.

"My King …" The woman bowed as best she could manage. "He looks to challenge you in the upcoming election, but I swear we do not intend to break our oaths."

"Good!" Victoria had pulled free a dagger which was now pointed at the woman. Jax held a hand up to calm her.

"Thank you for the invaluable information." Jax placed a hand on the back of her bowed head. "Your loyalty will be rewarded." He dismissed the woman and faced those he traveled with. "V, you are to take our soldiers and travel to the Burnt Oasis. Head off this newcomer. Do whatever you must to stop him from reaching the Tower. He cannot ask for a vote if he has not traveled the lands."

"Yes." Victoria dipped her head and raced away. The others followed, save Jeremiah.

"And us?" he asked.

"We travel to the Dunes. We must secure their vote as a precaution. We have the Tower and the Southern Passage. Once we have locked down a third clan we can deal with this usurper."

Jax clenched his teeth and headed deeper into the tunnels.

Five Days Earlier

The two men emerged from the Southern Passage a day later covered in sweat and grime. Their skin prickled beneath a blazing sun as sweat pooled up, dripped to the ground, and disappeared into the sand at their feet. A cool breeze rolled across the land and despite their current state, both men shivered. They had arrived at the Dunes, a vast land with great potential.

As they made their way through town Jax was pleased to see the clansmen hard at work. "This bodes well." He waved at several workers as they passed.

"I'm not sure." Jeremiah squinted through his glasses. "Something seems off. We should meet with the clan leader."

Jax nodded in silent agreement and made for the center of town. Here they found the man they had been searching for. He was surrounded by at least half a dozen others, all knee-deep in a giant mud puddle.

"Nathan!" Jax towered over the small man. "What is the meaning of this?"

Nathan looked up with a smile on his face. "Well, we're putting in a lake!"

"I did not order this!" Jax's face was growing hot.

"Nope." Nathan shrugged. "But we still wanted one."

"You can't just ..."

Jax then spotted several fortresses surrounding this new mud pit. They stood half complete, abandoned by the workers.

"I am your king!" he shouted. "I demand you finish my projects!"

"Paul said we didn't have to listen to you no more." Nathan went back to the mud. "I like Paul."

"Paul?" Jax turned to Jeremiah who shrunk back. "All this just for a name?"

Jeremiah said nothing. Jax balled his hands into fists and spun back to confront Nathan.

"This will not stand. I will deal with Paul first but let it be known I will restore order here!"

Nathan did not reply as the king turned on his heel and ran back to the tunnels. Jax had lost the Dunes and was now worried about the others. He had to gather support before it was too late.

Four Days Earlier

"You're joking." Jax sat on a tree branch with the Forest clan leader across from him. "You'd turn on me?"

Ethan shrugged. "Paul made some good points. I don't think I've ever enjoyed living here. I miss the Dunes sometimes. But with you in charge, I can't even visit."

"I brought order to chaos!" Jax was beet red.

"Nobody asked you to. Did you know I have a brother in the Southern Passage? Your order makes it so I can never share the sun with him. Explain that?"

"His time in the sun will come. You know this! We cannot just abandon everything we've worked so hard for."

"I'm sorry Jax but Paul has my vote."

Ethan gave a halfcocked smile, shrugged, and dropped from the tree.

"Not good." Jeremiah was standing behind Jax, his arms wrapped around a tree trunk. "Not good at all."

"No." Jax's jaw was tight. "Let's hope Victoria has fared better."

Two Days Earlier

Victoria ran across the plateaus at an impressive speed without fear. She darted across bridges and traversed tightropes with ease. Jeremiah hung back in the tunnels with a book pressed to his face, refusing to watch. Victoria crossed the last bridge, jumped with a twirl over a shallow stream of lava, and landed with a flourish. She winked at Jax.

"You bring good news?" He smiled as she rose to meet him.

"Just a name, Paul."

"We've heard the same. The Dunes and Forest are voting for him in the coming election."

"He was working to sway the Burnt Oasis as well. The clan leader stands with you, but his people do not. I've done what I can."

"And Paul still travels for the Tower?"

"He does. I tried to stop him, but he destroyed several bridges in his retreat. I could not follow."

"All we've worked for is coming undone." Jax pinched the bridge of his nose and sighed. "We march home and face this head-on."

Jax pushed past Jeremiah and ducked into the tunnels. The others followed in silence.

One Day Earlier

Paul was waiting for the king when he arrived home. He sat at the base of the Tower under the watchful eye of several soldiers. This foreigner was nothing like Jax had expected. He was tall, lanky, and had short blond hair. He wore a jacket of dark leather and his pants were filled with holes. He carried no visible weapons.

"King Jax!" Paul's voice was deep, laced with a thick accent. "The man I've been looking for." He smiled and held out a hand.

"Paul." Jax ignored his outstretched hand. "The foreigner come to steal my crown. Why?"

"Can't say I'm the biggest fan of the way you run things around here." Paul dropped his arm. "Seems like a few of the clan leaders agree with me."

Jax disliked this man more by the second.

"When I win this election, you will be exiled."

"If you win." Paul's smile widened. "And if I win, you're free to stay. Of course, things will be different for you. No more easy living for King Jax."

"You are not a citizen of these lands. You cannot run against me."

"Oh, I can!" Paul pulled a scroll from his back pocket. "The Dunes told me all about the upcoming election, so I got the clan leaders to sign off on my citizenship. You weren't around but your scribe took care of your approvals."

The king grimaced but did not bother with the scroll. "Victoria stay with Paul. Tomorrow I want you to personally see him exiled." Jax pushed past Paul and entered the Tower. "I've got a scribe to deal with."

Day Of The Election

"Paul ..." Nathan smirked as he cast the last vote cementing their new king.

"I believe this is now mine?" Paul pulled the crown from Jax's head. "Time to shake things up."

Paul strolled to the Tower's edge and looked out at the kingdom. He pulled in a deep breath, placed both pinkies in his mouth, and let free a strained whistle.

"Those who voted for me are welcome to stay." He looked over his shoulder. "The others should run."

Victoria fell into an attack pose. Paul did not bat an eye. Instead, he smiled as the sounds of a war cry reached their ears.

"That would be my people coming to take back what is rightfully theirs." Paul's smile curled. "The Exiled have returned!" He held his hands out wide.

Jax felt his body go stiff. This was far worse than anything he could have predicted.

"I said to run." Paul nodded toward the stairs.

Victoria grabbed Jax by the collar and ran for the stairs. He remained speechless. Outside they were met with a small army. The Exiled were pouring over the wall by the handful.

"Jax!" Victoria shook him by the shoulders. "You need to climb the wall! I'll hold them off, but you have to make it to the escape cruiser! Seek the help of the Ancients. They're the only ones who can help us now!"

Jax's eyes were glossed over. Victoria slapped him across the face and he finally snapped out of it.

"The wall, now!" She shouted.

"I'll come back for you; I promise."

He squeezed her hand and ran for the wall. An Exiled soldier came barreling at him from the left. Jax ducked beneath his attack and launched the soldier over his shoulder. He dared not look back and kept running for the wall. The sounds of war followed hot on his heels as he climbed up and over. His feet touched down on the other side and he ran faster than ever before. His cruiser was waiting exactly where he had expected it. He dove in, strapped on a safety belt, and told the driver to get moving. Jax sat in the back seat watching until his kingdom had completely faded from view.

"Jax?" A gentle voice in the cruiser broke his concentration. "Are you even listening?"

"Huh?" He looked up and caught his mother's eye in the rearview mirror.

"I asked if you had fun at the playground today? Quite a few kids today."

"It was fun." He shrugged. "Until the sixth graders took the big slide from us."

"Oh. That's not nice. I hardly think the sixth graders should be out there anyway. I'll have to speak to their parents."

Jax felt the worries of the day roll off his back. He would let the Exiled win for now but come Monday they would experience the full wrath of the Ancients. And then, Jax would take back his throne and hold it by any means necessary. After today he was done with elections.

Sweat drips down my back outside in the Arizona summer as I balance the heavy box on my knee. My mom fiddles with the lock on the front door for what feels like an eternity until she finally gets it. We both sigh dramatically when the first gush of air conditioning hits our faces, and then giggle as we shuffle inside.

"Set that by the couch and put something good on tv. I'll grab us some lemonade and be right back," Mom says.

"Okay," I mumble.

I let the box slide out of my hands, but don't immediately look for the remote. The couch is calling my name, and I just want to sit for a few minutes. My butt barely hits the overstuffed cushions before mom is breezing back in the room the way she always does. Her excitement is infectious as always, but I'm still tired from all the errands we ran this morning.

Her hand moves lightly to her hip. "You do want to do this right? Because this was your idea and I just spent a lot of money, kid."

"I do. I'm just hot," I drag the last word out even though I know it makes me sound whiny.

"We only have today to get all these buttons, posters, and flyers ready. Trust me, you'll have this student body president thing in the bag if we just get it done." Before she finishes talking, she has picked up the remote and is scanning the on-screen guide for something to watch. She settles on an episode of *The Simpsons* with a plot revolving around Lisa and I feel like it's appropriate; if Lisa ever got to be in eighth grade, she would definitely run for student body president.

Mom gives me some ideas for the posters but then backs off. Some parents try to live vicariously through their kids, but my mom really just wants to help me get what I want. She moves on to assembling the buttons while I start drawing out my first poster, carefully, in pencil.

If you had asked me at the end of sixth grade if I would ever consider running for student council, I would have laughed out loud. That was before I met Jessica Winstaff. Jessica was pure evil. She was the kind of girl who had to one-up everyone and always made you feel like you weren't enough. You would think in today's world even kids would know to be better, right? You see all these hashtag squad goals, and women's empowerment now, but Jessica obviously missed those posts. Maybe she's not on Instagram.

Two months ago, she moved into my neighborhood, where I learned to ride a bike, where I know every single person, and where I always felt safe. For some reason, her focus, from day one, was on making my life a living hell. So far, she's tried to steal my best friend Lizzy, kissed Mark (the first boy I've ever like-liked), and even though I can't prove it, I think she egged our front door. Those are just the big things; I could spend days regaling you with tales of all the little things she's done, but I won't. Basically, she always finds ways to make me feel small and helpless.

Anyway, school started three weeks ago, and she told Lizzy that she was going to run for class president. She doesn't want to be class president; she just doesn't want this girl Amy to get it. She actually said that. She is only running to beat Amy. I have no idea what she did to bring on Jessica's wrath, but Amy seems like a nice girl who is just shy and doesn't really talk to a ton of people. Now, listen, I'm not like, the most popular girl in school or anything, but I know these kids. We've all gone to school together basically our whole lives and given the choice of me, Amy, or some new girl, they're going to choose me. I think. I'm pretty sure. I know it's petty and not very girl power of me to run out of spite, but I just can't let her win again.

So, today, Mom and I ran out to five different craft stores and now we are going to create campaign supplies. I'm a little fuzzy on the details as far as the debates and voting happens since I decided to run so late in the game, but I know tomorrow I have to give a speech about why I think I'll make a good president, so I can't mess around.

After four hours, our living room is littered with paper, markers, and other crafting supplies, but we've finished over a hundred buttons and fifteen posters. It should be more than enough.

Mom goes to cook dinner while I work on a speech; it has to be epic. It has to inspire the entire seventh-grade class. It has to be better than anything Jessica has to say. I start and stop dozens of times before Mom calls me into the kitchen for dinner.

"How's it going?" she asks, around a bite of chicken.

I push my food around on my plate. "I dunno. I'm not sure what to say."

"Well, why do you want to be president?" she asks.

I almost drop my fork. She knows why I'm really running. "Huh?"

"Why do you want to be president? What do you think you want to do in that position? It's a lot of pressure, you know? If you can put into words why you want to do it and why they should vote for you, you'll be golden."

A light went on over my head. "Mom, you're a genius. Can I finish this in my room?"

She squints at me like she's going to say no. "Fine, but don't leave your plate in your room. And don't just work until bed. You gotta pack up all your campaign stuff to take tomorrow."

For two hours, I polish the most beautiful speech. It's humble, to the point, and a total winner. My fellow students will be in awe of me after they hear it. There's no way anyone could not vote for me. Even Jessica might give me her vote. I roll the posters and pack them and the buttons in my backpack before I get in bed way too excited to sleep.

In the morning, I eat two toaster pastries and dust a huge glass of milk for breakfast. Mom's eyes follow me around the kitchen over the cup of coffee she hugs to her face.

"Kick butt today," she says and kisses my forehead.

"I will! Love you," I reply before I run out to meet Lizzy at the bus stop.

Lizzy and I both proudly fasten Vote for Samantha! pins to our tops during the short ride to school. I tell her all about my speech in whispers, so no one else will hear. Jessica is sitting near the front of the bus since she was one of the last kids to get on. She didn't make eye contact, but she did flip her hair in my direction before she sat down. I hope it means she knows I'm running against her and she's nervous.

"Wow, I can't wait to hear it. And to see Jessica's face when you win," Lizzy says.

I nod in secret agreement and the bus comes to a jerking halt. Game on.

In first period, I get called to the student council teacher's room. I'm surprised but assume maybe she wants to let me know when all the debates are happening or to give me permission to put up my posters, so I bring my backpack with me. Funny, though, I don't see any other posters up in the halls.

"Samantha Greenwall?" Miss Callighan asks when I walk into her room. There are two other adults I don't know sitting on either side of her and for some reason, my stomach drops. My first thought is they know why I want to run for office. All three teachers are staring at me expectantly.

"Sorry, yes. That's me."

"Great," Miss Callighan says, "do you have your speech ready?"

"Oh, yes, I do," I answer. "My mom and I also made buttons and posters last night. When ... are ... we ..." I trail off as I notice all the adults are looking at me ... sadly?

"I'm sorry, there seems to have been some confusion, Samantha. You read your speech to us, not the student body. We're listening to all the speeches today and announcing who gets what position at the end of the day. No one explained that to you?"

My face is stone and tears are seriously threatening to spill over. "No, no one explained that to me. Um, so, I just read my speech now, here?"

Miss Callighan tries to shine sympathy through her smile, but I feel so angry and betrayed it falls flat. "Are you ready to do it now? We could give you a second to think about it."

"No, that's fine. I can do it." I start to reach for my bag, for the paper tucked inside with my winning speech but decide against it. "This might get me in trouble, but I want to be honest. I don't want to be president. I just don't want Jessica Winstaff to get it." I ignore the little gasps across the room and continue, head held high. "She's a mean girl. There's enough mean and bad in this world that wins all the time, and I just didn't want it to happen this time. She doesn't want it either, she just doesn't want Amy Black to have it. I don't know why, but I know Amy really wants it, and even though I don't know her that well, I know she would make a really great class president. I just ... I know you guys probably don't remember what junior high is like, but it's really hard sometimes and bullies like Jessica win more often than not. So, obviously don't make me president, but don't let her have it either. Or at least give Amy a chance. I'm really sorry I wasted your time."

Miss Callighan clears her throat and I feel like puke is coming up mine. "Thank you for your honesty, Samantha. We'll have to discuss how to proceed from here. You can go back to class."

"Ok," I whisper and turn for the door.

The hallways are long, and I feel like I'm going to cry all the long way back to my class, but I make it dry-faced. The day passes in a blur except for every time someone interrupts a class when I assume I'm about to be in trouble.

My last class of the day is art and we're working on abstract pieces with clay. I just mush a ball into my palm again and again until the classroom speaker buzzes.

"Hello everyone, this is Miss Callighan." Terror seizes me. What if she tells everyone what I almost did? "Mr. Jameson, Mrs. Gleaver, and I are proud to announce your student council." I relax a little while she announces the historians, treasurer, and vice president, but hold my breath when she says, "and your class president is ... Amy Black."

Sweet relief practically punches me in the face. It didn't happen the way I thought it would, but goodness won.

@David Cameron From 3 May 2015: "Britain Faces A Simple And Inescapable Choice—Stability And Strong Government With Me, Or Chaos With Ed Miliband."

The aliens touched down at precisely 13:06 on March 29, 2019. Brian knew this because he was unemployed. Ever since the Honda plant shut down, he spent his days on the sofa watching daytime soaps and sending off applications to various agencies. Anything would do—aside from picking asparagus—his redundancy package was worth practically zilch, Universal Credit was a joke and he had mouths to feed, rent to pay, weed to buy and his wife's part-time temp work wasn't going to cut it. At 13:04, Brian emptied a tin of baked beans into a bowl and microwaved them on high for two minutes. He scrolled through his newsfeed and paused midway over a shaky mobile livestream from Hyde Park as the timer dinged. He thought it was a hoax, the wind whipping the tree branches, the scorched ground beneath the saucer and the screaming passersby, nothing more than paid actors. That was until an emergency news bulletin cut in on Jeremy Kyle—'Paternity Test Reveals All: My

Son Voted Remain, Was His Mother Playing Away?'— and officially announced Earth's first invasion.

Reporters, journalists, the military, curious onlookers, and those just desperate for a selfie flooded Speaker's Corner as the spaceship's jets ceased and it settled on the grass. Like every good sci-fi movie, a ramp lowered with a hiss of steam and an extraterrestrial being emerged. Brian dropped his beans on the floor and swore out loud, not just because of the cream carpet but because there on television, waving at the cameras, was a real green man.

"We come in peace," it declared in garbled English.

It had a generally humanoid figure, but rounder in the middle, a curvy green blob, covered in a viscous liquid, a large oval head, several tiny legs, and several tiny eyes, only two of which were open. Two mouths smiled and a single tentacle molded into the shape of a hand and made the two-fingered peace sign to all the snipers and tanks trained on it.

"We come bearing good news. You've won the Intergalactic Lottery."

Coverage of the invasion interrupted the latest parliamentary debates over the newest final leave deadline and the preferred shade of navy for the new British passport. This was a national emergency.

Online they played the livestream footage over and over, politicians and journalists speculated on the nature of the visit, scientists on the power sources within their ships and everyone was left guessing what on Earth—or not—this Intergalactic Lottery was.

Facebook was full of it: everyone posting selfies, re-posting video links to conspiracy theories and sharing the word of the end-is-nigh preachers. Abductionists proclaimed a newfound legitimacy to their stories, some extended warm welcomes, and others paranoid, we can't trust them—who knows why they're really here.

An add for custom t-shirt printing popped up on the side of Brian's newsfeed. That was it. He set about trawling through the online images of the Hyde Park Landing, copy and pasting the best, and within a couple of frustrated hours using an Eastern European manufacturing website he'd placed an order for a thousand Intergalactic Lottery #winner crew necks and a thousand grunge-theme alien graphic tees. They'd be with him by the end of the week. He stuck them as his profile pictures and waited for the orders to pour in. So engrossed in his new business, he almost forgot to pick his son up from primary school. When he got there the caretaker was locking up. Marcus stood at the gate with one of his teachers.

"Hey little buddy," he said with a smile.

Marcus burst into tears as he hugged his dad's legs. "I thought you'd forgotten about me."

"Never little guy."

Miss Murray wanted a word with Brian, Marcus had pushed classmate Ayaan Hussain over in the playground, or something. Brian wasn't really listening as he shuffled from foot to foot, wanting to get away for a smoke. Then he just lit up anyway. He probably deserved it, he said. The teacher looked horrified. Brian spouted some spiel about grounding him. That pacified her. They walked home together, and he captivated his son with stories about the invasion. He nipped into the garage to buy another pouch of baccy and slipped *Alien* into his pocket on the way out.

Marie returned home to the screams of Sigourney Weaver vibrating through the surround sound. She switched the TV to standby.

"What you do that for?" Brian said over his beer and used the remote to turn it back on, the screen defaulted to the BBC.

"Are you out of your mind? He's seven; he can't watch that."

"He's mature for his age."

"You promised me you wouldn't just sit in front of that TV all day again. What example are you setting for your son?"

"I'm going to make us some cash."

"Did you get a job?"

"Better. I am my own boss." He showed her the t-shirts. "Aren't they great, I already have a couple of orders. And I could do keyrings and coasters, you can get all kinds of shit printed."

"Look, Dad, it's the alien." Marcus pointed at the screen. "He looks friendly."

Sure enough, it stood in front of the microphone outside Downing Street next to the prime minister. Cameras flashed and bodies jostled to get closer. Her haggard face smiled for the first time since the referendum and asked for quiet.

The alien addressed the crowd. "I am Gkrpian, King of the Gkripori. The Intergalactic Lottery is a tradition that my kind have upheld for millennia, for we have the power to turn any substance to gold. You, citizens of Earth, have won."

There were widespread oohs as he reached out and with the tip of his tentacle touched the door of Number Ten, and sure enough, it turned from black to gold. A reporter offered up his pen and, obliging with a gentle caress, Gkrpian transformed that too.

"We came to Earth to deliver your winnings; however, we leave with something far more valuable—a trade partnership."

"This the Final Solution to Brexit," the prime minister said, taking center podium, her eyes flush with gold. "Today, the majority voted in favour of my deal with the Gkriporieans, giving us the strength and stability to exit the EU with a no deal without hesitation, a welcomed end to the long-winded negotiations and political indecisiveness. We can finally deliver the will of the people. We celebrate not only the end of Brexit, but the birth of Britain's friendship with our new extraterrestrial allies from outer space."

There was raucous applause as May offered her hand and Gkrpian molded his tentacle into a mirror of hers. Cameras flashed and people cheered and clapped as they shook on it.

Brian joined in. "See, Marie, I told you something good would come out of this Brexit thing," he said, taking another swig of his beer. "We're going to be so rich the government will pay our benefits in bars of gold." He turned his attention back to the TV.

"And now we shake in the traditional Gkripori way," Grkpian said.

Put on the spot, May faltered. She turned to her press secretary—this wasn't on the script. He shrugged, just go with it.

"Relax. It won't hurt." Gkrpian sensed her unease.

The words reminded Brian of the first girl he'd conned into bed.

"It will all be over very quickly."

That had also been true.

Unlike Brian, Gkrpian lied. Brian couldn't tear his eyes away as, live on the BBC, in ultra-high defi-nition, Gkrpian's long protruding tentacle slithered between the buttons on May's blouse and penetrated her navel.

A collective shudder of revulsion rippled through the onlookers, and regardless of political party, social-ist sympathies or right-wing bent, all were unani-mously in agreement—not even the idea of Boris in a mankini nor Rees-Mogg's cum face came close—there was nothing more hideous than this. All of Gkrpian's eyes rolled back in his head and both of his mouths pressed into quivering lines, his globule body trem-bling. With a belch, he produced several white slimy orbs from the sacks at the base of his tentacle, in a sheath of mucus they moved like ants toward May.

"Wait, what are those?" she stammered.

But it was too late. The first white sphere disap-peared beneath her blouse, the bulge visible beneath the satin slowly moving towards the pit of her stomach.

"A fertilized Gkriporiean egg. Did I forgot to mention? As part of our new deal, the UK populous will act as incubators for the future Gkriporiean race."

Desperately, her hands clawed at the throbbing tentacle, fingers grappling, manicured nails digging in, anything to pry it out of her. It was futile.

"But we didn't vote for that!" she cried.

May screamed as her bellybutton was stretched and her flesh gave way to the egg, her hands flapping by her side like a salmon out of water and she was dancing once again. When she was full, Gkrpian withdrew. May slumped to the floor like an overstuffed bean bag. A dead overstuffed bean bag.

"Who will be next?" Gkrpian said.

Several other tentacles emerged from his body, all coated in the pulsating white eggs. Screams broke out and the audience tried to flee. But it was too late, fellow Gkriporieans surrounded them. Chaos, the camera fell over. Then the screen went blank.

Brian checked his Twitter feed. Somebody had already made a gif of May being struck by the tentacle. He screenshotted a still, it would make a great graphic for his next batch of t-shirts. The television flashed back to life. It cut to outside Downing Street, a reporter crouched down by a bush as cars were hurled overhead, people ran screaming from office blocks and the Gkriporieans marched freely through the street, impregnating whoever was in their path. They watched, numb with disbelief.

"The streets of London are overrun with the Gkripori aliens!" she shouted at the camera. "It is not known how many of them are here or the extent of their presence across the UK, citizens are advised to stay inside and await the response of the military and emergency services ..."

Her words were drowned out by a scream as she was hoisted into the air by a Gkripori sixteen feet tall and with tentacles thick as tree trunks. Her midriff imploded with a squishy sound as it punched into her, depositing huge white eggs the size of footballs that slowly filled her up like a balloon.

"Marcus, don't watch this!" Marie cried, covering his eyes.

Brian saw a flash of light outside his lounge window. He peered beneath the net curtain. The sky was filled with the Gkripori's spaceships, like the saucer that arrived in London, only bigger, much bigger. The Gkripori were throwing themselves from it and splattering on the ground. One landed on their road, a flat green puddle. It sucked it's mass together and re-assembled into a huge tentacle nightmare, with large razor teeth and mean eyes looking in all directions, one of which focused on Brian. A long black forked tongue emerged from one mouth and licked the lips of both as it lumbered up their driveway.

"Shit, they're here! Marie, get Marcus and run!" he cried, launching himself from his armchair and racing to the closet where he kept his Uncle's unregistered shotgun.

"Is this a game, Dad?" Marcus said.

Brian was strangely proud of him as he stood in his England replica shirt wielding a baseball bat that he was only just taller than.

"No, son. It's fucked up."

Their front door crashed down. Marie screamed. Any sense of pride was gone as Marcus was impaled on a tentacle and became the first in family to be an incubator.

"You bastard!" Brian shouted and fumbled with the cartridges as the thing then got Marie and began pulsating in pleasure depositing its eggs. "Fuck off back to your own planet."

Brian fired the gun. The shot hit. He expected blood and guts to gush out, for the creature to writhe in agony and fall to the floor, but instead he found himself staring straight through a clean circular hole. Rapidly, it closed up healing and resealing in front of him. He dropped the gun and turned to run, but there were another two Gkripori at the back door. The first tentacle hit him like a brick, then a second, then a third. He tried to struggle, but the pain was too much.

Brian floated in and out of consciousness, hearing their grunts and panting. Of course, he thought, there was never an Intergalactic Lottery. And nobody was going to buy his t-shirts now.

A MATTER OF PRIDE
IAN KITLEY

A clap of thunder rattled the window, echoed down the hall, and charged into the living room. A trumpet call, it pierced the drowsy calm of my nap before the fire, driving off the sandman coaxing me towards dreamland. Not even old bones warmed by the heat could keep me under and I mentally railed against the intrusion. But I could not for long, for it was a boon—a reminder I couldn't afford to wile away the night. Important matters were afoot and much still needed to be completed. Even in the foul weather currently battering the boards of my home.

Stretching, long and slow, I got down from the chair and padded across to the kitchen for a late dinner. The servants had kindly left a plate of fish, my favourite, out for me before they retired and, without anyone to scold me, I could feast at my leisure. So, I took my time, knowing this was likely the last luxury available to me for the rest of the night.

Before leaving the house on my errands, I made sure to get cleaned up and presentable. When one wished to impress, they needed to appear the part, act the part, be the part. I was already entering on the back foot—no need to make it any worse.

Entertaining one last thought of giving up and returning to the fire, I firmed my resolve and stepped out into the storm punishing my corner of town. The wind whipped my hair back and rain pummelled every inch of my body as I dashed past driveways and storefronts, heading towards the alley. The now-infamous alley. The one where we found Toby Three-Legs last week.

I say 'we,' but I wasn't actually there. Curly and One-Eyed Frank found him. The birds had already gotten at him, but it was clear what happened. A 'hit', an accident, something no one could have predicted, but it left our community rudderless, the two sides at each other's throats.

The Haves and the Have-Nots, that was the easiest way to think of things. Toby kept the peace while he lived, a Have who became a Have-Not; respected by most, feared by the rest. Our leader. Now he was gone, someone needed to step up, but no one possessed the support of both sides. Tonight, a necessary decision would be reached—had to be reached—and it didn't look like it would be an easy one.

I still smelt the copper tang of Toby's blood in the bricks and mortar of the alley. Even the gnashing, snarling storm couldn't wash it away. Some events tore a wound so deep in a community that the damage never fully healed. I feared this was one of those.

Shivering, mayhap from the cold, mayhap from the ghosts, I ducked into Pop's Grocery Store. The shop was dark as a tomb and twice as quiet after hours. As I entered, Moe and Maeve, the siblings from down the street, greeted me, glad I decided to make it. A little further in, I spotted Curly and the Tawny Twins, all from the Haves, along with a half dozen more. It seemed they heeded the call.

Unfortunately, apparently One-Eye had done his own recruiting. A quick count told me the Have-Nots were also out in force, meaning this would be a close-run thing. I needed to play my cards just right.

Weaving between the attendees, I rubbed shoulders and purred reassurances to those I could. Others I snarled or rebuked as required. I tried to do this unobtrusively but, from the tense way One-Eye held himself, he knew something was up.

Thunder shook the roof and cans rattled the shelves, sending the room into a reverent hush. As if this were his God-given cue, One-Eyed Frank hopped onto an overturned soapbox and surveyed the assembled throng.

"You know why we're here. The Have-Nots and the Haves. If it were up to each of us, we would live the separate lives we crave. But that cannot be. The servants do not understand our ways and, if they knew the frailty of our community, they would rise and cast us out. They would welcome our dreaded enemies, those mongrels who believe they should live in harmony with the servants. We cannot let this happen; we *will not* let this happen."

His words were a catalyst, a cry tearing through the souls of our people. I couldn't have done a better job myself.

"Thus, we must work together, as we did in the past. But the past has shown we need someone to guide us, to keep us all on the right path. Toby was that once, but he is gone. Now, we need another. Someone respected and followed by all."

There was a certainty there, an obvious hint to who he thought that should be. Therein lay the problem. He was too cruel, too ready to act without thought. This was why the Twins came to me. This is why we were all here.

Now came his proclamation. It thrummed in the air, counterpoint to the storm raging above, poised to fall upon our people.

"My brothers and sisters of the claw, this duty has been lain at my feet. I am the voice of the Have-Nots, those who do not live a life of pampered luxury. We, the ones who must work every day, bide our time to scavenge and hunt. We, the ones who understand sacrifice for the good of all."

You mean the good of yourselves, I thought, but my outrage remained contained. For now.

"Our laws say all must accept the one who leads. Thus, I ask for a show of faith. A show my words and deeds have gained that acceptance. What say you, my kin?"

The room filled with the hisses and growls of the Have-Nots, to no one's surprise. If they didn't love One-Eye, they tended to respect him. And, if they didn't respect him, they feared him enough to be cowed into accepting him. It made the silence of the Haves all the more prominent, and even One-Eye, revelling in the adoration, noticed. He trained his gaze on our corner of the room.

"Am I not acceptable?"

Openings like that didn't come along every day. My friends and compatriots padded aside, leaving a corridor between One-Eye and me. Stepping forward into it, I silently glided up to stand before his soapbox.

"No, Frank, you're not."

I showed my back to him, knowing this might be my first and last mistake, and faced the gathering. "You all know me. I am Wilbur Ellis III, and, as Frank would point out, am a Have. I'm a pampered dandy in his eyes and many of yours. But that's only half of it." Most of them didn't remember Toeless Will. I'd outlived almost all who did. I was lucky. It was time they remembered.

"Once, I was a Have-Not. I fought for every scrap, for the right to the best cardboard and the driest underpass. I ran with Toby before he became Three-Legs. Before betrayal and the authorities took me away. Before being adopted into the home where I now sleep." The Have-Nots didn't believe my words, but the Haves did. My past was the reason they never accepted me and, ironically, was why they so desperately needed me now.

I turned back to Frank. "You have the Have-Nots. I have the Haves." At that, my adopted family cried out their support. "Look about you, Frank. The split is equal. You know what that means."

My opponent climbed from his perch, growling to me as the watchers pulled back, leaving a circle around us. "I never liked you, Will. The day they took you away, it proved you weren't worthy of running with us."

"Oh, Frank, you think I forgot what happened that day," I purred, loud enough for only him to hear. "I remember you. I recall the claw flashing across my heel. Is that how Toby became Three-Legs. Was that the first time you made a play for his job?"

Fire flashed behind Frank's eye, and I saw the truth. This is for you then, Toby.

The storm sounded the bell once more, as it had all night, a flash of lightning blinding all. All except One-Eye, standing before the window. He sprung at me, claws outstretched, fangs bared, a blur of darkness against the light. I pivoted on my hind legs, the old injury almost resulting in failure from the outset, and barely evaded the ball of fury.

As he landed, my tail lashed across his face, the orange whip first a distraction and then a lance across his eyes. Letting loose a yowl dripping with pain and anger, he ripped the offending appendage away. His claws sliced, agony cutting through me, and I knew, deep down, he had drawn first blood in this fight.

Hissing, I continued my turn, a whirlwind raking at his side as I jumped away, preferring to hit-and-run rather than face him outright. He chased, hair on end, a clear sign of the anger he must feel, sight locked on my fireball silhouette. The air behind me tore as he pounced, and I dropped to the boards, flipping onto my back as he sailed past. In that moment, time slowed, my paws lazily paddling at the roof as if One-Eye were a ball of yarn. Claws hooked into his belly, trailing gouges down his length—a distraction.

With a crack and a crash, One-Eye slammed into his soapbox, he and it collapsing to the floor, broken.

And, just like that, the fight was all over.

I could follow through on our laws, but we both knew this was done. Limping away now gave him a chance in the future, time to regroup. Accepting defeat provided opportunities to try again, to wrench free the power he felt he deserved. But I needed him to keep the Have-Nots in line, a major to my general. The Not to my Have.

The storm was winding down, only the lingering wind left to buffet at the walls of the buildings around town. The Twins kept me company on the way back, but they peeled off to cuddle with their servants at the drive before mine, exiting with the promise to visit once my servants left for the day. I didn't mention I might need to sneak away before then to speak with Frank, to ensure the fish market was still a safe hunting ground. My life was more complicated now, but that was my lot. To be a Have meant I needed to look out for the Have-Nots, a duty I didn't regret.

Slipping inside, I headed for my favourite chair. The fire had burnt itself out, but the coals still glowed, and my pillow was still warm. Hopping up, I pawed at it, turned around three times, and only then settled. It was good to be home. It was good to be in charge.

☑ ☑ ☑

"Honey, did you forget to lock the door again?"

"No, Henry. Why?"

"Wilbur's fur is wet, and he's left damp paw prints all the way through from the kitchen."

"You mean the back door? Shoot, I forgot about that one."

"No worries, Honey. I'll mop it up in a minute. Though, if you forget Wilbur's cat food again, you might find yourself in need of new pillows."

"Don't you dare joke, Henry Ellis! Our little baby would never do that to his mommy."

Oh, my dear servants, if only you knew what I would do for me and mine.

Marisol blew warm breath on the funeral home's windows and drew smiley faces to replace the angry ones outside. The ceremony was well underway. Most of the attendees were sitting in pews or at the podium, paying their respects. Marisol, however, preferred to keep her distance. Her brain needed the extra space to think.

The world mourned her Grandpa Timon's death, though she knew many were outraged. She categorized them into two groups.

Like her, the first group was sad they had lost their respected leader; someone they loved and respected. These folks were hurt and looking for someone to blame.

The majority, however, including those outside the funeral home, fell into the second group. It had been discovered Timon Maldonado, President of the United States, was an AI, and they were furious.

Marisol imagined the freshly drawn smiley faces were cheering him on, the way a crowd cheers on a music performer, inciting an encore. It was only when the organ pipes took a breath that the real-outside would filter into the chapel, producing a sound so ominous and dissonant—a minor key. The real-outside made her stomach uneasy, like ghosts with harmonicas.

Amused at the ridiculous notion, she smirked. Her piano teacher would have enjoyed the quip if he were here. Louis, an acclaimed and talented AI pianist, not only trained her but doted on her to a fault. As annoying as it was, he was truly the only other person, aside from her grandpa, that understood just how much of her life was contextualized through music.

Louis called her a child prodigy and regularly basked in the adoration of being her mentor. Marisol felt undeserving of the compliments but couldn't argue the point further. Her technique and performances were impeccable.

Therein lied the problem.

It was too perfect.

Just out of her reach were the flaws that would impart character.

Perhaps that's why minor keys fascinated Marisol. They sounded darker than other keys. The distinction—or "major" distinction, as Louis would retort—was in the third note of the scale. Just a half step down and an otherwise melodic piece would sound unresolved, as if something waited around the corner. A trivial change, yet it altered everything around it.

Grandpa Timon was like a minor key. Only one person, but his changes rippled like soundwaves, and all who heard were changed by it. Marisol was heartbroken when news of his death reached her.

Her parents hadn't given details, though she'd picked up enough conversation from others to get the gist; a tragic industrial accident.

Grandpa had been lobbying for safer working conditions at a chemical plant. An explosion had happened, and, although investigations were still ongoing, they hadn't ruled out terrorism. Grandpa died before his doctor could arrive on the scene. She hoped he didn't suffer.

So, her grandpa was an AI. Big deal! Artificially intelligent beings were some of the kindest she'd ever met. Nancy, her babysitter, was an AI, and she was loads of fun. The chefs and waiters at every restaurant were AI, and they gave excellent service. The country's police force, doctors, and teachers were all AI. Marisol didn't like their dentist much, but she was pretty sure it would hurt even if their dentist was a human.

Marisol knew her cavalier attitude wasn't for everyone. In fact, she empathized with the public outcry. People, in general, don't like when they've been told one thing just to discover it's actually another.

☑   ☑   ☑

Recently, her parents had organized a backyard picnic, so they could reconnect after a long day of funeral planning. Marisol had looked forward to it because picnics meant ham sandwiches.

Mother smelled of gardenias, and Father's brown stubble tickled as they kissed her cheek. They placed a sandwich in her hands, and she beamed with satisfaction, legs dangling, as she took the first bite.

And then she froze.

Something wasn't right.

She stopped mid-chew to assess.

Bleh! Turkey.

Why didn't they just tell her it was turkey?

But then, she probably wouldn't have taken that first bite. They knew that. And she knew that.

Marisol slumped a little, though she continued to chew her food and swallow her disappointment.

If people would just be honest with themselves, they would eat their metaphorical sandwiches too. Because they're hungry, and it's good for them. She understood their anger. It didn't taste awful. It just wasn't what she'd expected.

A thought came to her then. "If Grandpa was born a baby"—crumbs hurtled from Marisol's mouth—"how did he become an AI?"

Her parents shared sidelong glances. Father swallowed his food, put his sandwich on the wrapper, and wiped his fingers.

Marisol eyed his sandwich contents to confirm it was also turkey. If she had to eat it, so did they.

"We're not entirely certain, hun. If I had to guess, I think Grandpa became an AI when I was about eleven."

Her father told her about the car accident Grandpa Timon had been in. He used a lot of medical jargon, but, as she understood it, Grandpa cracked his skull, and his brains almost fell out.

Fortunately, back in those days, one didn't have to find the greatest brain surgeon. They were all great because they were all AI.

Father said Grandpa wasn't the same after that. He was better.

Grandpa stopped drinking and took better care of himself. He seemed healthier, kinder, and just plain better. In every way.

He also changed career paths and moved into politics. That was when he fought for AI rights, even when the idea of AI rights wasn't really a thing.

Finishing the last of her sandwich, another thought occurred to her. "How did everyone learn he was an AI when he died? Grandpa didn't have the eye-lights."

It was easy to tell when someone was an AI, because a ring of light surrounds their irises. Personally, Marisol thought the light added some sparkle to their personality, the way cymbals or tambourines can add a little dazzle to an otherwise ordinary song.

She would often look in the mirror and wish her eyes would light up. They never did, no matter how she tried.

Her mother's smile wavered, and Marisol knew she must have struck a chord. Mother smoothed the bangs from Marisol's forehead, so they could see each other's eyes. "You know how actors change their eye color with contacts for different movies?"

Marisol nodded. She'd never considered it before, but she had noticed it.

"Well, unless the purpose is documented, like an actor's movie contract, AIs aren't allowed to cover or disguise their eyes in any way. Even to wear sunglasses." Mother sighed. "What Grandpa did. It was against the law."

"Oh." The disbelief stuck, like a frog in Marisol's throat.

Mother released Marisol's face. "Even though it's not illegal for humans, we don't cover our eyes either. It shows mutual respect to make eye contact. No one covers their eyes anymore."

Mutual respect? Marisol doubted it. People get the stomach flutters if they don't know who they're dealing with. They want to know it's a ham sandwich. Not that it should matter, but it does.

☑ ☑ ☑

In the moments leading up to the funeral, she heard many stories and memories of her grandpa. Father had told her about Grandpa's first election and how he'd won by a landslide.

Marisol thought that was an interesting choice of words. Landslides were usually caused by some kind of an event, like heavy rainfall or an earthquake. Gravity, however, was always involved. The year Grandpa Timon had been elected president, the world was like one big earthquake. As the AI population grew, violence followed, like aftershock tremors.

Back in those days, human-to-AI violence had practically been an unchecked epidemic. Especially, male assault against AI women.

"Another reason to keep your eyes exposed," Father had warned.

Not everyone treated AIs horribly. The world, as a whole, was still composed of good people. Simply put, the bad people found an easier target in AIs.

The unfairness of it all was that AIs were incapable of intentionally hurting anyone, not even to retaliate or defend themselves. In fact, Marisol had only ever heard of three times an AI had hurt a human. Once, a kid died because a bully pushed him in front of an AI-driven bus. The bully got detention; the AI got recycled. The other two times, AIs performed the Heimlich on choking humans in order to save their lives. Those AIs were lucky. The humans survived with bruised ribs, and the AIs avoided incarceration. Barely.

The rules were simple. If a human got hurt, there were consequences. If an AI got hurt, people might think badly of you, but no one ever went to jail for it.

Even the vice president—or president now, she supposed—shared stories of his time campaigning with her grandpa. Mr. Stevens was a burly man with coarse salt and pepper waves shaved tight on the sides exposing a scar just above his right temple. Just like Grandpa's. He'd had a brain tumor, she was told, removed about ten years ago.

He patted her shoulder, sighing. "Timon was a great man of purpose. Don't let anyone tell you different. His vision for the country will live on in me. And in you."

Mr. Stevens's eyes were a soft brown, also like her grandpa's, and, instead of choking back tears, she fought the instinct to ask if he wore contacts too. That would probably be rude.

Grandpa and Mr. Stevens had shaken the nation with their campaign—a platform aimed at safety regulations for AIs.

Since all the bad things happened to AIs, protecting them meant a safer place for everyone. It made sense to Marisol, and, if she could have voted for him, she would've. Grandpa Timon was very smart and had many ideas, but a clever campaign aimed at AI rights spun to benefit all human life? That was his best idea.

The nation must have thought so too because that's how they won by a landslide—with an earthquake. And gravity.

Her parents even reminisced about how excited Grandpa had been when they announced they were pregnant with her. Marisol hadn't been born yet, and he had involved himself in every doctor's appointment. Mother joked it was the only time she'd seen him abuse his influence and power, solely to provide her with the best prenatal resources.

"You'd think it was his baby! It was embarrassing, really. We all thought it was strange at first, but we couldn't fault him." Mother shook her head, and her lips smirked to one side. "It finally made sense after you were born. You loved him already too, from the first time you laid eyes on him."

Marisol had her own memories to fondly recount. Though no one believed her, she could remember the night he had won the first election.

Swaddled in Grandpa Timon's arms, he had paced and swayed about a crowded room. Though she was only a baby, she remembered feeling calm in the warmth of his presence, so the swaying must have been more for his comfort than hers.

She recalled long pauses of strained silence followed by news updates and phone calls. Electoral votes were announced periodically, met with hoots and hollers from those in the room.

One fourteen.

Then one eighty-nine.

Two seventy-two caused the whole room to erupt in chatter and handshakes, and there were still hours to go.

In the quiet moments, Grandpa swayed and whispered to her of change on the horizon. Humanity was an enormous ship, too big for him to turn quickly without help. He crooned to her about the course corrections he would make, so minor at first no one would notice.

Triumphant, his lips gently rested on her head, caressing her scalp with his secrets and brushing the wisps of her hair with promises of a healthier world.

A kinder world.

A world that was just plain better.

She thought about the last time they hugged. Grandpa had carried her into the house because she'd fallen, scraping her knees and palms. Actually, he had carried her into the house, because William "Buttface" Falton had pushed her and ran away.

"It's not my fault I'm better than him at everything!" She cried.

Grandpa cleaned and bandaged her scrapes then wiped the tears from her face with his handkerchief. "My little Merry-Soul." He poked her belly. "You could have pushed him back. But you didn't. How come?"

Marisol chuckled back tears at the nickname, covering his finger with her hands to prevent further tickling. "I wanted to. But then he'd just get mad and push me back. And then we'd just keep pushing each other."

He hugged her tenderly then pulled away. "That's why you're my model citizen! Won't it be nice when the whole world is full of people just like you?"

☑   ☑   ☑

Someone bumped into Marisol, and she was back in the funeral home. Disappointingly so.

The organ pipes had taken their final breath. Everyone was standing now, shuffling at a slow and steady pace. The funeral doors opened occasionally as people exited, and the discord outside made her scalp itch and buzz, like a kazoo in the summer.

She farewelled the smiley face windows to find her mother's hand. Stopped by every attendee who wished to convey their condolences, they made very little progress toward the door. With eyes locked in so many conversations, Mother was too busy to notice

Marisol dancing in place and crossing her legs. Impatient, she tugged her mother's hand and made eye contact, pleading.

"Go ahead, sweety," Mother whispered between handshakes. "I'll most likely be here when you get back."

☑   ☑   ☑

Marisol's black vinyl shoes clacked on the tiles as she entered the single bathroom and locked the door. Once she concluded her business, she righted her clothing and flushed.

The sink was a bit high for her. If she stood on her toes, she could probably reach the faucet. Instead, she spied a small end table between the sink and the toilet with an unhappy and drooping green plant atop.

Marisol placed the sad plant on the floor and tugged at the table bit by bit, so it wouldn't screech against the tile, until it met the front of the sink. Bracing herself against the porcelain, she climbed the table until she could rest her knees onto it and then rinsed her fingertips with soap and water. She could still hear the cacophony of minor keys even over the bathroom fan, and her stomach fluttered again.

Drying her hands, Marisol inspected her image in the mirror and checked her face for dirt. Her reflection shouldn't seem any different, but somehow, she felt bigger. More important.

She was honored to see Grandpa's smile in the curve of her lips. Though her eyes were not his eyes, they had a similar shape. She leaned in and tipped her head in different directions, hoping for that glint of light. There must be more of him in her somewhere to have been as close as they were.

There.

Just there.

As her chin touched her chest.

It was brief but distinct. A black dot on the white of her eye, hidden beneath the bottom lid.

Did she have dirt in her eye?

No, it was something else.

Marisol pulled down her bottom lid with her finger and found four tiny black dots. If she connected them, she could make a square. What were the chances this was a birthmark?

Curious, she checked the other eye. The dots were there too. Marisol had seen enough documentaries to know circles happened in nature quite a bit. Squares were less likely. She had stumbled onto something … unnatural.

"Marisol? Are you still in there?" Her mother knocked at the door.

"Coming!" Marisol skittered down the end table and gingerly put everything back the way it was.

☑ ☑ ☑

Mind racing, she allowed herself to be led to the double front doors currently closed. They waited as security officers took position around her family. She released her mother's hand. It was time to face the discordant outside and see what was waiting around the corner for her.

The double doors opened, and an orchestra of shouts and bellows accosted them. Marisol walked, feeling every eye upon her.

Blue eyes, brown eyes, and ring-lit eyes followed her procession. One boy caught her attention standing still amongst the clamoring. He wasn't just looking at her, he seemed to be looking into her. Then he pulled down his lower eyelid for the briefest moment.

The briefest and greatest moment.

Then the moment was gone. Security had ushered her past him, and he was just a normal boy clamoring with all the others.

Ahead, she caught a glimpse of another child. A girl of six, who went still amongst the outcry when their eyes met. Again, this girl pulled down her lid only long enough for Marisol to notice.

Past that, a boy her height.

And beyond him, an older girl with braces.

This happened again and again, like a recurrent verse to a masterpiece only she could see and hear.

The procession had reached its end, and she ducked into the sanctuary of the limousine with her family. Doors closed; the tumultuous chorus was reduced to a dull moan. Marisol sat stunned, neither ham nor turkey, sandwiched between her parents. As the limousine pulled away from the chorus and funeral home, her mind became calm, like the hush that falls before the concerto begins.

The minor keys sang of something waiting around the corner. Her voice longed to join the discord. In that moment of quiet, her grandpa's whispers resonated. *How nice it would be when the world was full of people like her.*

MRS MONROE'S CATS
MICHAEL J INGRAM

Bernard forced his face into a welcoming smile. That couple from the second floor were approaching, their matching strides heading straight for him. He put the brake on the trolley he was towing and waited for them.

"Good morning, Mr and Mrs Smith," the warmth of his greeting sounding insincere even to him, "what can I do for you today?" as if he couldn't guess.

"It's Doctor, actually," said the gangly man at the same time his wife said, "Ms."

"So sorry, Doctor and Mizz Smith." For a second, Bernard thought he'd overdone it with the emphasis. He also knew their titles but enjoyed feigning ignorance. Fortunately, today the Smiths had more important fish to fry.

"That woman"—the doctor's finger pointed upwards over Bernard's right shoulder, towards Mrs Munroe's apartment—"has gone too far this time."

Ms Smith nodded in agreement. "Too far."

Dr Smith sucked in air through his nostrils—a considerable amount, given the size of his nose. "I consider myself a reasonable man—"

His wife nodded, whilst Bernard hoped his eyebrows had stayed still.

"—but that woman takes the biscuit."

"Biscuit."

"I've had it up to here with her." The doctor indicated his shoulder level.

Bernard turned the corners of his lips down in appreciation. The doctor's shoulder level was well above average height. He nodded in recognition of how reasonable the doctor was.

"Here." Unfortunately, Ms Smith used her own shoulder level, which, given she was about two feet shorter than her husband, implied a much less tolerant attitude.

Bernard suppressed a sigh. "What's she done this time, sir?" He double tapped his mastoid implant to wake his wireless link.

"Cats. She hasn't got rid of the last lot, and I'm sure she's got hold of even more. I told her last time that I would take steps, and I told her again just now."

"You've spoken to her then, sir?"

"Yes. We've come straight from her apartment. I could see them all over the place, smelly little blighters. She's got hundreds in there, she has."

"Hundreds." Ms Smith nodded.

"Hundreds?" asked Bernard. It was only a two bedroomed apartment. They were cats, not sardines.

"Well, at least thirty."

"That's right. Thirty. At least ... forty even."

"Have you got a recording, sir?"

Stupid question.

"Of course, I have." The doctor reached behind his right ear for his own implant.

Bernard blinked to accept the retinal import. It did indeed contain video of cats in an apartment he recognised as Mrs Munroe's.

"Don't worry, sir." He patted the trolley beside him. "I'm just doing my deliveries, so I'll have a word when I pass by."

"Yes, well, as concierge, I would have expected you to take steps beforehand, as it is, I've called an extraordinary meeting of the Resident's Committee at two this afternoon."

Bernard ground his teeth and concentrated more than necessary on releasing the trolley brake. "Very good, sir. If you'll excuse me, I must carry on." He nodded to Ms Smith. "Mizz."

☑   ☑   ☑

Two o'clock arrived and the residents gathered in the communal office. Dr Smith, flanked by his entourage, had arranged the tables to hold court and the rest of the residents sat or stood wherever they could. Ms Smith was also present, either sucking on a sherbet lemon, or just disapproving of everything. It was hard to tell which.

Bernard leant against a far wall, imbibing the atmosphere of bored expectation.

Dr Smith rapped his knuckles on the table. "I call this meeting to order to discuss the problem with—"

"I'm sorry I'm late, I was just having a nap. Excuse me, young man."

Bernard smiled as Hilda Munroe entered the room. Rotund and bowed with age, everything about her seemed to have seen better days, but there was shrewdness behind the thick lenses of her glasses which Bernard admired. The resident she had spoken to jerked out of his chair as Mrs Munroe's walking stick prodded him in the back.

"Yes, well. The meeting was notified via the apartment's—"

Dr Smith's voice was drowned out by the sound of Mrs Munroe dragging a chair across the tiled floor. It seemed to take hours for her to cross the room until she could place the chair mere inches in front of Dr Smith's table, then several more minutes while she eased herself down into it. Eventually, she said, "What was that, dearie?"

Dr Smith's jaw muscles rippled, and he let out a very slow breath before saying, "The meeting was no-tified—"

"No, before that, young man. You said there was a problem. Someone very kindly told me about the meeting. I don't go in for that interweb thingy."

Dr Smith glared at Bernard, then looked to his wife for support before giving Mrs Munroe his most patronising smile.

Here it comes, thought Bernard, *the shit sandwich.*

"Mrs Munroe. You are one of our most respected and revered residents. In your day you were one of the world's leading veterinary surgeons, but we simply can't live—"

Hilda Munroe interrupted the doctor again. He had possibly been interrupted more times in the last five minutes than in his entire career.

"I call for a vote of no confidence," she said.

Bernard stood away from the wall. Wow.

Excited chatter broke out amongst the residents. Indifference had been superseded by a tangible air of anticipation. A resident's committee meeting hadn't been this interesting since Brian Hawksworth's heart attack over ten years ago.

"But, but you can't," blustered Dr Smith. "I'm the Chair. I've always been the Chair."

"Time for a change, then!" called one wag from the back of the room.

Derek Somersby was to the immediate right of Dr Smith. Red-faced and jowly, he hurried to activate his own mastoid implant through the roll of flab around his neck.

Bernard was quicker. "Yes, she can," he said, raising his voice over the hubbub. He slid a finger down his temple as he scrolled through PDFs visible only to him on his intraocular display. "Paragraph thirty-six of the Resident's Committee Constitution states: 'Any resident can call for a vote of no confidence if the Chair of the Committee displays conduct amounting to an abuse of his or her power.'"

"But I haven't." Dr Smith's voice rose in pitch. He turned to Somersby who had also managed to locate the correct paragraph.

Somersby nodded. "He's right. She can. According to the Constitution, neglecting to inform all residents of an extraordinary meeting amounts to misconduct. When upheld, a vote of no confidence automatically results in a ballot open to all residents to choose between the claimant and the existing Chair. The winner of the ballot is thereby elected to start a new term as Chair."

Dr Smith and his cronies gave Somersby a look previously only reserved for Judas Iscariot.

"Thanks a bunch, Derek. That's the last time I treat your gout for free," whispered Smith, so quietly that only Somersby could hear.

☑ ☑ ☑

The following afternoon, Bernard towed a heavily laden trolley up to Mrs Munroe's apartment. The closer he got, the more he could smell it. He rang the bell outside and waited.

After a long while, she opened the door, releasing the full odour of cat faeces and kitty litter which was potent enough to make him take a step back.

"Err ... Hi Mrs Munroe," he said, trying to disguise the action of covering his nose by wiping it with a handkerchief, "here's the stuff you ordered. Did you mean to get all this?" He patted the boxes beside him. "Are you sure it's not just an error with your ancient laptop? You really should get an implant you know."

"Oh! Hello, sweetie, no it looks perfect. I like the old-fashioned ways. Just bring it in, and put it all in the kitchen, will you? Ach, don't mind Montague, he's just an old sourpuss right now because he's not had his cuddles. Now, steer clear of Sebastian and Gwendoline, they've each been like a bear with a sore head all morning. I don't know what's got into them ..."

Mrs Munroe kept up a running commentary of her cats' behaviour and moods as Bernard threaded his way through the apartment. The cats, for the most part, either ignored him or stared with disdain. He couldn't tell which particular cat she was talking about at any one time and didn't really care. The stench was making his eyes water and he just wanted to get out. He was very careful to move slowly and not make any threatening moves. Small as they were, he did get the distinct feeling that he wouldn't get out alive if Mrs Munroe came to any harm.

"There you go Mrs M.," he said, once the boxes had been stacked in her tiny kitchen. "What's all this for then?" He tried to read the writing on the labels, but it was all in Chinese.

"Never you mind, young man," she said, ushering him out by gripping his arm.

He grabbed his trolley and used it to part the sea of cats in his way.

"Are you going to be okay for the election next week, Mrs M.?" he asked. "Dr Smith has a strong following, and he's been canvassing hard."

"I'll be fine, thank you, dearie, don't you worry about old Hilda. There're a few bites left in the old dog yet, you'll see. Besides, my darlings like it here."

"Yes, well, if Dr Smith gets in their opinion won't matter. Just to let you know; Mr Carter, the IT guy from apartment twenty-five, is writing the software to handle the voting. You'd need a mastoid implant to vote, but as you haven't got one, I can cast your vote on your behalf."

"Oh, that's very kind of you, young man, but I won't be voting."

"But Mrs M.! If you don't win the election, Dr Smith will make you get rid of your cats, and there's nothing I can do about it, this time!"

She half pushed him into the corridor, and he turned to plead with her some more, but was met by the door shutting firmly in his face.

Bernard shrugged and pulled on his trolley, rubbing his arm where she had gripped him much harder than an old lady her size should be able to do.

☑ ☑ ☑

The day of the election came around quicker than Bernard would have liked. He wasn't a fan of cats, but Mrs Munroe was one of the few residents who treated him as a human being, and not some slave for their every need.

The election results were going to be shown on a cast from Bernard's implant onto a viewing screen in the communal office.

All thirty or so residents, except Mrs Munroe, had filtered in, and there was a low murmuring of discussion. Whilst Dr Smith was certainly not popular, and no-one actually disliked Mrs Munroe, there was an overall desire to be without the cats in her apartment, or at least the odour from them that permeated the whole building.

"Are we ready yet?" Dr Smith's odious tones called from his usual place. He was surrounded by most of his usual sycophants. The poor Derek Somersby was relegated to the general population, and he sat with one swollen foot propped on a chair in front of him.

Taking a last look toward the entrance door, Bernard sighed and activated the screen. On it was a large blank pie chart.

Mr Carter spoke up, dabbing his forehead, his voice trembling to be speaking to people, especially to so many at once, "Okay, so once you've accessed the app, scroll to toggle your highlighted choice, then long blink to vote. Your votes are anonymous, obviously, but will show up immediately as red for Dr Smith, and blue for Mrs Munroe. The figures in the bottom left." He moved up to the screen and pointed to three words next to flashing zeroes. "TVC stands for total votes cast, and the numbers are the percentages of TVC, red votes and blue votes respectively. Once the TVC reaches one hundred, voting is over and the higher of the other two percentages wins." With that, he almost ran back to his chair and the protection of his wife, Irene, who put a protective arm over his shoulders.

"Right, let's get on with it then," said Dr Smith. He tapped just behind and below his right ear, ran a finger up and down his temple, then closed his eyes for a second, before looking up at the screen.

Everyone in the room turned to follow his gaze. The white circle of the pie chart turned red, and the figures in the bottom left changed to read:

TVC: 2.86%
Red: 100%
Blue: 0%

There was a flurry of activity as his supporters followed suit, and the TVC percentage rose rapidly, then slowed as the pace of voting reduced. Some people struggled with navigating the software, others just weren't as enthusiastic.

Eventually, the room became still again. On the screen the pie chart remained completely red, with the figures showing:

TVC: 97.14%
Red: 100%
Blue: 0%

Applause broke out from the top table and those able to reach slapped Dr Smith's back.

"Well. That's that," he said, rising. "I'll take great pleasure in telling the old biddy to get shot of those cats myself."

"Err ... it's not accepted by the Constitution unless the voting reaches one hundred per cent," said Mr Carter, wide-eyed. He leant closer to his wife as he spoke. If he could stand behind her, he would have.

"Bloody poppycock!" shouted a puce Dr Smith, "stop being so ridiculous, man. We've won. There's no way she can win the vote now."

"Nevertheless, she must vote for the election result to be valid." This was from Derek Somersby, gloating written all over his face. "If she abstains, then the result is null and void."

"I'm afraid that's not true," Bernard spoke above the noise. He hated himself for what he was about to say. "I've just checked, and if a resident wishes to abstain in matters where voting is compulsory, then I have to vote on their behalf, and vote as I believe it is in their best interests to do so."

Dr Smith opened and closed his mouth several times. His eyes flicked from the pie chart to Bernard and back again. Slowly his face returned to its normal colour and he sat down.

"Go on then, man. Vote for her and be quick about it."

Bernard sent a silent apology to Mrs Munroe. She thought she had found a loophole in the system, but it was not to be. Even worse, it was to be he himself who finished her off.

He highlighted the blue rectangle in his intraocular display and prepared to close his eyes.

"There we go. Good lad," he heard Dr Smith say.

"Hang on," said Mr Carter. "What's going on?"

Voices came at him from all around the room:

"Who's voting?"

"It's going blue!"

Bernard looked around in confusion, then at the screen. The TVC percentage was flickering so fast he couldn't make it out. What was more obvious was the thin wedge of blue that appeared in the pie chart and rapidly expanded until it shared exactly half of it.

The figures at the bottom left of the screen now read:

TVC: 98.6%
Red: 50%
Blue: 50%

Everyone was silent, mouths open.

"Cheating!" said Dr Smith, standing and glaring around the room as if he could gain a confession through sheer will power.

Mr Carter shot to his feet, his jaw was set, and the heat of his gaze cowed the taller man. "How dare you, you pompous oaf! I programmed that app, and it is impossible for anyone to vote more than once, or for anyone outside this building to vote!"

Irene Carter stood up, looking at her husband in wonderment. She clasped his face in both hands and gave him a passionate kiss on the lips. Mr Carter smiled back, gulped, then sat down heavily.

"What do we do now?" asked someone.

"I've not voted, yet," said Bernard. The blue rectangle was still highlighted. He gave a long blink and checked the screen again:

TVC: 100%
Red: 49.3%
Blue: 50.7%

☑   ☑   ☑

"Mrs M., Mrs M.! You've won!" Bernard was hammering on her door, breathless from having run up the stairs to tell her.

Inside, Hilda Munroe sat smiling in her armchair. Mister Tiddles, a large tortoiseshell, lay in her lap, purring as she stroked him. All around the apartment lay the detritus of surgical equipment, anaesthetic drug vials and empty boxes of a certain electronic gadget.

And cats. Thirty-five cats. Just enough to give her a majority.

It had been a busy week, but she had managed to get them all done in time.

Mister Tiddles stretched, and Hilda was careful to avoid touching the stitches behind his ear, where the bulge of a freshly inserted mastoid implant could just be seen.

NOT READY TO FORGIVE
GABBY GANNON

Chilling air causes the four sisters to huddle closer to each other in a small family consultation room of the hospital. Dr. Miller slowly enters the room with his head down, not looking them in the eye until he takes a seat across the table from the sisters.

"Sorry for the wait. As you know your mother, Louisa, was brought in unresponsive suffering from an overdose. She is in organ failure due to long term substance abuse and is not showing neurological signs of improvement. She is currently on life support, meaning a ventilator is breathing for her and it is solely machines keeping her alive." The matter-of-fact tone in the doctors voice is contrary to the sympathy in his eyes.

A whimper escapes from Hailey. The sisters grasp hold of each other's hands. Hannah steels herself. "Is our mother showing any signs of brain activity?"

"I'm afraid not." Dr. Miller closes his eyes briefly allowing the severity to set in.

Lily's small voice holds hope, "How long until she recovers?"

Before Dr. Miller can answer, Claire scoffs, "She isn't going to recover. No brain activity means no chance of recovery. Right, Doctor?"

"Sadly, yes it means that medically there is nothing else we can do to help her. I'm very sorry. The damage is too severe to repair. There is one more thing to discuss. When she was brought in, we asked if there was a living will, and we were instructed there was not one. With that being the case, life support can only be terminated by the next of kin."

Hannah's flinch causes Hailey and Claire to look up at their older sister. "Dr. Miller, mother is an only child and a widow." As the words leave her lips, she knows his response before he says it.

"Hannah, as the oldest child you are legally her next of kin. The decision to terminate life support falls to you."

"I cannot be the one to decide. I won't. You don't understand what you are asking of me. I can't." Hannah fumbles over the words as the spew from her.

Claire's steady voice breaks through, "You have to be the one to decide. We will have to live with the decision that you make." Her words feel like a challenge to Hannah. Years of abuse and torment flash through Hannah's mind. Hailey, Lily, and Claire rose from their seats and exited the quiet room to go back to their mother's room.

Dr. Miller's voice brings Hannah back to the current conversation and away from years of memories.

"Hannah, I know what I'm asking of you. I also think I have a pretty good idea of what you have been through and understand your reluctance to be the one to make this decision. I have seen you in the emergency department enough times to know that you are not just a clumsy person. I know the weight of this decision. I can assuage any guilt in the sense that I do not believe it is possible for your mother to recover. This can potentially be the best way for you to achieve closure."

"What about a vote? Can we vote to take her off life support? Can we all make the decision together?" Desperation is evident in Hannah's voice. Looking at her sisters, she knows that they will judge her and resent her decision to essentially kill their mother. They will consider it selfish of her to get Louisa out of her life.

"It is unprecedented. All I can really tell you is that you are the next of kin. In terms of medically, the choice is yours."

Shortly after those final words from Dr. Miller, Hannah collects her siblings, and the Loughty sisters leave the hospital.

> *Dear Diary,*
> *Today was not a good day. I missed a spot cleaning one of the windows. When mom saw it, she slammed my head in the glass. Luckily, the window didn't break, and the bruise is easy enough to cover up. Mom immediately told me that I better be glad the window didn't break, or I would have to come up the money to fix it. Then she told me to redo all the windows before I was able to go to bed. Lily tried to help, which made mom even madder. She sent Lily to bed, turned to me, and said since I needed help with such a simple task, I needed to wash the outside of the windows as well to make*

sure I learned how to do them properly. I mistakenly turned away and she grabbed my arm and slapped me in the face. I thought she was done talking to me, but I guess she wasn't. Her eyes glazed over, she let go of my arm and went to her room. I assume she needed a fix.

    Dear Diary,

       Today was a bad day. Dad died five years ago today. Claire, Hailey, and Lily went to dad's sister for the weekend, leaving me alone with mom. Every frustration she took out on me. I tried to cook dinner and it wasn't what she wanted so she dumped the scalding food on my legs, told me to clean it up and quickly get her a glass of wine. Taking deep breaths to hold in the tears I got her wine as quickly as I could. I was shaking from the burning on my legs and knocked over the glass before even pouring any. She took the broken shards and cut my palm stating that would be my reminder to learn to fill a glass without being clumsy. As tears poured down my face, she yelled that I had nothing to cry for and that if I wanted to experience real pain I should imagine everything she goes through.

    Dear Diary,

       Today was a really bad day. I graduated from high school today and was running late because mom wasn't home, and I had to get the girls ready. My teacher Mrs. Taylor barely hid her frustration as she said that she would watch the girls so I could get with my class. I shouldn't have been surprised that Mom didn't come. It was nice hearing my sisters and friends cheer for me when I walked across the stage. For a brief moment, I felt proud of myself. That only lasted until we got home. Mom was on the couch when we all walked in. Lily ran in happy and announced that she got to watch me walk across a big stage and got to eat food at Addison's house when we stopped by there. Mom just looked at me expectantly asking where her food was. I told her that I was sorry there were no boxes to take anything with us. She sent the girls to get ready for bed. She called me over to her. When I walked up to her, she grabbed my arm, put the burning end of her cigarette to my skin and told me not to scream. Luckily, after all the times she has done that, it doesn't really hurt anymore. She asked what happened today. I told her that I graduated from high school. She scoffed and said it's not like I was valedictorian or going to be anything special. Something came over me and for the first time I wanted to stand up for myself. I told her that I was going to make something of myself in spite of her and everything that she is. I will leave this place and never look back. I then told her that I didn't give a damn about her. She flew at me and began to strangle me with my graduation cord. As she pulled the cord tighter, I could smell the alcohol on her breath and see the dilation of her pupils. I tried to claw her hands away, but I could feel myself beginning to black out. Claire came screaming into the room and pulled mom back.

Reading through her old diaries reaffirms the need for Hannah to not be the sole decider. Hannah's decision will be selfish, biased, and most of all judged if she does this on her own. Hannah finds a lawyer to have a consultation with. She needs to know the legalities of the sisters voting.

"I'm sorry, Ms. Loughty, did you say that you want to have a vote between you and your siblings to determine to take your mother off life support?" Mr. Roper's look of shock was to be expected.

"Yes, sir. I do not want the decision to be mine alone."

"Does your mother have a will or a power of attorney, any legal documentation giving someone authority over her?"

"No, she has nothing. She has never been the most prepared person. The doctors said because she does not have a Will the decision must be made by her next of kin. Mom was an only child. My father died over ten years ago. I have three younger siblings, but I am the oldest, making me the next of kin."

Mr. Roper turns his head slightly to the side. "Ms. Loughty, I do not mean any offense here, but you are an adult, and you seem intelligent. What prevents you from being able to make this decision on your own? Do you feel that you are not mentally competent?"

A wave of apprehension grips Hannah. "No, sir. It has nothing to do with competence. I am mentally stable. I just do not feel it is in anyone's best interest for me to be the sole decision maker in my mother's case." Looking down, Hannah fidgets with the bracelet on her wrist.

The simple silver wrapped around her wrist has not been removed since the day it was placed there. The plain engraving simply boasts the word, *YOU ARE*. The words would have no meaning to anyone else, but they mean more to Hannah than anything in this world.

Gathering an inner strength, Hannah feels generates from the tiny bracelet, she straightens her back. "Mr. Roper, my mother mentally and physically abused me my entire life. I cannot say with certainty that I would be making the best decision for her. I cannot say with certainty that I would not be making the decision out of spite or selfishness. I cannot be the only one to determine if my mother is taken from life support because I'm not sure I can forgive her."

"Ms. Loughty, in this instance, no one can blame you for the way you feel, and if a doctor is approaching you regarding terminating life support, you cannot be negatively held responsible for doing so. Please let me know if there is anything else I can do for you and your family."

Leaving the lawyer's office, Hannah is more determined than ever to speak with her siblings about voting. Claire, Hailey, and Lily were all old enough to know what was going on. Lily, the youngest at fifteen, would have the hardest time with things. Claire, nineteen, was already distancing herself from the family and attending college classes at the nearby community college. Hailey, seventeen, was more concerned with graduation and the approaching prom. Each of her sisters reacted with sincere concern when they received the call Hannah found their mother unconscious.

Hannah, only physically twenty-three, had already taken over being the provider for the girls. She raised each of the girls with little input from Louisa. The girls' father passed away over ten years ago, leaving behind enough money to support them and, unfortunately, their mother's drug habit. Robert Loughty was a kind and gentle man that would have never allowed his wife to behave the way she has in his absence. The few times that he saw her degrading or getting rough with Hannah when he was still alive were the only times Hannah ever saw him upset or raise his voice. He always apologized to Hannah and told her to come to him if her mother ever treated her badly. As much as Hannah loved her father, she knew that she couldn't tell him about all the things that her mother did to her. She could never break him in that way.

After parking her car in the driveway, Hannah slowly walks up to the house with a weight in her chest. She knows, on the other side, her sisters are waiting for her. She did not tell them she was going to meet with a lawyer, simply that she had a meeting to attend. Reaching her hand towards the doorknob, light twinkles off the silver of her bracelet.

Her dad gave her the bracelet before he left on his last business trip. Hannah thinks part of him knew she would need something tangible to help get her through things. Of course, he could not have known that was going to be the last time he would see his family. There is no way he could have known three miles down the road he would be involved in a fatal accident that would forever alter the lives of his four daughters by leaving them only in the hands of Louisa Loughty.

The small trinket holds so much importance to Hannah because her father always told her, you are. It has so many meanings. You are enough, you are kind, you are worth everything. The delicate jewelry is always able to bring a smile, sense of strength, wave of calm, whatever Hannah needs it provides her.

Calling on that strength she goes inside and calls out to her sisters. Gathering around the dining room table, she looks to each of them. Thankfully, Louisa spared Hannah's sisters her wrath and disdain, taking it out solely on Hannah. She claimed it was because Hannah is the one that ruined her life, and Hannah is the one that would never be beautiful or become anything in life. Claire, Hailey, and Lily were not physically abused, but they have had to deal with a neglectful drug addict for a mother in the years since their father's death.

"Y'all know that Mom is not doing well. She has been in a coma since I found her passed out in the yard. The only thing keeping her alive is the machines that she is hooked up to. Y'all heard Dr. Miller say her body and mind will never recover because of the damage of the drugs and the lack of oxygen when she overdosed. Unlike Dad, Mom never wrote a will. The decision is supposed to be mine, but I think we should vote, because it affects all of us." Hannah rushes through the words before she can chicken out of saying them.

Claire is the first to speak up. "Hannah, I don't think we can take a vote. I don't think it would be legal. You have to do it."

Hailey looks uncomfortable as tears pool in her eyes but says nothing.

"I think that we should vote; it's not fair to Hannah to be the only one to decide. Especially after everything Mom has done to her. If we all vote, no one can say that she did it to be mean or cruel or vindictive. If we all vote, we all have a say. Just because Hannah is the oldest doesn't mean she should be the only one with that put on her." Lily, despite being the youngest, has always been the most intuitive. After saying her piece, she looks at Hailey and Claire, almost daring them to say something to her.

Hannah clears her throat. "I figured we could just write yes or no on a piece of paper. Yes to take her off life support, no to keep her on it. I'll put a bowl in the middle of the table, and as you decide, write your vote on a piece of paper, fold it, and place it in the bowl. Tomorrow we will take the bowl to the hospital, and in front of the doctor, we will read the votes together."

As her sisters left the table Hannah, remains seated. Lost in thought, she does not notice Hailey beside her.

"We wouldn't blame you for pulling the plug on her. She hasn't been great to us, but she was always horrible to you. You did your best hiding things, but we knew the beatings she gave you. The horrible things she has always said to …none of it is true, by the way. You are beautiful, you are smart, and you are going to accomplish great things." As Hailey walks away, Hannah freely let tears fall from her eyes for the first time since their father's death. For the first time, Hannah feels an appreciation she's never experienced before, and a small piece of her heart heals.

Splinters and fractures remained from the lifetime of damage from her mother, but with whispered acceptance, Hailey began to allow Hannah to heal.

The next day, Hannah, Claire, Hailey, and Lily take the small clear bowl to the hospital.

Dr. Miller takes it from Hannah's hands and pours out four small scrap pieces of paper. With gentle understanding, he takes each piece, unfolds it, and reads each one. "Yes, yes, yes, no." His clear voice holds clarity as he makes eye contact with Hannah.

Claire, Hailey, and Lily look at each other before their eyes land on Hannah.

"I'm not ready to forgive her."

THE OLDEST
KAGAN DOOM

It came over the hill like a languid freight train, full of power and momentum. A line of burly motion beckoned by the rustle of a feed bag. Nostrils were as smokestacks, steam billowing out in the cool of the early morning. Hooves trudged down the muddy paths that sprawled throughout the pasture like arteries. Three dozen pairs of eyes, bulbous and black, regarded us in their approach. My dad shook the half-empty feed bag again and wiped off the sweat that had matted his forehead.

"Come and get it. Come on, now, come and get it," he called out.

We stood behind him and watched that bovine caravan stream toward us with confounding grace. My mom stepped to the pen and unlatched the gate then opened it for my dad. His boots collected mud as he went through and to the pen's center.

"Come and get it. Come on, now."

Honeydew was first, as always, but my mom slid the gate closed and the confused heifer kept the same speed and skirted the exterior of the entire cattle pen, energized by the rustle of the feed bag inside. Next to be excluded was Idaho. She bunted her head to the horizontal slats and that state-patterned mark across the bridge of her nose jostled the gate on its hinges, but it did not give. Mom shooed her and the heifer turned away but behind her came Ginger and Pancake, followed closely by their ungainly calves who were ignorant to the reason for the sudden activity, but the young pair studied the scene with the intense inquisition of creatures not yet hardened into indifference by their new world. My mom kept the entryway closed and the four followed the others in disappointment around the pen then scattered into the open area around the pond.

My brother, looking particularly tired and young in the early morning daybreak, climbed up a section of cattle gate and balanced on the top edge. Now taller than I, his dishevelled hair caught the sunlight that poked through the stand of oaks and his dark strands were recast in a brilliant bronze. Dad's old boots fitted him like clown shoes, and they scraped the metal beams like mud-caked irons as he positioned them on the lower rung. He scratched his temple and spit next to an empty feeding trough. "Get up here. From this spot you can see him."

"I ain't got to see him," I said. "I know he's coming."

"Better keep an eye on him."

"Why's that? He's got his eye on *you*."

He turned to me, the action almost whirling him off balance. "No, he don't. He's coming for you."

My dad rattled the bag. "Here he comes. Get ready."

Through the mass of brown withers sprang a massive head, fur as black as shadow, haunches pumping in accordance with their corded muscles, transforming caboose to vanguard locomotive as it headed the herd; a beast having utter dominion over the pastoral landscape from fence line to fence line. It raged on with tremendous will. The herd obediently flared open to give the bull a wide berth then closed back together like a curtain in its wake.

A memory came to me. My brother had been watching a toddler's show on television about the alphabet while my mom cooked a large breakfast in our newly remodeled kitchen. The show didn't keep my attention as I was too old, so I joined my mom. She let me try some of the pancake batter but mostly my job was relegated to waiting. During that time, I peered through the bay window—the one that aimed to the north and revealed the spanse of pastureland near the county road—and idled in the rich glow of an August morning, feeling the already sweltering heat through the glass, waiting for Dad to come back from his routine fence inspection. Several cows grazed about but one in particular, white with brown spots, wandered off, only stopping at intervals to bellow. She disappeared into the tree line, reappeared then revisited the thick bramble. Toiling through visible exhaustion, she oscillated her head back and forth in a panic.

Then I saw the Great Danes.

Our newlywed neighbors had kept three Great Danes in their home, massive dogs that made a habit of escaping their backyard fence only to terrorize neighborhood cats. That day their target was in our pasture: a young calf, days old. Dominant in wit and agility, the trio of dogs herded the young one into the corner of the pasture near a felled tree and snapped at its thin legs and bit at its tail. The dogs were so devoted to this torment they didn't see the bull.

In one swift motion, 150 pounds of German-bred canine were transformed into a brindle, wingless, floppy-eared bird. A second charge sent the brown dog, the more ferocious of the three, sailing ten yards to the south until it smashed into a wilted limb of the felled tree. The third, apparently the smartest of the three, fled and was followed soon by his limping cohorts.

The next weekend I noticed our neighbors had installed a taller fence in their backyard and placed bricks around the base to prevent tunnels from being dug. Between the slats in the new fence, I saw three large dogs pace back and forth. Two walked in a bizarre gait because of casts plastered on their forearms. Cats in the neighborhood have become more social since then.

Now, as the bull comes to us, I'm reminded of that ungodly power. The power to lift a heavy load into the sky with a flick of a neck. I could picture myself as one of the trio, knowing I too was about 150 pounds and without the understanding that some movement of mine could enrage the precarious beast and I would find myself in the limbs of a nearby tree or tossed amongst the herd.

"Who's doing it?" My dad asked.

"Momma?" My brother suggested.

Mom opened the entry gate wide. The bull's girth expanded with each step in the pale light. We could hear the heavy tread of it now. "Not me. I've got the gate."

I turned to my brother still perched on top. "You do it."

"Why?"

"Well, because I'm the oldest. And I said so."

He spied the unpredictable bull, watching with an uncertain glare. "You do it."

"I'm the oldest."

"Someone grab the drench gun," my dad said. "Get ready."

The beastly shadow whipped into the pen and my mom snapped the gate closed. Large hooves kicked globs of wet, rural soil into the air which landed around the pen and dappled my brother's shirt. Dad shook the bag and backtracked through the cattle run, steading himself before each step in the greedy mud. This led the bull through the pen; it paced through the open chamber then snaked around the alleys in a hungry trance like a mouse maneuvering around the confines of a maze.

"Get ready, boys," he called again.

"Get ready," I told my brother.

He hopped down and picked up the drench gun and fed the nozzle into the bottle of antibiotics then pulled the plunger. The plastic tube filled with a viscous, white medicine.

"Hurry," I told him.

"I don't want to do it."

"I'm the oldest. Go."

He proffered the gun to me. "But I'm the youngest."

The wide animal was in the narrow alley now. Black fur rubbed against the metal tubes. The tail, thick as a rope, swung instinctively at flies. The fence narrowed and concentrated the wide girth of the bull into an uncomfortable channel where the only motion allowed was forward. A string of mucus dribbled loosely then was shot out at cannon speed when the creature snorted. My dad arrived at the end of the alley and tossed a few feed pellets into the blue squeeze chute. The bull went on.

"You boys better decide."

My brother gave a cursory glance to my mom then stalled on me. "I vote that you do it."

I shook my head. "I'm the oldest."

My mom turned to me, grinning. "I vote that you do it too."

"I'm the oldest, though. I vote no."

"Two against one," my brother said and stuck the gun in my hands. I refused to claim it.

"No, no," I said. "Dad ain't voted yet. He's the swing vote."

My dad clambered up the alley fence and spun a leg over then landed in the safety of the empty feeding side, his boots sending a spray of mud out like an indecent flower. The bull surged past him on the alley side and erased the comparatively small boot prints with hooves. My dad ran to the exterior fencing and hopped over then got into position and placed one hand on the lever of the squeeze chute.

"Daddy, you gotta vote who does it," my brother said, then chuckled. "You get a vote that swings."

My dad looked at me, then my brother, then me again. "Then I vote for you. You're the oldest."

I stopped kneading my hands and took the drench gun from my satisfied brother. My sighs went unnoticed, or ignored, and I took position near the head of the squeeze chute. My brother and mom stepped back.

"Here he comes," my dad said.

The bull had finished the alley and was neck deep in the chute, following the trail of tossed pellets that had scattered in the crooks of the steel mechanism. One hoof in. Then two. The chute moaned from the new weight. Waiting for the entirety of the animal to enter, I saw a printed label on a support beam of the chute that guaranteed the manufactured piece of equipment could accommodate up to a 2,500-pound animal.

This guarantee is about to be put to the test, I thought.

Three hooves in.

I was reminded of the painful howl the dogs had let out after their failed assault. Through the bay window, I had heard their whimpering cries as they retreated back under the barbed-wire fence and across the county road to their own yard. Even then, after the attack, the bull loomed its head over the fence near the road, watchful and cautious, caring not for the stick of a barb, but showing force by mere presence to prevent a secondary attack by the dogs.

I too am about 150 pounds.

Four hooves.

Dad lifted the lever, and the head gate pinned the jutting front of the bull, holding it in place. There was a violent storm of thrashing and lowing as the animal validated the strength of the steel enclosure and its welds. My father flipped another lever that pressed the ribbed squeeze plate into the black fur. The animal was pinned but the head still jerked and pivoted in its metal collar.

"Get him," my dad called out, his body weight on the squeeze lever. "Get him, now. Hurry."

Those mad eyes rolled in fist sized sockets. Teeth snapped around a protruding tongue. The entire unit jostled against the furious weight. I stepped forward and put the nozzle to the bull's lips but a jerk of its rageful muzzle sent my hand back.

"Don't break the nozzle or we'll have to start all over again," my mom said.

"I can't hold him long, son. Hurry."

"Yeah, do it," my brother said with his hands cupped around his mouth. "You gotta do it. We voted for you."

Clouds of hot breath steamed out of my focal point, my target. My aim needed to be precise. The bays had alerted the other cattle, and as I drew the nozzle forward again, I had three dozen extra pairs of eyes, bulbous and black, watching my movement. The bull paused briefly in his flailing, ostensibly to let me do my elected duty, so I plunged the curved nozzle into the open mouth of steaming breath. I thrust the plunger down then brought the device back to myself. The bull flipped his tongue in and out then went about thrashing again.

My dad still held the lever. "Done?"

"Yeah."

"Easy?"

"Yeah," I told my dad, shaking.

"Stand back."

My mom, brother and I retired to a corner between an old oak and the cattle fence then my dad released the squeeze lever then hoisted up the head gate and the bull shot out of the chute in a terrible display of power. It bucked once, then twice, spraying us with ribbons of mud and severed grass, then trotted with belligerent priss around the attentive brown mass, before the patriarch joined his herd and led them all uphill toward the ascending eastern sun.

I was given a brief applause by my brother who I subsequently thumped on the shoulder.

"My term is over," I told him. "The next election you'll run unopposed."

ONE FINAL DIFFERENCE
STEVEN MORSCHAUSER

Arnie Sumwalt stared at the full moon the way he always did when it was low on the horizon. It was sinking fast as the sun rose quickly behind him. He stood on his balcony, hoping that the early morning mist wasn't soaking into his best jacket and tie, and sipping his lukewarm coffee to push back the cold, crisp air. It didn't matter how hard he tried, it never tasted as good as Jennifer's. Even after fifty years of marriage, he never bothered to ask her how she made it. Back then, it had always just been there in the pot each morning, waiting to be poured into his chipped Pittsburgh Steelers cup. The coffee may have changed, but the cup was still the same. A lot of things were still the same. A lot wasn't.

A quick gust of cold air brought him back into the moment and away from his self-pity. He looked at his empty cup and decided to go back inside. The morning air was replaced by lavender. His living room always smelled like potpourri. While Jennifer was still a part of his life, it reminded him that she wasn't home anymore, and was in a hospice bed. When he was in a good mood, he didn't really notice it at all; but when he wasn't, the smell left him depressed and angry. He had been smelling a lot of lavender lately.

Arnie was noticing it very much at the moment.

He looked at the clock on the stove. Quarter past seven. It was time to go. The polling location in the middle school wasn't open for a few hours yet, but he still had to get some breakfast. It wasn't going to cook itself with just him around. He stopped and looked at himself in the hallway mirror. It never seemed appropriate to vote looking like the people standing in line on the news. Civic duty should always be paired with civility. Making important decisions wasn't meant for t-shirts and jeans. He straightened out his green and gold striped tie, checked it for coffee stains, grabbed his keys, and left.

The morning paper was sticking out of the hedge under the front window. Better there than in the pile of dog shit like yesterday, Arnie thought. Jackson Phelps was a good kid. He really was, but he was doomed. He had dreams of being a baseball pitcher one day. Arnie laughed and opened up to the front page. The Democratic candidate for mayor, Damian Samuels, was ahead by even more points than he was the week before. Jennifer would have loved that. He looked at his picture. Typical Jennifer-type guy. Long hair, glasses, and a tweed jacket. Also, no doubt, dumb as a stump. Why else would he be a Democrat? Arnie liked the other guy much better. You can always count on an ex-trucker-turned-politician to do the right thing, he mused. Phil Mulligan might not have a fancy degree, but he did have one thing: Arnie Sumwalt's vote.

He opened the door and threw the newspaper on the passenger seat. Damned car smelled like lavender, too. It was everywhere today. With his windows rolled down all the way, he backed out, narrowly missing the Phelps kid riding down the other side of the street. Tomorrow's paper is definitely going to be on the roof, Arnie figured.

☑ ☑ ☑

Arnie looked at his toast. It was burned beyond recognition. He obviously knew that it had been bread at one point in its past, but that time was long gone. It was a square piece of carbon covered with apple jelly. He couldn't resist the temptation to take a sniff and wondered if that was what Pompeii had smelled like the day Vesuvius blew its top, a lovely fragrant combination of burning ash and fruit. Welcome to breakfast, he thought to himself. He looked around at the other customers in the Brickhouse Diner. They had beautiful toast, perfectly made and lovingly covered in butters and jams. He again looked down at his, black and dead. Perfectly typical. Delores had his table again. Ten seconds later, right on cue, he asked himself again why he kept eating there, only to find the same answer he always did: The diner was cheap and so was he. It was also the place he had met Jennifer, a very long time before, when the place was just a dump dive bar called Pickerman's. The jukebox was long gone now, along with Joe Pickerman himself, but the place looked exactly the same, right down to the red and white tile flooring.

Delores didn't try too hard to shed the image of the stereotypical diner waitress and always came across as the love child of Flo from "Alice" and a construction worker from New Jersey. Perhaps it was an image she cultivated. She was shaped like a dumpling, wore far too much makeup, and, with the exception of her horrific prowess with a toaster, was fairly good at her job. She was requested more often and tipped far greater than any other employee in the diner. The only thing that was missing was the pencil behind her ear. She took customer orders with an app on her phone and beamed them straight to the kitchen. Arnie wondered if there was an app for making toast.

He picked up the newspaper and read the headline again as he finished his bacon and eggs. Maybe Mulligan will pull off an upset. It's happened before. With a grunt of disgust, he tossed it onto the empty table next to him. Delores looked over the head of the man she was pouring coffee for and smiled. Same old Arnie, she thought. The older lady who used that table for lunch really appreciated the service she got and tipped an extra buck each time she got a free copy of the *Daily Journal*. The worse the news, the more papers Arnie tossed, and the more money Delores got.

She put the coffee pot back on its heated base, grabbed a fresh one, and strolled over to Arnie's table. He was staring off into the air. His skin looked older today, she noticed, and his eyes were a touch waterier and more stained with time. She liked his eyes. They were a soft blue and gave away a gentle side that he wasn't going to show anyone anymore. Today, though, those eyes weren't happy.

"Anyone home?" Delores asked. "You gave that paper quite the fling there. Betty will be happy to read it later on." She refilled his coffee cup to get his attention.

Arnie looked up. "I don't want any more coffee." He pushed the cup away.

"Too bad," she replied. "Everything okay?"

He looked shocked that anyone would even care to ask him. "No. Yeah, I'm fine. I have a lot to do today."

"I don't see your 'I Voted' sticker on your lapel. You always have one on Election Day. Didn't you go yet?"

Arnie instinctively looked down at his jacket where the sticker would have been. "No, that's later."

Delores looked over at her other customers and decided that they were okay. She pulled out a chair and sat down. "Is this about Jennifer?" No point in dancing around the issue, she thought, go right at it. You never know when someone would be asking for a piece of pie.

Arnie just stared at her. "It's just not the same, you know?" He tried to smile and stared at his toast. "We always used to joke around about how we canceled each other's vote out. I'd vote for the Republican, and she'd vote for the Democrat. Didn't matter who was running. Now, it's just me today, and I really miss her. I'd even take her telling me why my vote was wrong if she could be here."

"You talk like she's dead."

Arnie realized that he had gone too far. "I'm sorry, I didn't mean it that way. Ever since I took her to that hospice, it just feels that way. I was there yesterday, and she didn't even know it. Wide awake and she had no clue I was even there. I'm going to see her after I get done voting. The hospice doesn't let people visit before ten." He stood up and pointed at the plate. "That's some bad toast, Delores. You could weaponize that. The Pentagon would give you a fortune for it. No nukes required, just drop your toast on the enemy." He smiled and left a nice tip on the table.

"Go vote, you old fart,"

"Yes, ma'am," he replied, saluting, suddenly realizing that he had never done that to a woman before.

"Tell Jennifer we're thinking of her, okay?" she added as Arnie headed for the door.

She began to clean up the table after he left, wondering why an old man like Arnie Sumwalt would ever use lavender scented aftershave.

☑ ☑ ☑

The polling location for his district was in the gym of the middle school. In fact, it was the same school he went to as a boy. He always regretted never going far from his birthplace. Even salmon had a more interesting life than he did, Jennifer used to tease. He pulled into the parking lot of the three-story red brick building and noted the line that had formed outside. His watch said it was just a few minutes until the doors opened. Arnie joined the end of the line and waited.

The young man in the t-shirt and jeans standing in front of him turned. "I heard there's a problem with the machines. Somethin' about the computer being down. It might be a while."

"Did they say how long?" Arnie instinctively looked at his watch. He wanted to get to the hospice and help Jennifer eat her lunch later on.

"Nah."

He looked at the young man. I know exactly who you're voting for, Mr. T-shirt and ripped pants, Arnie thought.

Arnie craned his neck to see if the line was moving at all. So were a lot of other people. It didn't appear that it was going to be moving anytime soon. He pulled out his phone to see if he had gotten any calls. It was still turned off from the day before when he had visited Jennifer. He really disliked being bothered while he was spending precious time with her and usually shut the phone off altogether.

One voice mail. He held the phone to his ear and listened. It was from the hospice. He was being asked to call them back as soon as he could and ask for the RN on duty.

His hands began to tremble. He called the number back and waited, feeling the sweat forming on the back of his neck. Seven long agonizing rings.

"Meadow Cliff Hospice. This is Melinda, how may I direct your call?"

"Um ... I'm supposed to ask for the RN. She called me."

"Name, please?"

"Arnie Sumwalt. My wife is there. Jennifer."

"One moment, please."

A click. "First floor nurses' station."

"Hello, this is Arnie Sumwalt. I got a message to call."

"Oh ... um ..." The nervous voice belonged to a young lady. He could hear the phone being handed off.

Another pause. A different voice. "Is this Mr. Sumwalt?"

"I believe I just said that. Yes, this is Mr. Sumwalt."

"Mr. Sumwalt, this is Carla at Meadow Creek Hospice. We spoke a little bit yesterday when you were here."

Now it was Arnie's turn for a long pause. He gripped the phone tighter as his fingers started to get sweatier. "Yes." Please let me have forgotten something at the hospice, he begged inside. Please, please, please.

Another pause. Pauses were never followed by good news, he thought. Win the lottery, and people came out and told you right away. Too many pauses and you needed to start worrying. He suddenly felt bad for Carla. Getting bad news was never good, but having to deliver it over and over again each day must be downright awful.

"She's gone, isn't she?" Arnie decided to soften the blow for both of them by coming right out and saying it. While he desperately hoped it wasn't true, he knew what she was about to say.

"Yes, Mr. Sumwalt. Yes, Arnie."

He was glad she used his first name.

"Can I ask when?"

"About an hour ago. She went into cardiac arrest not long after breakfast. We followed the order not to resuscitate on the chart like she wanted." Carla took a breath. "I'm so sorry."

His knees began to turn to rubber. This day was always going to come but that didn't make it any easier to accept.

"You've called the funeral home?" Asking that question squeezed his chest. "We had everything pre-planned. It's the Morgan and Kelly funeral home. They're the ones with that really bad commercial." His attempt at humor helped a bit and so did Carla's gentle laugh on the phone.

"No, not yet. The nursing assistants are getting—" she stopped, knowing that the rest of that sentence would come out as being too clinical and cold. "They are finishing up some last details and then we will contact the funeral home."

Someone tapped Arnie on the shoulder and pointed to the end of the line that had begun to move away from him down the sidewalk. "I'm sorry." He walked down the sidewalk to rejoin the line.

"Everyone there was great," he said. "I don't think she could have gotten better care anywhere else."

"Thank you. We really enjoyed getting to know her. She was quite a nice person. Again, I'm so very sorry for your loss."

Arnie turned off the phone and put it back in his pocket. In that instant he realized that the world suddenly looked different. Everything appeared the same, but something had changed. It was a world without his wife, and he didn't like that world. Every sunrise and sunset from now on would be one she wouldn't see. The line moved ahead several paces, and he was close to the entrance. Even this little act, voting, something she dearly loved to participate in would be denied her. All of it. He felt sadder over her loss of experiences than he did over his own loss. Jennifer loved her life.

At the table inside, a row of poll workers sat checking IDs and handing out large paper ballots. He was directed to the right side of the table and got in the line based on his last name. He pulled out his driver's license and handed it to the elderly gentleman who checked it against a list and spun a large binder around for him to sign. As he was putting his ID back in the wallet, a very old picture of Jennifer fell out and landed on the table. So pretty, he remembered. Still so pretty. He fought back a wave of emotion and put the photo away.

"Arnie Sumwalt," the poll worker said to the woman sitting next to him.

She double checked his name against her own list, crossed it off, and handed him a ballot. "You are number nine-hundred and fifty-seven. You can pick any empty booth to your right."

Arnie quietly took the ballot and found an empty booth. He scanned the list of names and referendums that he had to vote on. There was a new school being considered, an athletic field for the football team, and a bridge to be built over a marsh full of endangered frogs. Then there was the vote for mayor: Mulligan versus the hippy. Wonderful.

He stood there for several minutes. These were easy choices. No on the new school. No on the stupid football field. Most definitely no for the stupid frogs. As for the mayor, screw that damn hippy. Arnie thought about it again. These weren't easy choices. Not anymore.

He pulled out the picture of Jennifer again. She had her entire future ahead of her the day it was taken. Everything was possible then. What a wonderful life she had created since that day despite the constraints that the world tried so hard to apply. He was very proud of her. She should have had more time to finish all the things she so passionately wanted to do.

Arnie stared at the ballot a little longer before picking up the pencil. His mind had gone completely blank. It was just a meaningless list of names and empty circles to be filled in.

He set her picture next to the ballot. Her smile helped him decide what to do. It was as though she had whispered into his ear.

YES, on the new school.

YES, for the new football field.

YES, for the frogs and their bridge.

YES, to a hippy over the truck driver for mayor.

He smiled to himself as he looked at that old photograph taken so long ago. One more chance to make a difference.

RENTAL AGREEMENT 
LA HARPER

"So."

My mom's voice pierced through my thoughts. I was a million miles away—thinking about everything and nothing all at once—and like a rubber band, she snapped me back to the table. We had finished eating now, and a cup of coffee sat in front of me, mostly untouched. She looked tired but interested.

"Tell me, Laurel, what have you been up to?"

"Well, Sean moved out recently. He must be busy getting settled; I've been calling him to see how he's doing but he hasn't replied." I took a sip of my coffee and regarded the man sitting beside Mom. She'd had so many new boyfriends I couldn't even tell if he looked familiar or not, and I'd already forgotten his name. Kevin? Kyle? He smiled politely. He appeared tired, too.

Gross.

"Oh, that's too bad. Sean was a nice kid." She trailed off into awkward silence. 'Kyle' cleared his throat and folded his hands on the table.

"Can you afford the rent on your own?" he asked.

"Well, not really." I hesitated, thinking about what happened earlier today. "Maybe we can."

"We?" That was Mom. She never cared about my friends and couldn't be bothered to remember their names. Bringing them up was a polite conversational formality for her.

"Yes. Me, Travis, and Hailey. We took a vote about getting a new roommate."

I looked down into my mug, the pale creamer swirling in invisible eddies.

"What did you decide? Tell me everything." 'Kevin' had leaned forward in his chair, listening intently. He was kind of creepy, and I hoped Mom would dump him soon. I swallowed and took another sip.

"Well, Sean hadn't gotten all his stuff ..."

☑ ☑ ☑

Sean hadn't gotten all his stuff yet. There was a wall of reused liquor store boxes piled up by the door and in his bedroom when we talked about it. Hailey was crying, holding a box of Sean's things like a life preserver, the bright yellow background of an 'Espinoza for Congress' sticker peeping through her splayed fingers. I knew why she was so upset, but it seemed overdramatic, even for her. Travis was trying to console her, and he looked over at me with those pleading, puppy-dog eyes. Crying girls aren't something he's equipped to handle, but if we are being honest, that applies to pretty much *any* girl. I think he may have the hots for Hailey— *who doesn't?*— but he is one of those nerdy-geeky types, with too many Funko Pops, who can hole up for an entire weekend in his bedroom, surviving on energy drinks and video games.

Anyway, I had to take over for him to try and get Hailey to calm down. Otherwise, I wouldn't have enough peace to do my Art History homework.

"I'm just going to miss him *so much*," she blubbered into my shoulder. I patted her, unsure of what to say, so instead, I took the box from her. She was wallowing, and I wasn't going to allow that.

"We'll see him again; he just got his own place with his brother." At my words, she burst into a fresh onslaught of misery. Travis just watched from the kitchen doorway and shook his head.

"I don't know about you guys, but as a starving programmer and game design student, I can't afford to pay a third of Sean's rent, and since we all work at the same damned place, I'm pretty sure neither can you."

It was true, I got them both jobs at the store. Such a huge retailer meant that, even though we worked in the same building, we never saw each other due to shift scheduling, and the same went for at school. Except for Sean, who I shared a few classes with, but he worked at his dad's men's retail shop on most nights and weekends.

"No more roommates." Hailey's grip on my arm was viselike. "They never clean up after themselves."

"And never love you back?" The sardonic tone of Travis's voice wasn't lost on Hailey, who got up from the couch to confront him.

"Oh, and you're the guru of romance? All you do is sit on your ass and play Fortnite with ninety-nine other lonely dudes every weekend." She jabbed him in the chest, and he stepped back. Hailey was kind of scary when she got mad, and Travis wasn't much of a fighter.

"Guys, can we please not argue? Let's take a vote. All for having a new roommate?"

"We don't need a new roommate, you guys!" Hailey's sentence ended in a harpy-like screech of frustration that made my eardrums rattle.

"Yes, we do. My friend Nathan has been looking for a place anyway, and he's a chill guy. Won't bother anyone, and we don't need to worry about making the rent." Travis's reply was immediate; apparently, he had been considering Nathan for a while. He did have a point, but it kind of bothered me he was so quick to replace Sean. He was our close friend and roomie for three years!

☑   ☑   ☑

"And that made you upset?" 'Karl' broke in, interrupting my story. I glared at him over my mug of coffee.

"I mean, not really. It's just Travis being, well, *Travis*." I shrugged. "Sean was more than free to leave; his brother needed help paying his own rent, and it was closer to the school for him, so it just made sense. The only one mad about it was Hailey.

"What's Hailey like?"

"Don't you want to know what the vote was?" Mom butted in, her face gaunter than before. Was I staying too late?

"Mom, if you're tired, why don't you go upstairs to bed? I can go home. You look pretty awful." She flinched as if I moved to hit her, and I frowned. "I didn't mean it like that."

"I know, honey." She patted my hand, and it was ice cold. I hoped she wasn't getting sick, that would be terrible with everything happening in the world lately. "Finish your story; it was very interesting."

"Okay ..."

☑ ☑ ☑

Okay, so Hailey was about ready to hurl Travis through the front window, I swear it. He's not exactly a little dude, but she sure would have tried. She's kind of a firecracker anyway—always the one doing spontaneous things and making wild decisions because of her mood—but that's what makes her so fun to be around. Travis is more cautious and reserved, and they butt heads a lot. They're pretty good friends, but being polar opposites creates a lot of static sometimes. Especially this time. Though, I'd never seen Hailey so upset over something so dumb before.

"That's a 'no' on the roommate. We can make it work if we pull extra shifts and cancel the cable. No one really watches real TV anymore anyway," she said, sitting back down next to me.

Travis groaned, instantly firing back with never having any free time, and then they were back to fighting about how much time he spent playing 'those dumb games.' It was like watching a married couple argue and I could feel our friendships cracking. I had to defuse this, and quickly, before either of them said something they would regret forever.

"Stop it! Hey!" I had to practically shout over them to be heard. "Don't I get the deciding vote?" They both paused and looked at me like they forgot I was even in the room. That tends to happen a lot with those two, but it's okay. I'm pretty quiet.

"Of course, you do, Laurel." Hailey was all honey and innocence now, trying to sweeten me into siding with her. "Go ahead."

Travis said nothing, just stared at me. He had already appealed to my more logical mentality, and working extra shifts in that retail hellhole didn't seem at all fun for me either, and he knew it. He gave a curt nod as if to say *go on*. But I also really didn't want to make Hailey sad again, so I was torn.

"If no one moved in, we could stop sharing a roo-oom." Hailey cooed in a sing-songy voice. Dammit, she was getting to me. I'd wanted my own room for a while, no offense to her, but she was a neat freak and constantly poked me to be tidier. I hesitated, thinking about it.

"But what about having to work so much?"

"I'll help you study so you don't spend so much time face-down in a textbook. I'm taking art as my minor, remember, so I'm sure some of our studies cross paths."

"What about me, Hailey? What about *me* having to pick up extra shifts? Just because Laurel is the swing vote doesn't mean I shouldn't also get a say." He had made it back to the kitchen door frame, leaning against it like a chubby James Dean impersonator.

"I'll break your computer and then you won't have to worry about it, will you, since you'll have nothing better to do." There was venom in her voice, and I could almost taste the acidity of it on my own tongue.

"All that really matters is that Laurel is happy because her name's on the lease," Hailey continued, smiling at me and patting my shoulder reassuringly. "It'll be totally fine. You get your own room *and* a study buddy *and* nothing even changes!"

I didn't have to say anything before Travis knew he wasn't going to win this one and stormed off to his bedroom. The slamming door rattled the kitchen cabinets as Hailey nearly tackled me in a hug.

"Thanks, Laurel. You're the best." She squeezed me and I gasped a little as she continued, "I never get what I want with you guys."

"Hailey, you *always* get what you want," I said, pushing her off lightly and sighing in defeat. She grinned like a cat in a fish market.

"I guess that's true," she said, before leaving me alone in the living room.

☑ ☑ ☑

"So, you voted 'no,' then? How do you plan on paying the rent?" 'Karlos' asked. I shrugged.

"I'll just work extra shifts and cancel the cable, like Hailey said. With the three of us working toward it, we can do it."

Mom exhaled sharply.

"Are you okay, Mom?" I looked over at her, and she appeared absolutely exhausted, defeated.

"Oh, yes, dear." She tried to smile but it ended up more disturbing than comforting. "Just please answer Officer Kellar's questions."

Wait, Officer Kellar? That was her boyfriend's name? My confusion must have been clear, because Kyle, no, Kellar, regarded me with a neutral expression. I stared more closely at him, this definitely not a face I recognized. He was dressed in a white button-up, open at the collar, with a loose, drab tie ornamented by a tiny 'McLellan for Sheriff' pin, probably forced on him by his boss.

"Laurel?" His voice sounded muffled and far away, and I realized the mug I was drinking from was actually a Styrofoam cup. The table, that before had been in my mother's dining room, had swum out of view, replaced by one of those cheap excuses of furniture with wood veneer and plastic sides that made you think of school dances and bingo halls.

"Wait, we were having dinner. How did we get here?"

Mom gave me an apologetic smile. "After dinner, we had come to the station for questioning." She looked over at Officer Kellar for help, discomfort lining the creases of her face.

"Your friend, Sean," he started, tasting the words before speaking, choosing them very carefully. "He's been missing for a while, and we've talked to all his friends. We already talked to Travis but haven't found Hailey yet."

The pit of my stomach dropped.

"They can't find him? Do they know anything?"

"Only that he never showed up to his brother's house with his stuff."

I immediately thought of the wall of boxes back at the house and felt so sad about them, like, why didn't I notice it had been so long? Was I that deep in my studies? I hadn't even remembered we weren't at my mom's house anymore. Where was my head?

"Well, anything I can do to help. Please, ask me anything."

"Where is Hailey?"

"I don't know. Home? She was home when I left."

"Okay. What were you doing before you went to dinner at your mother's?" Officer Kellar asked. This felt like a proper investigation now, and my breath caught in my throat. I had absolutely nothing to do with Sean's disappearance, but the idea of saying something *wrong* was absolutely terrifying. I thought back, but there was only empty space.

"I ... can't remember. Studying for my Art History exam, I guess. That's pretty boring stuff, and I can't ever seem to remember it."

"What about before that?"

"Arguing with Travis. He was mad I sided with Hailey again, mad I always side with her just because she's pretty and fun and interesting. All the things I'm not."

"Oh, honey—" my mom started, but Kellar stopped her with a small hand gesture.

"So, this Hailey girl, she's kind of like the boss?"

"No one's really the boss, I guess, but they both seem to listen to me a lot. Most of the time. Sean was the smart one; they liked to listen to him, too."

"You're a college student, Laurel. Do you engage in drug use? It's not uncommon."

"Whoa, wha— no!" I turned my head toward my mom, but she wasn't looking at me anymore.

"Mom? What's happening?"

"I'm sorry," she whispered, still unwilling to meet my gaze.

"Why ... Why won't you look at me?"

"I'm sorry." Her eyes glazed over as she repeated the words, and she sniffled. The room started spinning, a slow, dizzying waltz.

"Mom?" I heard my voice crack, felt the catch as a wave of sadness washed over me. My mother couldn't bear to focus on anything in my general direction.

"Laurel." It was the barest hint of a whisper, a shadow of her voice. A shadow's shadow. "Honey, with Sean moving out," she paused, as if she was uncertain she should tell me whatever she was thinking. She inhaled and closed her eyes, "you live alone now."

☑ ☑ ☑

The world went quiet. It was like cosmic forces violently shoved cotton balls into my brain, everything turning all soft and muddled and muffle-y. Kellar was talking to me; his lips moved but I couldn't focus on the words.

"Alone? I don't live alone. I have *two* roommates! Hailey Espinoza and Travis McLellan, ages twenty-one and twenty, college students like me. Hailey loves rainbows and parties, and Travis loves energy drinks but hates coffee and is loyal to a fault, most of the time."

"Laurel, did you hear me?"

"Did you hear *me*? I don't live alone!"

"Laurel, this is going to be a bit of a shock to you, but I want to be completely honest. Sean isn't really missing. We've found him, but he … he died, Laurel. Someone killed him."

You ever break a mirror or a glass and follow the cracks, trying to find the point of the initial blow and end up just following the cobwebby lines across it? I felt like that. I felt like those fragile lines, barely holding together, surrounding that sharp, shattered point of impact: my heart. Sean was gone? Dead? No, not my Sean. Not the Sean I knew was all smiles and tan-lines, who was so smart and dedicated he was putting himself through a dental degree and helping his dad out and still made time for the three of us when we wanted to hang. I refused to believe it.

"Mom, tell him he's wrong. About everything." She shook her head and I reached for her hands, only to notice blood spattering my knuckle. I stopped, staring at the ugly red slashes along the tops of my hands, fine cuts and bruises that were fresh and just settling in.

"Mama," I breathed, unsure of what to say, fear gripping my insides with icy fingers. I pulled up my jacket sleeves, exposing more cuts, more bruising. Looking down, I found my sky-blue hoodie was covered in blood spatter.

"Sean was stabbed to death, Laurel, and those look like he was very much against the idea." Officer Kellar's voice was deadpan as he indicated the defensive wounds on my arms and my ruined jacket. I couldn't look at him, couldn't focus on anything. I tried to speak, but the words wouldn't pass my lips. My mind froze, and a tingling sensation washed over me. "I'm gonna pass out. Or throw up. Or both," I warned, before falling out of my chair and into the waiting darkness.

☑   ☑   ☑

I came to with Officer Keller carefully picking me up, helping me back to my seat.

"Laurel? Are you okay?" he said, looking at me and touching my head. I hissed and pulled away. It *stung*.

"Laurel? Say something if you're all right."

I looked over to him, a sneer creasing my face.

"That hurt! Don't touch me, jackass. And stop calling me Laurel—my name is Hailey."

RETURN TO DEMOCRACY
DON MCENERY

I wander the empty streets. The security forces have stopped their patrols. The guns are finally silent. After three long years, the rebellion is over. It's a peculiar feeling; I feel safe and worried simultaneously. I'm lucky; if the rebellion lasted any longer, I would have reached the age of maturity and been conscripted. Now, as an adult, I have a task that haunts me more than the thought of fighting, more than the thought of death. My mind is so occupied with this, what was it? I look down and check the information booklet in my hand, this election. We choose our leaders; it's a difficult concept to grasp. It's mandatory; they have lists with everyone's names. One hundred percent participation is being ensured jointly by the security and resistance forces' leaders.

I watch the road as I walk.

"Breathing in fresh air without the stench of gunpowder is refreshing," I hear behind me.

"Peter, how are you?"

"I'm well; I assume you're preparing for the voting line?"

I nod as we walk. "I just wish I could talk to someone about this. I need insight, guidance, but discussion of the election is forbidden; they deem it a necessary measure to prevent coercion."

"I feel the same," Peter says. "Hal, we have no information, we've never done this before, and we're supposed to ask nothing, say nothing, and just carry on like our lives haven't been overturned."

I stop and flip through the election information. "A firmer understanding of the process would make this so much easier. The booklet uses terms I still don't comprehend. What does it mean by ranked ballot?"

Peter stops and points to a section on the page. He reads and I follow along. "The goal is to create a ruling council. Five council members will be chosen by us. There's a pool of ten candidates. We rank our top three choices on the selection paper. They have a point system; five points for the first rank, three for the second, and one point for third. The five candidates with the highest point score will be our council."

"It sounds complicated yet somehow simple at the same time," I say

I continue to flip the pages feeling blind; having to make this choice but knowing nothing about these people. I see names and small amounts of information, but somehow it seems too brief for the decision I must make.

Peter has his pamphlet in his hands. He flips to the candidate list. "The pool of candidates is mainly security force officers and resistance commanders from among the country's sectors. Two sector governors are also listed. There are a few citizens of high esteem ..."

"Before the resistance, we called those people informants," I interrupt. "We've spent years regarding them as treacherous scum."

"Some of the resistance commanders are security force defectors. I feel like they're forming a new government with old leadership. How do we keep whatever new freedom we now have if all our leaders know is the tight military control which sparked a rebellion?" Peter asks.

"We shouldn't discuss this," I whisper. "There could be ears all around us."

Both our heads tilt and our eyes scan the buildings and alleys for signs of security forces. There are no uniforms to be seen. No drones fly overhead with their cameras trained on us.

We continue to wander the streets. The sun is higher in the sky, brighter, warmer. Shops are opening. Children are out to play. The viewing screens are off; the broadcasts the government provided with constant information on citizenship and civic duty have stopped. I had ignored the same handful of messages, repeated all day, a long time ago because they bored me. They became the same background noise provided by a fan left on while you sleep, unnoticed until absent.

The election station opens at midday in the town office. The shops will be open for only a short time. The entire country will shut down for this. Even those in the hospital are having arrangements made for a security detail to help with their voting. As I near the town hall, I see hip-high poles and ropes being erected. They're the same ones used for government relief pickup.

On gift day security forces herd everyone into this temporary pen; treated like cattle and waiting for their meagre scraps. Some people are lined up already. Waiting a long time is never pleasant; the square is open with no cover or shade. In hot weather, without water around, it can be brutal. In the winter the wind whips through the square, chilling us to the bone as we wait. On relief day we try to arrive early to have a spot close to the front. Security forces patrol the line, enforcing the silence statutes. Since there's to be no campaigning or discussion, I can only assume today will be no different.

"Well, Hal, shall we get this over with?" Peter asks.

"Lining up now means less wait later," I reply.

I walk into the pen, Peter behind me. Passing between the ropes we march back and forth, inching closer to the town office.

"Best to just be in line and done quickly," Peter says. "I loathe feeling penned in and standing still."

"Agreed," I say, checking the information booklet again. "All these names, almost none are familiar. No real information, just titles or ranks, names, and where they come from. I have no idea what they claim to stand for."

Peter points to his pamphlet. "General Hargrove is a candidate. He's the security forces general here in

Canton Sector. He's known to be lenient but also endorses curfews and civil disarmament. He's an old stock general."

I flip to the section he indicates and start reading. There's another general on this list; Claig from Dorvar Sector in the west. And there's Lieutenant Bortas from Shuron and Lieutenant Anashay from Mushkan. I've heard they were the most senior officers left in their sectors after the rebellion ended.

"A pool with four officers," I mutter. "Would life change under old stock officers?"

I hear a throat clearing growl behind me. There's a tapping on my shoulder. Slowly, I turn to see a patrolman from the security forces glaring at me.

"Silence," he orders.

I nod and return to the booklet. Peter and I breathe a sigh of relief as he walks away. On gift day that could have meant being yanked out of the line and beaten in front of the crowd, before being ordered to enter the line at the back and wait even longer. Hargrove personally oversaw the lines back then. He always wore a sadistic smile during beatings, many of which he administered personally.

There are two civilian governors on the list. There's Clurban from Shuron, the heart of the resistance. Governor Parlond from Mushkan Sector is listed. Being the central sector, Mushkan was ravaged the worst by fighting during the rebellion.

There's Commander Zernon from Shuron; a security forces defector who became a key leader in the rebellion. There's another resistance commander listed; Belgrade, from Preslatt Sector in the north. Those leaders stood strongest and the longest against the government.

Last, there are two former leading citizens; nothing but informant scum, turning people in to the security forces to get themselves ahead. They're the lowest form of survivalist; getting ahead at the expense of others. They destroyed lives and careers just for favour with the governor, or here in Canton, with the emperor.

"Torrell, from here in Canton," I whisper, "he would turn in his own brother to get ahead."

"Would," Peter scoffs. "He did."

"I can only assume Karleas from Dorvar is the same type of man," I whisper back, watching for the patrolman.

The open square is hot with the sun at its midday peak in the clear sky. Sweat trickles down my face, but it's a nice heat. Such a beautiful day for what we are told will be a new beginning.

Shops close. Lights turn off. Shopkeepers lock their doors. People file into the human cattle pen erected for us. I look around. My friends, neighbours, the shop owners and workers, they all stand with blank looks. I wonder if everyone is as confused and clueless as me.

I need to rank three choices. Resistance and security forces troops arrive and patrol. My vote is supposed to be a secret, but uniforms make me uneasy. Will they look? Are they being bought by someone? Growing up in constant fear of the security forces, and the wrath they brought down on us, raises the question about voting based on conscience versus safety. As the pen fills with people and more uniforms arrive it isn't safe to even whisper anymore.

My conscience says vote for resistance leaders like Zernon, and for Governor Parlond, who would be concerned with rebuilding and freedom. Those uniforms compel me to rank General Hargrove first, to avoid a beating, or worse. None of the candidates are allowed in the square; they're in special isolation with special voting arrangements made. At least the absence of Hargrove's sadistic smile is a welcome change.

Sweat runs faster down my face. My chest feels tight. I'm breathing heavily. I wonder if anyone can tell. I look around. I see many panic-stricken faces in the crowd. Most have their information booklets open. Several chests heave as people inhale; I'm not the only one trying to hide their discomfort.

The doors to the town office open. People are brought in ten at a time. The line moves, then stops. The patrolmen circle like vultures, stopping to peck at anyone making a sound. The line moves again, then stops. The patrolmen and resistance soldiers silence the line, but nobody is being hauled out for a spectacle. This is a glimmer of positive change.

Nobody exits through the front door. This must be the same as gift days; you go in the front, receive your government rations, and exit through the rear door.

I swallow hard followed by a mild dry cough. I close my mouth and make chewing motions. A small amount of saliva collects in my mouth; I swallow it, wetting my throat. It's hard to breathe, but there's no leaving this line. I must remain here, enter the town office, have my name checked off their list, and cast my vote. But what if the wrong vote means there's no leaving the town office?

The line moves and stops again. With each movement, I draw closer and closer to the door. The moment approaches, and I can't stop wrestling with the question of conscience versus fear. If only I were a few months younger, I'd be spared this duty. I'm sixteen now, considered grown in the eyes of the law and responsible to act like an adult. All those years I wished to be grown up, what was I thinking? I'd give anything to be fifteen again, to be spared this ordeal.

After an eternity in the scorching sun, I'm rethinking my assessment of the day's beauty. I shuffle closer to the door. The square outside the ropes empties as people file into the corral. The latecomers will be in this sun all afternoon. Nobody is coming out and returning to the square. It's unfortunate; I'd like confirmation that everyone who goes in comes out unscathed.

I step through the door. The building is dark compared to the bright square; it always seems gloomy in the town office. I blink until my eyes adjust to the dim light. My heart pounds in my chest; it's so loud I wonder if anyone can hear it. I'm handed a piece of paper with the ten names in alphabetical order. Beside each name is a blank line.

A woman is handing out the papers. She sits behind a table with a resistance soldier on one side and a security forces patrolman on the other. She raises her arm, both handing me a paper and pointing behind me, and says, "Take this paper behind that curtain and cast your vote." I glance at where she points.

Behind the closed curtain, there is a small table and a pencil. I examine the paper, no serial number or identifying marks that I can see. The edges are not torn, no folds nor creases. I look up, no visible lens for a camera. I listen, no rustling. I look around; the curtain is still and closed. I look down, no feet or shadows at the edge of the curtain. I think I'm alone in here. This may actually be a safe place. I pick up the pencil and set the paper down. My hand hovers over it. Hargrove and the old ways, or Parlond and new hope? Zernon hoping for freedom or Torrell to avoid being snitched on? My mind doesn't know what to tell my hand to do.

This is the most freedom I have ever had, and yet I feel just as shackled as before. My hand hovers over the paper, trembling. The tip of the pencil inches closer to the paper; my twitching hand switches its course from one box to another.

The curtain shakes. "Are you all right in there?"

"Just a moment," I call out, terrified of what I just said.

"Please cast your vote soon, citizen. Others are waiting."

A please? I can't believe my ears. Please is a word people use to beg the security forces, I've never heard any of them say it.

After hearing the use of please my hand steadies. I look down at the paper. There is a new world starting, and I must ensure that it starts well; my only choice is to vote my conscience. I rank the box next to the name of Parlond first, Zernon second, and Commander Belgrade third.

I fold the piece of paper and bring it out. The resistance soldier standing there points to a box on the table. It has a lock on it and a small hole in the top. "Ballot goes through that hole in the box."

I walk over and shove the paper into the box.

"Out the back, the same as gift day," the security forces patrolman instructs.

I walk out of the town office; it feels weird leaving without a ration packet. I look up at the open sky and the bright sun. My eyes shutter as they adjust. I see Peter standing with a crowd of friends. It seems that everyone who voted left the town office safely. We truly are starting a new world for our people.

"We could just kill them all and be done with these stupid votings," Lyyra said. Her eyes wandered around the ample space that was filled with tiny glass spheres. She took a few steps closer to one of the orbs and tapped her fingers against the cold glass. The ball contained dense fog, which made it impossible to see inside. "At least these losers here," she said and tried to shake the orb," I'm so bored with them. This must be the worst one we've ever created!"

Her face was buried against the sphere. She opened her mouth and blew a few breaths against the surface. The three others observed her like she was a wayward circus animal trapped behind bars somewhere on the wrong side of Uranus. The smallest of the group approached Lyyra and the tiny glass ball she was mistreating.

"I don't understand how you can be so coarse! Kill them all, like they are some pests that need to be wiped out!" Otava said and leaped closer to the sphere, "and stop that right now! You will cause another quake if you are not careful!"

Otava took the glass ball out of Lyyra's reach. He looked like a museum curator that managed to snatch a Fabergé egg back from a petulant toddler. He placed his fingers around the sphere and waited for it to stabilize. Otava turned his head against the others but kept the tiny glass ball close to him. His eyes were fixed on Lyyra, who was busy picking her nose.

"We should let them be, see what happens, and how they evolve."

Lyyra took out a big booger and snorted.

"Where is the fun in that? If we can't blow them up, we should then do something drastic to create a major disruption. Remember the last time–"

"Oh please, don't bring up the asteroid again! We all remember what happened after that, and we all remember it was your idea! I don't see how we could forget since you bring it up every time we have this conversation!" Otava said and rolled his eyes at her.

"At least that was fun to watch! Now we look at them doing idle things; perhaps they blow up a few of their kind, destroy their planet at a steady speed as always, but nothing interesting ever happens!"

"Yes, and do you remember what happened after the asteroid?"

"No? Let me remind you! Nuclear winter, mass extinction, and a prolonged time of extreme boredom! Don't tell me that it was fun to watch as well!"

Lyyra set her jaw and looked out from the window. Otava tried to establish eye contact with her, but it seemed like her neck had turned to concrete.

"You have never understood the finesse in observing how a world unfolds a little piece at the time, how civilization matures towards a greater understanding.

No, you want to blast everything! I'm surprised you haven't suggested the xanerians already!"

"The xanerians! What a great idea! I'm sure they would wipe out your precious little world before you can say 'evolving civilization'!"

Feeniks moved past Lyyra, Otava, and Vaaka and placed herself in front of them. She had a great posture, almost regal, and she was ten inches taller than the others.

"Stop bickering! We will vote like always."

There was a short silence in the group. Otava was still hiding the sphere behind him. His eyes were watery, and his loud swallow echoed through the room. Lyyra looked like she had smelled the liquid from a *martian sphinx's* anal glands.

"No, I hate voting for it! You three always want to do something radical, and I always lose! It's not fair! Why won't you listen to me? We should step back and enjoy the little things, see what happens without altering the world," Otava said and stood up as straight as he could. He reminded Feeniks of a mother hen trying to save its chicks from the big bad wolf.

Feeniks looked at Otava with a wide grin on her face.

"So we should do as you say because you are smarter than the rest of us and understand world building better?"

Otava's face was swarming with tiny twitches that he tried to subdue.

"Well, uhm, yes. I wouldn't put it as bluntly as you did, and perhaps I'm not smarter in every aspect, but when it comes to constructing a universe, my way is the only decent way to go."

Feeniks and Lyyra laughed; it reminded Otava of his grandmother's herd of two-headed donkeys that always brayed at him when he walked by.

"Aren't you the little dictator, who would've known! And soon you will start telling us what we should wear, what to eat, and what to think!"

"No, I—"

"As amusing as this is, I've had enough. I don't have all day, none of us do. No matter what the little dictator says," Feeniks said and glanced at Otava, who felt his face go all blue and looked at his feet as if they were the most fascinating thing in the galaxy– "we will vote. Everyone has one proposal and one vote since this planet still was democracy the last time I checked! Lyyra, we will start with you. What is your suggestion?"

There was a pause before Lyyra spoke, Feeniks and Vaaka were staring at her, but Otava was still focused on his limbs.

"I'm not sure. Before all this nonsense," she said and pointed her finger at Otava, "I was thinking about giving a second term to the Big Orange One, but he hasn't done anything drastic, has he? The last time when I voted to put him in charge, it seemed like a hilarious idea. I thought they'd be fighting all over their world for the third time in a nanosecond, but he has made a lot of noise and not any real disturbance. He is entertaining, but I want something more."

Lyyra rubbed her palms together, and a smile lit up her face.

"The Short One with The Silly Moustache, now he was a real disruption! 85 million dead, metal, flesh, and land burned down around the world! Oh boy, that was a great time! I'm sure the Big Orange One will never create anything like that!"

"How about another virus?" Vaaka asked, "it was fascinating to see how they altered their behavior to stop the disease from spreading, how all of a sudden they were trying to work together and not against each other. It always amazes me why they need a global threat to do that!"

"They need a joint enemy, that's what it is," Otava said behind the others and lifted his face a few inches.

"I have hoped they would have evolved and learned to live in peace and work together, but it seems they are still in the stage where they must always oppose and hate something. When there is a virus going around and threatening their existence, they hate the disease together, and for a fraction of time, they forget to hate each other."

Feeniks looked at Otava, who tried his best to keep his head up.

"Perhaps we should settle for modifying the old virus a little so the vaccinations they've been developing won't work. I am not sure if they would have the strength to fight a new disease so soon after the first one. I've noticed my pet *cochleatix* often has more endurance and wisdom than they do," Vaaka said and looked at the tiny terrarium on the other side of the room where a ball of slime was gliding around.

"A bit harsh, but I must agree with you," Feeniks said and turned half of her eyes at Vaaka and half of them at Lyyra.

"Lyyra, have you figured out yet what to suggest? We could give them some advanced technology and see what they make of it?"

"No, thank you! Remember what happened when we gave some technology to Tall One From The South? And what did he do? Fucking space rockets and electric cars! And now he plans to travel to the fourth rock from the sun even though we gave him the coordinates and technology to come and say hello!"

"But you made him promise he would name his next born offspring after the burger joint in one of Orion's moons, didn't you?" Feeniks asked.

Lyyra chuckled and struggled to answer.

"Yes, I did! And it was the shitty place on A-12, the one that always serves its food cold and drinks warm!"

Feeniks and Vaaka joined her laughter, but Otava looked like Lyyra had told them she had cancer instead of a comical anecdote.

"I will go with xanerians, since they've never failed to cause havoc wherever we've sent them!"

"Ok, Lyyra suggests the xanerians. And Otava, I assume that as always, you propose we will do nothing?" Feeniks asked.

"Yes. I wish you would see that often the best and most interesting results will come when you give the world time to grow and mature on its own."

Feeniks looked at him and nodded.

"Ok, and Vaaka, have you decided what your idea is for this little planet?"

"I will go with alternating the virus. I'd like to see them working together, not against each other."

"Now we have our options, and we shall vote," Feeniks said.

"Wait, what about your suggestion?" Otava asked.

"I do not have a proposition. I will pick one of yours."

Otava looked at Feeniks and lifted all his eyebrows at the same time.

"But if we all have suggestions, then it's safe to say we will vote for our own choices, so it's a tie. Doesn't that mean you alone will choose what we will do?"

A sly smile built up in Feeniks' face.

"No, it means democracy will win as always."

Feeniks walked to the other side of the room. She passed a dozen glass spheres, which each contained the whole world and reality for their inhabitants, each planet equally sure of its own uniqueness.

"Ok, let's hurry, I should be back at my quantum gravity theory already, and you know how professor Aurinko can be! Please cast your votes on my mark: three, two, one!"

As soon as she had counted the numbers, Otava, Lyyra, and Vaaka were glowing in different colors.

Feeniks closed her eyes, wrinkles formed on her forehead, and her mouth narrowed to a thin line. Her head mimicked the colors from the three others until there was only the faintest hint of green color left on her cheeks. There was an odd silence floating around the space; Otava was not sure if they waited for ten seconds or ten minutes. Feeniks opened her eyes and smiled.

"I have gathered your votes, and I thank you for the fair election process."

She looked at the tiny sphere and the three other simulation runners.

"A fascinating choice, I must say!"

It had been nine billion years of bickering since the last Big Bang signified the new cosmic farming season. According to league rules from The Board of Celestial Overlords, the BCO, three consecutive scores of 25% purity or less resulted in being condensed to a pure ball of failure and resentment so dark and heavy it would explode into a black hole. *This* solar team was zero for two.

Jupiter, cockiest of all, sat sullen and bored, flexing its massive magnetic field and fidgeting with its red spot. "To recap," Venus struggled, "I am always at a steady temperature. I am the brightest, and although I share a lot of the same features with Earth, I *actually* have the gumption to substantiate my qualities."

"Steadily uninhabitable," Jupiter jeered. "Your atmosphere is too pressured for life to survive, why bother toots? You just want all the prestige that comes with being a host planet." The crowd gathered, circling in to catch the reaction from The Sun.

"Big bad Jupiter is going to come at a free spirit like me," Venus scoffed. "Good thing I have a strong, gas-giant to planet-splain things to a little ol' terrestrial like *me*."

"Don't blame me because I'm richer in gas ..." Jupiter chided.

"Gas you inherited ..." Venus clapped back.

Concordia listened amiably, waiting until the conversation reached an awkward pause then lowered its voice to relieve tension. "We have to focus on proactive measures to satisfy the BCO. The host planet won't receive any fame if we're all turned into a black hole."

Jupiter seized momentum, glaring at Venus, "In my day, independent orbits meant you were weird or uncooperative, not an independent thinker."

"Yea!" Uranus shouted, "Gas Giants first!"

Jupiter pressed, "Venus's climate is such a mystery, eh?"

"It's complicated ..." Venus fumbled.

Jupiter constricted, "Saturn, you've been in the league the longest. Ever seen a climate change in *just* a few million years? - Venus should turn a trail sample in for analysis, unless I'm the only rule follower?"

"... Pass," Saturn groaned.

Jupiter continued, "Neptune? Something to say?"

"What do I gain?" Neptune alluded.

Jupiter pivoted. "How about *freedom* from fear? We can't invest our time developing a planet like Venus, among others, with their feeble magnetic fields. I alone can keep us safe using my massive gravitational pull."

"How do we retrieve resources from a stormy, gaseous abyss?" Earth patronized.

"We can't deliver a winning crop of sentient beings if they have nothing to grow on," Venus addressed.

Uranus said, "Jupiter may blow a lot of hot air around, but what about Venus's volcanoes?"

"I'm still new at this," Mars chimed in. "Didn't we try the whole magnetic-field thing already? Maybe we need an independent idea?"

"Independent ideas might work if everyone pulled their own weight," Jupiter interrupted, glaring at Earth. "Stay in your orbit, newbie."

"Haven't you only been on one other team?" Concordia clarified.

"I was dealing with more pressing matters!" Jupiter erupted, "What's a *plain-Juno* like you going to know about it?"

Mars added, "Pressing matters include the time you just weren't big enough to trigger that fusion reaction you guaranteed?"

Jupiter seethed, "That's a nasty question … asked by a nastier planet."

"Jupiter may not have the experience I do, but his service in those years is exemplary," Mercury drawled out, latching onto Jupiter's gaze.

"High praise from a planet caught mapping out its surface for resource harvesters," Venus spoke again. "Harvesters who happen to be campaign donors. Ask about the Caloris Basin incident."

As if reading from a cue card, Mercury droned on, "The BCO has acquitted me of all collusion with black market resource barons. Furthermore, the incident at Caloris Basin was found to be an accidental collision, not a planned demolition."

Uranus shouted out, "I did my research on this! We're a league of laws, and the BCO wouldn't allow Mercury to participate otherwise!"

Jupiter gushed, "Both Mercury and I have some of the deepest, strongest core's in the universe. Some say they've never seen cores like ours!"

"Don't listen, I've watched for billions of years and below the superficial layer of lush ammonia crystal, Jupiter's just hydrogen and helium. No substance," Earth corrected.

"Maybe I'm too tired for substance. We're all left too tired, Earth. Unfortunately, we all have to fight because *someone* ... is too lazy, or afraid, to accept the role they're perfect for."

"May I intercede?" Concordia interjected. "We're doing a lot of spinning, without any real rotations to show for it. Earth, There is nothing wrong with being passionate and goal-oriented."

"Finally! Some sense," Jupiter teased.

"However," Concordia continued, "passivity is easier on the group than obstruction." Jupiter's frown returned, "We're too focused on previous mistakes to see opportunities for quick and easy production. Earth, you and Jupiter may not like each other, but the fact is, Jupiter and the other gas giants can cut transportation time in half using their collective pull to create a resource jet stream."

"That's true?" Pluto piped up.

"Who cares? Cooperation is a loser's white flag," Jupiter scorned.

"I care," Concordia declared.

A solar flare blasted off of The Sun, "Silence! This debate has turned to bickering. This campaign has been strong and challenging. Know what is at stake. No voting for yourself. Tie's will be met with a runoff."

While the Sun spoke, Jupiter used a passing asteroid to send a secret message to Uranus. "Vote for me and I'll vote for you. Together, we can win. Trust me."

Each planet fell into line one by one and voted as it passed the sun. Each planet knew, deep inside their core, failure to provide a quality host planet, and subsequent cosmic crop would provide a fused existence for the foreseeable eternity.

☑   ☑   ☑

It took several million years for The Sun to collect, tally, and authenticate the votes. "Jupiter received three votes, Mars: two votes, Mercury: one vote." Jupiter began to rise, ready to accept. "Concordia wins with five votes!"

Concordia greeted its peers for a victory speech, "Friends, thank you for your confidence. You could knock me out of orbit with a spec of cosmic dust. I don't wish to speak often, and there is a lot to do. Let's get started!"

"Wait!" Mars shouted, cutting the fanfare. "How are there eleven votes?"

"Indeed!" Venus agreed, "Only ten planets were here to vote?"

Mercury, arbitrating as slowly as time turned, "Oh, I'm sure it's nothing. Probably just a simple error."

The Sun bolted upright. "I make no errors! If anyone remembers making this *grave* mistake, *you must* come forward!" The Sun allowed a few thousand years wait time, but no one chimed in. "So mote it be."

"Pardon?" Venus admonished. "We need to look into this further! Someone tried to cheat." Uranus looked at Jupiter who wouldn't return the gaze.

Mercury's drawl added a sweetness to every accusation. "Elections were conducted in accordance with BCO regulations. Do you have a problem with BCO procedures? I'm sure there's always room in The Outer Realm for cosmic communalism if you do." Venus fell silent and Mars took a stern look from Jupiter.

The Sun rested the issue, "Let's move on and forget about these unorthodox circumstances. Plants, I present to you, Concordia, your new host planet!"

Concordia began delegating ideas and creating breakout sessions immediately while Jupiter's rage hid under a smirk. "Even crusty Saturn dances around while working," Jupiter mumbled.

Trouble brewed during the planet breakout sessions. The Sun reported to the BCO while terrestrial planets discussed resource packaging. The gas giants, however, weren't so engaged.

"Happy with how that went down?" Jupiter asked.

"I've seen worse," Saturn gripped.

Jupiter saw Pluto listening in. "Don't you think we could be doing more? We're gas giants, not gastesimals."

Pluto took the insult and hid among the other planetesimals.

"I say we stage a coup. We can use our strength and magnetic fields to pull gravity in our favor!" Jupiter looked at each gas giant, "In or out?"

Saturn was first to speak before returning to orbit. "Concordia works smarter, not harder. Not happy? File an appeal."

"What's in it for me?" Neptune asked. "I'm farthest from the action, the fewest moons and I'm polluted with methane. I don't want to be a gas giant in name only."

"Siphon resources, for starters." Jupiter smirked.

"Will that increase the likelihood of us failing again?" Uranus asked.

"The overlords never stuff enough cosmic crops into their brains to throw away a chance at more," Jupiter assured. "We'll be fine."

Neptune spoke up, envisioning himself with a new set of debris rings. "We can live like cosmic overlords."

Jupiter smirked.

"What's the hydrogen split?" Neptune asked.

Jupiter leaned in, "I get fifty percent, you and Uranus split the other half."

"Try again."

"Forty-five is as low as I'll take for *my* plan." Jupiter sat.

"The reward just isn't worth the risk. As bloated and apathetic as it can be, the BCO would not appreciate this, no matter how much extra product is discovered." With that, Neptune returned to orbit.

"Just you and me old friend," Jupiter said, cozying up to Uranus.

"Maybe," Uranus murmured. "I have a question. You said we'd vote for each other, but I didn't get any votes. Did you lie?"

Jupiter feigned hurt. "What baseless accusations. *I* voted for you. But, eleven votes? Come on. Someone, like Venus maybe, messed with the voting."

"Or Mars!" Uranus shouted.

"They never liked the gas giant class, Uranus. They hate our success."

Uranus nodded. "Those bastards. What's the plan?"

"We wait. Let them think we're good little planets."

"And then?" Uranus asked.

"Then we flex a little. The important thing is to spin around and around as fast as we can."

"Why?"

"It allows us to look like we're hard at work while allowing us the chance to manipulate gravitational pulls. It wastes time and resources. Mainly it makes Concordia look bad."

"Ohhhhhhhh," Uranus said slowly.

"Changing gravity allows us to skim resources for our advantage, Uranus ... you get that?"

"Of course, I do. We flex at the same time?"

Before they returned to orbit, Jupiter reminded, "In exactly one million years. We do it right, and no one will ever know."

☑   ☑   ☑

As it does, 750,000 years flew by. One day, an attractive, voluptuous celestial body, with craters in all the right places, burst from the void. Radiation danced behind it causing Jupiter's storm to swell in size. Thinking only of caressing that sweet, gyrating coma, Jupiter lost control and hyper-flexed its magnetic field, causing a chain reaction of epic proportions.

Saturn felt Jupiter's influence immediately. In just a few thousand years the slight tugging turned to a flattening assault. Saturn screamed to Uranus for help, but the amplified pull was simply too much. Uranus watched helplessly as Saturn was wrenched to the side, spinning upwards of 1,100 miles per hour, flattening its poles and bulging at its equator. The resulting combination of Saturn and Jupiter's gravitational pull upended Uranus to its side, pinning it forever sideways.

After the cosmic carnage was over, Saturn, though lazy before, was now catatonic. Uranus demanded answers and contacted Jupiter for a meeting.

"Did you even think about the consequences before you started flexing?" Jupiter lamented, indicating to poor, lame Saturn.

"My plan? This was your plan! Why would I irreversibly flip on my side?"

"That was the first question I asked you, don't you remember?" Jupiter gaslit, filling in the details until Uranus pictured it happening.

"I messed up. You'll help me through this, right?" Uranus pleaded.

"Of course," Jupiter reassured, turning to the expanse. "Hey ... do you see that out there?"

At that moment, a massive piece of celestial rubble pounded through the solar system, scream-crying as loud as its harsh, metallic core would allow. "Something's pulling me in, I can't stop!"

"It's going straight for Concordia!" Uranus deduced.

"Yea, we really ought to ... maybe someone should ..." Jupiter waited until the rubble was within moments of impact. "Hey, Concordia, heads up!"

Concordia turned just in time for the celestial rubble to burrow deep into its dense, organic core, exploding a foundation of rock and metal from its crust into space. Concordia imploding slightly, taking a sharp breath before exploding outward into trillions of pieces of terrestrial shrapnel. Its remaining planetary viscera floated into a belt shape between Earth and Jupiter.

It wasn't until the shock waves of destruction stopped raining Concordia bits did Uranus finally speak. "What did we do ...?"

"Deny everything. Stick with me and no one will ever know what you did," Jupiter reassured Uranus.

They made a very public scene to help root through the Concordian carnage. In the end Jupiter stood tall and proclaimed, "As the next in planetary succession, I'm honored to accept the role of host planet."

☑   ☑   ☑

"Despite this setback"—Uranus and Mercury shared a smile as Jupiter spoke—"I know we will rise together to continue the work Concordia started."

Venus, tired of waiting for a censure that would never come, interrupted, "Why would you get to be the home planet now?"

"Jupiter was the runner up ..." The Sun ruled.

"At a time like this, Concordia would want us to think about cooperation ..." Mercury droned.

Earth cut through the rabble. "The BCO may have issued an acquittal, but the facts remain about Jupiter. Storms? Lightning? Does quality product grow in such *harsh* environments? I say we give the newbie a try."

Everyone turned to Mars.

"Can you handle it?" Earth asked.

"I think I—"

Jupiter leered at Mars. "Careful now, wouldn't want you to *implode* under the pressure of handling something of this magnitude. Concordia was strong, and look what happened there."

Mars blinked. "I ... reject nomination."

The Sun finally chimed in, "Clearly there is no way Jupiter can continue as host planet. Mars concedes, Earth … it must be you."

The solar team held their breaths.

"I accept!" Earth lamented. "What choice do I have?"

"It is re-decided," The Sun declared. "I shall inform the BCO immediately."

In a last minute drive for attention, Jupiter had Uranus release a statement. "Although we wish the best to our planetary siblings, Jupiter and I will be requesting formal consideration of section nine in the black hole clause and recusing ourselves from this season's competition, for dogmatic reasons. We wish every planet our cognitions and invocations."

It took many millions of years, but Earth, despite everything, managed a team that produced stellar results. After being engaged by Earth, Neptune became quite the cheerleader. Pluto and its planetesimals were taken seriously filling in the gravity void left by Jupiter and Uranus. Saturn regained health and aided Venus and Mars in developing new ideas together. Even Mercury worked just enough to be noticed.

After ten billion years of cultivation, the BCO came to test the team's cosmic crop. The crop consisted of small, spastic, carbon-based life forms covered in a fur like substance comprised of keratin. They scurried around on two feet, engaging in various pleasure-seeking behaviors while fully doubting themselves in the process.

"Is this it?" The leader of the BCO grimaced while calculating the results."

Another member snarled, "Get the destruction team ready."

The machine buzzed and whirled until it spat out the results. "52% ... You passed."

An eruption of cheers flew from the planets. They would not be condensed to a pure ball of failure and resentment so dark and heavy it would explode into a black hole. Not today.

The team began to cheer and celebrate while Jupiter hung on the outskirts, close enough to hear an invitation to celebrate and far enough to pretend it never came. The planets waved to Neptune who was far away and alone.

"Join us, peers!" Saturn slurred.

"How can a once mighty gas giant debase yourself to start hanging out with that terrestrial trash?" Jupiter asked Saturn.

Seeing the once zealous giant reduced to a husk by Jupiter's insults, Neptune boiled over and shouted, "Jupiter killed Concordia! I was there!"

"What is this?" The BCO members took turns shaking the solar system's foundation with their bellowing. "What do you insinuate?"

"It's true!" Pluto added in. "I saw it! Jupiter tried to convince the rest of us ... to ... manipulate gravity."

The solar system was awed. "These charges are serious," they whispered among themselves.

"Have you any proof?" the leader of the BCO boomed.

"We saw it!" Neptune and Pluto pleaded.

Venus and Mars watched helplessly.

After taking a few hundred years to investigate and discuss, the BCO's chair being for propaganda spoke. "There is considerable evidence to show Jupiter committed some … possible infractions. But was Concordia not responsible for its own problems? For everyone's sake, we need to move onward and forward, putting time and energy into the next cosmic crops for consumption. It may be hard to swallow, but the implication of removing gas giants like Jupiter and Uranus would change the solar system team too much. They're just too big to fail."

In the end, the BCO left with their product. It wasn't great, but it was enough to feed the need for now. Jupiter still spins and pouts, using its mass to influence conditions from time to time. Pluto was downgraded by the board for breach of trust. Neptune, because of its size, was given a warning for frivolous whistleblowing.

One day, after a few million years or so, Mars saw Venus cry. "What's wrong? Can't you see we won? Sit back, we're in charge now."

"I can see. But can you?" Venus wiped tears away and replied, Earth's just coasting. It could be doing so much more. Sure, we may not have been condensed this season … but what about the next?

Earth pretended not to overhear Mars and Venus. Earth was just so busy being a host planet there wasn't time for self-improvement. In the meantime, Earth kept spinning and rotating, and rotating and spinning. On and on. And on.

THE TASTE OF VICTORY ✅
VARADHARAJAN RAMESH

April Sun scorched the black soil on the crust and painted a splintered modern art on dry earth. The bovine and the porcine sought shade in desperation. A nervous energy had engulfed the tiny village of Periyakulam; Something that had been brewing for years, nay decades, was about to overflow like milk that had been simmering over a burning stove and now had reached its boiling point.

Rasu sighed as he walked barefoot on the road leading up to the Angala Parameswari temple. The muddy road was like a balding head with the tar resembling sad little tufts of hair on it. Though the soles of his feet screamed in protest, Rasu smiled as he reached the locked doors of the temple.

"Amma, Maariyamma!" he bellowed with passion and devotion interspersed in his voice, "Today is the day. I seek your blessings, O! merciful mother. Make me the President of the village panchayat, and I'll satiate your parched tongue with the blood of a hundred goats."

Rasu rummaged through his bag and produced a coconut with a flourish. With an exaggerated movement of his hands, he lifted the coconut and deposited it to the ground with a crash that echoed across the barren land.

"Accept this, my mother," Rasu intoned to the Goddess. "I've waited far too long. Make me the President! I know you've been hungry for a long time. Allow me to satiate your hunger."

Rasu knelt and circumambulated around the temple on his knees. The rough granite floor of the temple was not kind, and skin met the hot and abrasive surface and started breaking. Blood seeped from the scraped skin and drenched his white veshti. He closed his eyes and focused on the Goddess inside, willing his senses to ignore the pain and discomfort. Only God can support the helpless. I'm your helpless child, O! Mother.

By the time Rasu had finished his bloody circuit around the temple, a small crowd had assembled at the entrance. Men and women looked at him with awe and respect in their eyes.

"Ayya!" Muthukkalai, Rasu's aide, walked up and pronounced in a loud voice so that the crowd could hear, "Please don't worry. You will win the election this time. The Goddess is with you, the people are with you, and justice is with you."

Rasu smiled at his right-hand man. Muthukkalai was almost like a son to him. No, he was better than that wretched son of his. Rasu's blood boiled as the thoughts about his son came to him, uninvited. He spat on the ground, stood up, accepted a drink of water from Muthukkalai, and looked towards the south.

Greyish-black wisps of smoke rose from the remains of the erstwhile Lenin Colony and vanished into the clear blue sky.

"What time are the results declared?" Rasu asked Muthukkalai.

"By five in the evening, ayya," said Muthukkalai as he opened an umbrella, unfurled it, and held it above Rasu's head with obeisance.

"Hmm!"

"Ayya, why do you worry? You are going to win this election, and you are going to become the President."

☑ ☑ ☑

Rasu smiled at the confidence he heard in Muthukkalai's words. Sometimes, he wondered if he had committed a mistake by devoting his entire adult life to attain the position of the Panchayat President. Periyakulam, with its two thousand impoverished inhabitants, was just a small ink stain on the map of the seventh-largest country on the planet. A minuscule ink stain which possessed no tourist attractions or mineral deposits to make it interesting or viable to anyone outside its limits. The village's name, Periyakulam, was a portmanteau of two Tamil words—Periya meaning big and Kulam meaning pond. Whenever he thought about the name, Rasu felt the urge to laugh; Periyakulam was neither big nor did it have a pond.

What the village had were scores of able-bodied men and women, most of whom worked as daily wage labourers in the cement factory located twenty kilometres to the east. Every morning, they assembled near the temple and waited for their transport to the factory. Ten dirty, noisy lorries would arrive at six in the morning to ferry nearly half of the population to work. Once they deposited the labourers at the factory gates, the trucks would head towards the godowns where they would be filled with bags of cement and sent on their way towards the nearest railway station. By eight in the evening, the lorries would be back with their distinctive rumble to spit out the cement-coated residents of the village.

Small businesses littered the village—there was a blacksmith who made hammers and sickles that were used predominantly to settle disputes. Rangamuthu's family was involved in masonry; their family built most of the buildings, including the Angala Parameswari temple in the village. The main road had three grocery stores run by quarrelling brothers whose mother spent half her time scolding them and the rest crying for them. The village was a liquor-free zone. So, Muthukkalai opened his alcohol shop exactly one foot outside the village limits.

The other thing Periyakulam had in abundance was its deep-rooted social inequality and frequent caste-based clashes. There were two main residential zones in Periyakulam; Periyakulam Main, where the upper caste resided and Lenin Colony–a sprawling slum that housed five hundred huts where the lower caste people lived. Rasu was counting on the upper-caste votes to win the election. They were his people, after all.

His fucking people!

Rasu cursed and spat a gob of saliva on the road. His fucking people, who never voted for him before. Seven times! Seven times, Rasu had contested the elections, and he had lost every single time. Thirty-five years of debilitating defeats. Rasu's father had extracted a promise from him on his deathbed. Win the election and become the Panchayat President. Rasu's father served as the President for thirty years—he won six elections, unopposed. Before his father, Rasu's grandfather was the President from the time India became independent, and before that, he was the village's Mirasudhar.

Rasu felt like spitting on his own face. If only it were physically possible! I'm the failure, the hapless black sheep destined to bring disgrace to his family. Rasu's first taste of defeat came in the by-election, organised just after his father's demise. Unfortunately for him, the ideology of communism spread like wildfire amidst the youth of the nation. Translated works of Karl Marx, Friedrich Engels, Mao Zedong, and Che Guevara were consumed with fervour. People started naming their children Lenin, Stalin, Trotsky, and Che. The impoverished and oppressed populace started raising their voices and their fists against the powers that be.

Rasu's dreams of succeeding his father were crushed to dust by the socialist revolution. Comrade Samathuvam, the man with the strongest fist and the loudest voice from Lenin Colony, became the Panchayat President and remained in power until his death twenty-five years ago. To rub further chilli powder in Rasu's wounds, Samathuvam's daughter succeeded him in winning every single election. Nepotism defines true communism! Che Guevara would be proud, Rasu thought bitterly.

Rasu had harboured hopes to win the election after the great socialist rule of Samthuvam turned out to be no different from his father's times. The upper caste still viewed the lower caste as untouchables, people of both castes still lived in poverty, and there were no discernible developments in the infrastructure. It should have been his year and his election when Samathuvam died. But something that had never even heard of before in Periyakulam's history happened—Samathuvam's son, Karki, eloped with a girl belonging to the upper caste. Bloody Karki, and his bloody comrade father! The idiot didn't even know the spelling of the great man, after whom he had named his brat. It is Gorky, not Karki. Useless swine, the lot of them.

The young Karki, with his wavy hair, sparkling eyes, and a natural, almost haughty charm—a result of college education had won over the girl's heart with ridiculous ease. Knowing that the entire village would oppose their relationship, the star-crossed couple decided to run in search of a better life.

What followed next was a bloodbath that had not been seen before; The enraged upper-caste men entered Lenin Colony and went on a killing spree. Men, women, and children were hacked to death, Comrade Samathuvam included. The Reserve Police force from Thirunelveli had to get involved. Thavaputhalvi, Samathuvam's daughter, rose from the cinders and rode the sympathy wave to win the election and become the Panchayat President, a post she held till date.

☑ ☑ ☑

Muthukkalai noticed the look of concern on Rasu's face and said, "Ayya, my grandfather used to tell me that the taste of an easy victory is not as sweet as the one that is attained after a struggle. You have waited for thirty-five years with dignity and bore the insults and ridiculous whispers. Today, you are going to taste a victory so sweet that you'd be forgiven for thinking it is divine. Mark my words."

Rasu smiled and said, "One shouldn't think about the price of ghee even before buying a buffalo. I have decided, Muthukkalai, this will be my last election, whether I win or lose. I have lost everything in my life—I wasn't there when my wife needed me the most; I never saw my son growing up or his many achievements. You once said that it was unfair my son resented me. I understand his position." He picked a stray pebble from the road and considered it for a moment. "Of course, I wish things had turned out differently. Why couldn't my son understand how important this election was to me? Why couldn't he understand the dynamics of the people here? And, why oh why was he so naïve?"

"Ayya, what happened has happened, and it had to happen. It was for the greater good."

Rasu sighed and nodded. He felt like he was two hundred years old. The past week hadn't been kind. He had to make certain decisions, tough decisions, decisions that split his heart into a thousand jagged shards ... yet, he made those decisions. Rasu cursed his fate; why did he send his son, Mugilavan, to study in Singapore? Why did he have to meet that witch there? Why should he fall in love with her, of all the people in the world?

☑   ☑   ☑

Despite the resentment he felt towards his father, Mugilavan had returned to Periyakulam a month back to help Rasu with his election. Rasu was touched; His son had taken the first step in breaking the ice. The young man had come with a big smile, wide eyes, and a file full of campaign strategies.

"Appa," Mugilavan had said, "Times have changed and so too, have the people. You can't expect to win the election by singing the same old songs."

"Same old songs?" Rasu had bristled.

"Your ancient election strategy, Appa," Mugilavan had said with an exaggerated roll of his eyes. "How long will you keep promising these people about the road that will never come and the temple festival that will never happen?"

"There is no road because the bitch daughter of that untouchable bastard is sitting in the seat that should have been mine. The temple festival hasn't happened because the untouchable swine is refusing to release funds," Rasu had said, his nostrils flaring. "If I had been the president, I would have ensured the road was laid, and the temple festival had been organised every single year."

Mugilavan had shaken his head and said, "That's the wrong strategy, Appa. Why do you think you have lost every single election so far? That's because you have been focusing on these two issues and these two issues alone. You've been crying foul at every opportunity, but the opposition has used your own voice against you. They have portrayed you as an embittered, entitled old man who is still trying to bask in the legacy of his family. It's high time we changed that."

"You don't understand these people," Rasu had said. "You have seen cultured people in Singapore and have become one of them. We are a different breed. We still have a strong sense of what's right and what's not. I know what our people want."

"Yet you've lost every single time." Mugilavan's calculated barb had hit the mark. Grumbling, Rasu had accepted to follow his son's strategy. Mugilavan's plan centred on using technology and helping the residents of the village to start a cottage industry focused on manufacturing bamboo furniture fit enough for export. There were business plans and go-to-market strategies. Rasu had smiled; his son had come prepared.

"Empower the people," Mugilavan had said, "and they'll back the person who was responsible for that."

The lad had also drawn plans to introduce dry-land farming to make the people's lifestyle self-sustainable. This is true revolution, Rasu had thought. My son is going to change the fate of this village. Rasu knew within his heart that a change was coming and he was the one to spearhead it. He campaigned long and hard, trying to educate the people about the importance of stepping away from old traditions and into a future where the youngsters wouldn't feel the need to run away in search of a better life.

Things were going according to plan until two things happened in quick succession. First, Thavaputhalvi, the Panchayat President announced a cash loan of five thousand rupees to every home in the village. The queue that formed outside the Panchayat office to avail the loan made it clear to Rasu that the villagers were more interested in an okay-ish now than a glorious future. The headway he'd made was undone as his campaign lost steam. Mugilavan, his wonder boy, for once had no answers.

"It's over," Rasu had lamented one day. "Why did I listen to my useless son?"

Muthukkalai poured country liquor into a steel tumbler and handed it to Rasu. "Ayya, I told you that Chinnavar's plan wouldn't work. These people are uncouth and ungrateful dogs. You don't build a bungalow for dogs and feed them good food. No! You have to chain them up and throw a bone at them. Do that, and you'll see how they come behind you, wagging their tails."

Rasu took a deep swig from the tumbler. His eyes were red with alcohol-induced fury, and his addled brain was a vortex of despair and self-pity. "You are right. I shouldn't have listened to that naïve idiot. Now, my defeat is confirmed. Muthu, eight defeats in a row. I'd rather die than live to see another day of that untouchable swine holding the position that is mine."

The ancient pendulum clock chimed once and, somewhere, an owl hooted. Rasu was pacing the length of his garden in an agitated state.

"We have to do something, Muthu ..." he said as if he was a tape on repeat mode. Muthukkalai and a few of his men were lounging in a corner in a comfortable stupor. The sharp note of a car horn brought them back to their senses. Rasu squinted his eyes as the Ambassador car entered the compound. Mugilavan got out, followed by a young woman dressed in a pair of skin-tight jeans and a Blue Oyster Cult T-shirt. Rasu bit his tongue and hissed. He had forgotten that Mugilavan's girlfriend arrived that day.

"Appa," Mugilavan said, "Meet my girlfriend, Daisy."

A Christian?

"Vanakkam, Uncle." The girl said and smiled. She was beautiful. No wonder my son has fallen for her. Rasu nodded and looked at his son with a question in his eyes.

"Daisy's parents are from our village, Appa. I never knew before today."

"Really?"

"Yes, Uncle." Daisy said, "My parents left this village twenty-five years ago because of some issue. They settled in Singapore. I grew up there, and I'm extremely thrilled to return to my roots."

"What were their names?"

"My mother's name is Dhanalakshmi, and my father's name is Karki. My aunt is the Panchayat President of this village, uncle."

A fiery rage bloomed inside Rasu, blinding him. He grabbed the alcohol bottle and smashed it over his son's head. Before anyone could react, Rasu had stabbed his son with the neck of the broken bottle.

"How dare you?" Rasu spat at his son who was gurgling to his death. "How dare you bring the daughter of an untouchable pig into my house? You are not my son!" He kicked Mugilavan's face.

Daisy started screaming. Muthukkalai and his men grabbed her and dragged her away. Rasu knew that the feral dogs that masqueraded as his loyal men would tear that untouchable wench to shreds.

The next morning, Mugilavan's dismembered corpse was discovered just outside Lenin Colony. Instigated by Rasu, the upper-caste people waded into Lenin Colony and burned the place down. They laid the blame squarely on Daisy and her aunt Thavaputhalvi. Police claimed the duo had absconded as soon as they had lured Mugilavan to his eventual demise. Fifteen days later, people queued up to vote in the election.

☑ ☑ ☑

The clock chimed five times. Rasu sat on a rattan chair in his garden and stared into the distance. He could hear the burst of crackers and the sound of trumpets. Didn't Muthukkalai say that victory would be sweet? Why wasn't he able to taste that sweetness? A boisterous crowd led by Muthukkalai entered the compound. They were shouting victory chants.

"Am I not untouchable now?" Daisy's last screams rang louder than the chants in his ears.

Rasu closed his eyes. There was no taste to his victory.

Glossary

Ayya – Sir
Appa – Dad/Father
Amma – Mom/Mother
Maariyamma – Goddess name
Veshti – a lower garment, usually white, worn by men
Vanakkam – Hello

TWO BIRDS, ONE STONE 
MELISSA S RODGERS

Some believed in angels—a tiny cherub sitting on the right shoulder ... and a little devil crouching on the left. But not me. I forged my own path. Rocky and rough, just how I liked it.

☑ ☑ ☑

The techno beat hummed along every nerve, even through my hair. Each strand pulsed as if alive.

It thrummed.

Pounded.

Burned.

It was amazing what a few blue capsules could do, washed down with an energy drink, chased with a shot of vodka ... or two. A little Molly never hurt anyone.

The throng of dancers moved close, bodies pressing tight ... but not tight enough. I tingled in anticipation of every graze.

My costume glowed under the blacklights—a beautiful angel, wings and halo included. With each sweep of the strobe, the glitter on my skin sparkled.

The colors, the taste, the sound, the smell, all wove together, creating a tapestry of sensation.

"Megan?"

My name's not Megan. Tonight, it's Lilith.

"Megan!"

Hands gripped my shoulders and whipped me around. Wobbling, I squinted, trying to focus on the face zooming in and out.

My brother searched my eyes, slowly shaking his head. "Damn it, Megan. Emmy's waiting at home. You promised to take her trick-or-treating tonight."

"What are you doing here, Tom?" No matter how hard I tried, I couldn't hold back the giggle rising from my throat. It had a hollow wind-chime pitch. So heavenly.

Tom shook me so hard my head snapped back, knocking my halo askew. "What are you on this time? His gaze flicked over my shoulder. "Are those Emmy's wings? She's been looking all over for those."

"I'm only borrowing them." I snuck a look over my shoulder, watching the crowd gather around the ballot box. First place at this costume party would get me some attention. "I promise, as soon as the votes are in, I'll head home." I gave him my sweetest baby-sister smile; it always worked.

"Sure, it's not like I haven't heard that before." He pushed his fingers through his hair and pulled. "What's wrong with you? You'd jeopardize your daughter's happiness"—Tom dropped a hand, holding it out to the party—"for this?"

"I said I'd bring the wings home in a bit." Didn't he understand? I gave up everything seven years ago. Couldn't I have this one night?

"That's not what I was getting at. Emmy doesn't care about those wings. She cares about you, and maybe, just maybe, you'll grow up someday and understand what that feels like … before it's too late." Without a glance back, Tom stormed away.

Guilt. I should've felt it, but the line around the election box grew, pushing those heavy thoughts away.

I spread my wings, allowing the twinkling lights to enhance my beauty. I'd give everyone a show. That trophy was mine. I rocked on my heels and closed my eyes, losing myself in the music again.

Lilith.

The raspy voice sent a hot flash through my body, and I scanned the crowd, frozen in place.

Lilith—three caws echoed through the room, and a dark chuckle followed—*how fitting.*

The voice scraped me from the inside. But not painfully. No. An erotic stroke. Sensual yet tormenting.

The mob of people parted, and the air stilled. Standing across the room, dressed in a foreboding black robe, a mysterious stranger held my gaze.

The lights flickered, and with each flash, his face intensified—high cheekbones, full lips, a straight nose, and a broad chin, all covered in makeup. Dark paint marked his prominent features, giving the illusion of a skull.

Icy fingers traveled up my spine, and I shivered, even though my skin flushed.

"Ten minutes left to vote!"

I jumped at the voice over the speaker but didn't take my eyes off my latest prize. Yes, I wanted to win, but I had no problem taking a second trophy home. Licking my lips, I lowered my head and peeked up, waving him forward with a curling finger. I turned the corners of my mouth up, slow at first, ending with a seductive smirk.

With his first step, the floorboards shuddered, and wisps of fog drifted around each booted foot, snaking up his torso. The cloak took to the air, rippling in ghostly silence behind him.

His scent wafted under my nose, and my nostrils flared. If hotness had a smell, this would be it. A faint hint of cedar and sandalwood ... smoldering.

The closer he came, the stronger my heart pounded. With each of his movements, a cool breeze caressed my skin, and every hair stood on end, goosebumps spreading.

He stopped, not touching but stripping me to the bare bones with his eyes alone. Everywhere his gaze lingered, I burned.

"Hi." I leaned close, taking in his breath—a mixture of cinnamon and danger.

He didn't acknowledge me but stared deep into my eyes, as if searching for something.

"Aren't you going to say anything?" My voice trembled. There was something about him—something overwhelming ... overpowering.

The second I couldn't bear to hold his stare any longer, he smiled. His expression softened, eyes darkening to the color of a summer sky.

"Hello." I thought his voice would be deep and commanding, but instead, a gentle timbre fell from his lips. He pushed back the long fringe of black hair hanging in his eyes. "I've been watching you."

Close up, his face held youth, yet his eyes reflected wisdom, which only came with age. Something familiar hid within their depths, but I couldn't put my finger on it.

"I've noticed." I edged forward, but he stepped back before our bodies brushed. "What's your name?"

"Ankou."

Such an odd name. Hands cupping my mouth, I shouted over the music, "Ankou?"

He shrugged. "It's Celtic." Ankou licked his lips. "And you?"

"Megan." I purred the last syllable, turned, and smiled over my shoulder, working my magic with a backside bump and grind. Every time I moved near, Ankou eased away.

"And here I thought your name was Lilith."

He intrigued me. Had I said that name out loud? I pressed a hand to my fluttering stomach and faced him. "Why would you think my name was Lilith?"

"Isn't that what you said earlier?" He leaned close, his breath tickling my ear, and whispered, "Lilith, one of the Fallen, a warrior of Hell, Satan's second in command. Big shoes to fill with such tiny feet." The side of Ankou's mouth turned up as he reached over and twisted a lock of my hair around his finger. "Tiny yet beautiful."

My cheeks warmed, and I played coy, pulling a wing forward and shielding my face. Ankou was turning me into a silly schoolgirl, who blushed over sweet words and sexy smiles. I cleared my throat and fanned my face. "Have you voted yet?"

Ankou dropped my hair and turned toward the ballot box. "No need. In the end, I always win."

"That's some ego you've got there." I smirked because baring my teeth would be rude. "What are you supposed to be, anyway?" His costume consisted of black clothing and a matching hooded cloak. The paint on his face appeared professional, but the whole package lacked originality ... lacked thought. He had no chance.

"Me. Only me."

"Only you, huh?" Through the corner of my eye, I glanced at the last handful of voters waiting in line. They stared back, but I couldn't tell who they gawked at, him or me.

I had to do something to up my chances. My feet moved, deciding for me, and I swayed to the music. "Dance with me." I hadn't seen him on the dance floor all evening. In my experience, most men had two left feet and watched from the sidelines. And this time, I counted on it.

I'd made a mistake. Ankou mirrored me, move for move, as if dancing with his reflection. If I slid right, he'd glide left. The crowd of onlookers forgotten, I inched closer, needing to feel the thump of his heart against mine, but he kept his distance, if only by an inch.

Long ago, my grandmother claimed, "The eyes are a window to a person's soul." If this were true, I was in trouble. One moment, Ankou's eyes shimmered blue—the next, black as the dead of night. Not that it mattered. I liked my men bad.

"Tell me about your daughter."

"Who?" Here I stood, burning with need, and he wanted to talk ... kids. Gritting my teeth behind pursed lips, I counted the seconds until they checked the votes and announced the winners. This party was growing old.

"You have a daughter, right?"

I turned a saccharine smile his way, fluttering my lashes. "What ever gave you that idea?"

Ankou tilted his head, brows furrowing. "But your brother said—"

"Brother? Were you spying on me?" Not giving him time to answer, I turned to leave.

In one blurring motion, Ankou blocked my escape. "I'm trying to give you a chance here. Just say her name."

"What chance, and whose name?" I crossed my arms over my chest and sneered. "Listen, you don't know anything about me, so get out of my way, freak." Swinging around him, I made for the door.

His whisper beat me to the exit. "You won't leave. Your fate lies here."

His words couldn't bring me to a halt, but the intercom did. "All the votes are in and counted, so we're ready to announce the costume party winners."

It was my destiny to win, and Ankou somehow understood. Swiveling around on the tips of my toes, I faced him. A smug smile pulled at his lips—lips I desperately wanted to kiss and slap simultaneously. My drug-induced sexual attraction still lingered because, pissed or not, Molly didn't care.

"I guess I'm up." I slid around him and shouldered my way through the crowd, heading to the front of the stage. A flurry of black feathers blocked my path, and I pushed the costumed guy aside. He squawked, playing the part of a crow down to flapping his wings.

My high was fading, and I clenched my jaw. "Damn you, Ankou."

"Quiet. Bring it down a level or two, guys." The announcer stood center stage, microphone in hand. "First up, best female costume. Can I get a drumroll, please?"

The tapping of drums erupted from the crowd, mixed with laughter and loud conversations.

"Shh, be quiet! I can't hear!" Taking clipped breaths, I clutched my gown. Pressure built in my chest, and my heart raced at an unsteady pace.

"And the winner is ... Angel Prescott, wearing the sexy devil costume."

My heart sank but continued its chaotic rhythm in the pit of my stomach. How? How did I fail again?

"Kind of ironic, isn't it?" He was back again ... Ankou.

"How so?" Why was I talking to him?

He stepped close. No longer having an alluring fragrance, he reeked of rampant forest fires. "A girl named Angel won. And dressed as the devil, no less." His shoulders shook as he snickered.

Heat ran up my neck, and sweat trickled down my back. I gnashed my teeth, sucking in the hot sticky air." Let's see if you win, skeleton boy."

Ankou kept his eye on the announcer. "You'll see. I'll win." His open cloak fluttered as if caught in a breeze, but that didn't make sense; the room was stifling … stagnant.

"We'll see."

"Next up, best male costume." The emcee riled the mob by pumping his fists.

The drumroll echoed around the room, and with fingers crossed, I prayed he didn't call Ankou's name.

"The winner is Daniel Morrighan, the crow in the back, making all the noise." The announcer's laughter blended with the caws of the victor.

Giggles started low in my gut, slipping out in snorts and gasps. Mr. "I always win" stood there motionless, expression vacant. "I'm so sorry. How rude of me." I couldn't keep the shake from my voice. "I'm sorry for your loss."

Ankou met my gaze. The blacklights blinked, illuminating the white makeup on his cheeks, chin, and forehead. A skull, empty and eerie, blazed in the dark before his youthful face took shape. "I never lie." His flat tone and icy expression sent shivers up my spine.

"And now for the couple's costume."

The microphone crackled, but Ankou's gaze sizzled.

"And the winners are"—stomping and shouts boomed through the room—"Lilith, the fallen angel, and the Grim Reaper!"

At the word *Lilith*, something inside, deep and dormant, burst to life, but I pushed it back down, concentrating on the task at hand. I hunted for another set of angel wings. Not a pair in sight. "I won ... I really won." Giddy and lightheaded, I lurched toward the stage, staggering as tiny lights winked in my periphery. "Sorry, skeleton boy. Maybe next time."

Whistles and catcalls swirled around as I spun and showed off my winning outfit. My moment had come ... finally.

The crowd roared, and my heart grew full, close to exploding. A sensation of needles ran down my arm, and I loved every prick, every stab. At last, I could feel again.

"Come on over here and stand next to your partner, darlin'." The announcer took my arm, directing me to center stage.

The scent of brimstone and ash burned my nose, bringing me back to my senses. Ankou was there ... on the stage ... with the other winners. Although he appeared unchanged, they didn't.

A large crow perched on Ankou's shoulder, and a horned, red creature hunched near his left. All with flat black eyes fixed on me.

The crowd screamed from behind but deadened with a swipe of Ankou's hand.

"I don't understand." Either Molly was messing with my head or the alcohol finally kicked in.

"Megan." Ankou strode forward as the crow and demon dissipated into a smoky haze. "I was the only vote you should have worried about, and you only had to say her name to win. But you couldn't. Or shall I say, you wouldn't. Your daughter deserves better."

"Who are you?"

"I could ask the same of you."

"Excuse me?"

Without saying another word, Ankou reached up and slipped the hood over his head. His face sunk into the blackened depths, fading into nothing. Smoke swirled around his flowing cloak, taking the form of a scythe. Ankou grasped it with a skeletal hand, and his boney fingers clicked against the charred handle, one at a time.

"I go by many names. Ankou. Thanatos. Father Time. The Grim Reaper." His voice dropped to a rasp. "Death."

I had to get out of here. I searched for a stage door, and when finding none, I spun to run. Ankou didn't stop me, but the crowd swarming around a lifeless body brought me to a standstill. They frantically worked, giving CPR, and I had no doubt the girl wouldn't make it. Her wings, Emmy's wings, lay trampled and broken beneath her—beneath me.

No, not me, but …

"Have no fear, my wayward friend. They can't see you … but I can."

I stood there dumbfounded as my mind cleared, and for the first time in years, I remembered who I was. With what should've been a heavy heart, I turned to face my fate.

"How did you find me?" I brushed myself off, ruffling my ebony wings, and remnants of Megan flew in a dusty cloud, thick in the air. "Can't a girl take a little vacation and forget who she is without interruptions? I mean, I wasn't hurting anyone. I didn't have to do anything but sit back, relax, and enjoy the Megan Show." Kind of true. But the Fallen made a habit of lying.

"Lilith, it doesn't matter how I found you, only that I did. You've had enough time leeching off Earth's miserable. You've been summoned, and I've been sent to escort you home."

"Summoned, huh?" Well, what if I'm not ready?" I huffed, studying my nail polish. "Lucifer doesn't care. Doesn't give two shits about what I've done for him over the years."

Ankou advanced, his bone-white hand reaching out.

I hesitated, staring at each of his fingers, and it came to me. Throughout the night, Ankou only touched Megan's hair, and I should've realized why. With one brush of flesh against any part of his body, she—I—would belong to him. Trapped. His prisoner. The sly dealer of death had actually given me a chance to turn myself in.

I sighed and smirked, accepting I'd made my bed, or rather, I'd dug Megan's grave. I placed my hand within his, and the stark chill of the contact pierced me bone deep. It felt good—more than good—compared to the unbearable heat I'd soon reencounter. "Did you have to kill her, Ankou? She was entertaining ... in a pathetic kind of way."

Ankou drew me forward until our chests pressed together. Deep inside, I knew his mouth turned up at the corners as he leaned in and whispered, "I wasn't sent for you alone. The proverb, I believe, is 'killing two birds with one stone.' And you of all should know"—he chuckled—"I always win ... in the end."

VOTE SADIE, UNLESS YOU SHADY

RAYONA LOVELY WILSON

"Yeah, no, I'm not voting for shit."

"Why not? You want Sadie to be class president, again?" My best friend Keke sits to my right, and my girl Nique sits to my left, a flyer flowing back and forth in her hand as the wind picks up around us.

"Nah. I don't do politic shit," I state, staring at the text from my boyfriend.

"Come on, sis, Chrissy is trying to make a change here, and Sadie just wants her name on everything. I know you don't want that," Keke says.

I roll my eyes way too hard and shake my head. "I hate Sadie, but I hate politics even more. That shit is all the way rigged. How they count four hundred ballots in a damn day?"

"Ugh ..." Keke is a little annoying when she wanna be. "I don't want her representing us, again. She think she the shit and don't do shit." She snatches the flyer from Nique and waves it in front of my face.

"Move, Micha wrote me the cutest poem." If my cheeks could turn red, I know they'd be red right now.

"Damn, girl, is he all you care about?" Keke play-shoves my arm, and we bust out laughing.

"Look, I'm not callin' you a sheep, but people who vote are exactly that. They know who's gonna be class president before we even vote. I don't wanna be a part of it."

"Please." She draws it out.

"Damn, Keke, you desperate or nah?"

"Or nah, but I'm trying to get change at this stupid school. Since I gotta go here, I can at least get some fun going on."

"Like what?"

Keke's smile spreads across her face. "Okay, besides getting us out these ugly ass uniforms, she's going for less homework, better lunches, and even letting us Doordash our own food. Aren't you sick of these fake ass tacos?" She pokes the weird looking tortilla with her fork, her lips curling, disgusted like everyone else. "My favorite thing is more dances and letting us hire better DJs. You love going to dances."

"I do, yeah."

"Exactly, remember the music at the last dance, it was booty." She reminds me, "If you woulda went to the debates you woulda heard all this, now I have to relay it to you before lunch."

"Why before lunch?" I send a winky face to Micha and put my phone down.

"'Cause we have to go vote, today."

"Today? I was gonna go meet up with Micha," I say, knowing he'll be waiting for me like a lost puppy.

"You seriously just met up with him yesterday after school, you saw him this morning before school, and now you skippin' school to go see him again?" Nique smirks. "Getting' more serious, huh?"

"Whatever. I like him. Sue me." I look around the cafeteria and see Sadie walking with her clique. She really does think she the shit 'cause her daddy's a rapper and buys her what she wants. She tries to act better than all of us and only runnin' for president so she can get all the recognition.

"Boo, freak." Her and her girls laugh and stop in front of our table. "What are you lookin' at?"

"I dunno, trash."

"Ew, trying to be cool in front of yo ratchet-ass friends."

"Brah, don't stop over here if you gonna insult us. I will beat yo ass." Nique is a fighter, she don't give a fuck who it is.

"Whatever. Make sure you guys go vote for me at lunch. I promise, you won't regret it." She winks, and they walk off.

I want to slap her. She's a bitch. Queen Bitch if you ask her.

"Imani?"

I stand from the cafeteria bench and grab my stuff. I'm sick of Sadie and her shit. She exactly like us. She let her daddy's fame go to her damn head.

"Let me think about it."

☑ ☑ ☑

I can't believe I let Keke talk me into this. I can't believe Sadie got under my skin callin' me a freak. I should be with Micha, listening to his sweet poetic self, but here I am, with my girls, voting for class president.

"Don't forget, vote for Sadie." She's at the end of the hall, handing out store-bought cookies. Shame.

"If you vote for me, you're invited to my party next weekend."

"Vote Sadie unless you shady." Her girls are lame for that one. It was plastered on almost every poster.

I roll my eyes as we stand in line waiting our turn. Chrissy better fight for the things she says she wants to change. I don't want to regret this.

"Next."

I step up to the student-made polls, and the girl sitting at the table gives me a paper.

Class president has three nominations: Sadie Desmond, Chrissy Montana, and Jessica Andrews.

I circle Chrissy's name and next to Sadie's write, *Bitch*.

I already know Sadie's gonna win. She likes to buy her votes, and it's pathetic; it's the person she is. She's literally throwing a party if people vote for her.

"Thanks, girl," Keke says as we meet up outside the hall, a huge ass smirk on her face. "You wanna know something?" She giggles.

"What? Spill the tea," I say as she puts both hands over her mouth.

"I dunno, you might say something." She looks around, and I do the same, making sure nobody's being nosey.

"Keke, what the hell did you do?" I ask, grabbing her arm.

"You might tell—"

"I ain't no damn snitch and who the hell am I gonna tell?"

"Sadie. I mean, she is your sister." She smacks her lips and flips her newly straight black hair over her shoulder the way the white girls do.

"First of all, she's my half-sister, and I ain't tellin' her shit. She don't even live with me," I correct her.

"Fine, okay ..." She looks around us again before leaning in toward me. "I may or may not have rigged the vote."

"Oh my god, what?" I whisper, hunching toward her as students begin to walk outside.

"Yeah, I found one of the ballots and made hella copies," she tells me, trying not to be the loudmouth she is. "Nique worked some magic with, uh, Jared and got him to help us switch them. If you thought last year was a mess, this year is worse." She giggles, throwing her hand up in the air doing the Nay-Nay. "Sadie won't be class president this year."

"Oh shit." I never thought she'd do anything like this. She's always the nice girl. "Okay, I'll definitely be watching this shit show."

WELCOME TO PLUTO
CARL D JENKINS

"Welcome, everyone. We see some of you struggling to understand. For those who do understand, please direct those struggling to the pentangle badges before you. Attached to the lapel, these devices ensure clear communication, including translation. We do not all speak one language, so even if you currently understand us, please ensure you are wearing your own."

"Now, again, welcome to Pluto, and thank you for answering our call. This is a historic occasion. We do not often have openings within our ranks. It has been centuries. All of you are here because you successfully promote the plutonomy of your primary nations. We are proud to recognize you among the global economy's one percent. Those who are most successful this week will leave able to do so much more than you can currently imagine.

"Additionally, you each participate in governing those nations, visibly or discretely. We hope you have left people you trust to carry out your wishes in charge of your affairs. You'll have no outside contact until your flights home. Your attention here will be solely on your campaign. Your fortunes are at stake, and some of you will finish with nothing.

"An interesting word—campaign; it means different things in different places. You all call countries with elected officials home. Your first round plays upon such principles. Other contestants come from states where political campaigns follow ... different paths. Competition occurs for them in other parts of the compound. Keys given to you on arrival access those sectors. However, only your own abilities and those of your security officers guarantee your safety while there.

"Security officers may not enter the Election Booth, and facility police will protect you from uninvited threats in your own quarters. Security officers will receive their instruction in The Guardhouse concurrent to your own. The Guardhouse is likewise off-limits to those without a badge granting individual access.

"Your officers will participate in various voting opportunities that arise, so treat them with respect appropriate to their stations. Their voices and your own will be the only ones able to influence our decisions.

"Lastly, we are five. We are usually six. One of us will always be near. The victor, after three rounds, will become number six and complete The Plutocracy. Three from each first round competition will move on to round two. Seven others among you will finish with far greater affluence than you enjoy today. As on the outside, you may beg, borrow, or steal in whatever fashion you find advances your position.

"Any questions? We see several hands. You already have all the information we need to share. Discuss anything you wish amongst yourselves. Your security Officer will come to escort you to your rooms as they finish next door."

☑   ☑   ☑

"Assembled officers, your attention please. We see your Masters' differing interpretations regarding security. Unfortunately, your jobs are no longer simple. Brains and brawn. Alliances utilizing both are advisable.

"Your access to the outside world is limited to financial statements and accounts, but you'll find internal communication capabilities here exceed your norm. Your skills to enhance, disable, and embrace such services have potential to work both for and against your employers. Workstations are located in each of your master's quarters, within the barracks, and in the central lab—where assorted tools and equipment are also stored. All keys, however, are simple metal types.

"For those of you with brawn. Be aware there are other campaigns active in the compound that are less diplomatic than you are used to. Your employers' keys can access those areas. Assorted weapon stores in various parts of the compounds contain defensive and offensive tools that will make your jobs more and less comfortable. Ordinance for firepower is plentiful but will not be replenished. Predicting the needs of later rounds is important.

"Security Officer keys open all labs, weapon stores, communal areas, and your individual master's suites. They will not give you access to other campaigns on the compound. The contestants alone can open those doors and gates. Employees answer only to those employing them. In this contest, you can still be hired, fired, lent, or contracted. You are limited only by your own ambition and loyalty.

"One last piece of information is available to you. Should you kill someone here, their wealth and responsibilities become divisible between yourself and your master. During challenges, most will go to the employer. In defensive altercations, most will go to your employer. In offensive altercations, the majority will go to whomever was coordinating the offense. Teamwork introduces more complicated scenarios, but you understand. Greater risk yields greater reward.

"Spend whatever time you require for discussion, then proceed next door and show your employers to their rooms. Maps of this bunkhouse are beside the door. A general outline of the sector on the reverse shows locations of assorted facilities. You are your employers' guides. One of us will be monitoring to consider appropriate level questions that arise."

☑ ☑ ☑

"To all in the compound, an evening meal will be served in compound facilities at nineteen hundred hours nightly. Other meals are available twenty hours a day. The private dining chambers attached are available so long as the door is unlocked. We recommend you get a good night's sleep. Your scheduled activities begin at seven hundred hours on The Golf Course."

☑ ☑ ☑

"Good morning gentlemen. It is a lovely day to play a round, isn't it? It's rhetorical. There are only three holes. You can play them after we finish if you wish. But first, election business. Several of your nations enjoy electing entertainers, while comic book heroes are the rage this century. For today's festivities, campaigners will choose a random package from the table and wear the costume enclosed for the duration of the day. Your security officers will be delivered associated sidekick costumes.

"You must wear the mask at all times in community rooms. You may take them off in safe spaces and private dining rooms. Today will be about networking. We encourage you to discuss key issues together. We have unlocked an extensive selection of newspapers, legislation, geographical detail, political and corporate intrigue, and other material in the workstations for those of you who engage in research. The election tonight centers on these issues. Rest assured, your favorite realities are all represented.

"Telescreens in various parts of the facility will update to include your costume, as well as your current wealth values along several markers.

"You may select packages now. Place your badges over the scanner until the green light flashes. This allows pairing of sidekick costumes.

"One last thing. Five different heroes appear. Some heroes experienced variation in appearance over the years; some did not. As a result, many of you will look alike. This will be more noticeable among side-kicks. Until tonight."

☑ ☑ ☑

"Good evening, gentlemen. We trust it has been a productive day for you here at Pluto, and that you have begun to refine agreements you previously enjoyed. Watching you on the monitors has been amusing. Superman and Batman had predictable scuffles in the hallways. Robin face-planted someone onto a concrete floor, but otherwise, only egos appear bruised.

"In sadder news, a pair of Green Arrows decided to check out telescreens in the South compound with their security officers. One died, but two attackers were killed. Some of you no doubt noticed the change in statistics on the telescreens. Both security officers gained enough wealth to place on the screen—you'll have to scroll if you didn't realize you could. Neither gained contestant status, but the week is young. The newly unemployed Officer can be hired. Please find the stage with your hero's logo above it and find your seat. The logo is on your costume.

"On to voting. You see several selections on the ballot. Our favorite: you'll select the top three menu items you would like to see our chefs prepare for the rest of the week. Soylent Green is a historical favorite, although we created our own recipes. Your officers do not get to vote on this one.

"Next you'll see the chance to vote for best and worst portrayal of the campaigner in each costume. The contestant earning best will get a small bonus, as will their sidekicks. You can still vote for the dead man in these contests.

"You will next identify your most important three platform issues. Don't rank them, and write-ins are welcome in if you are unsatisfied with the list. You know how useful that can be.

"Lastly, please do write in your favorite supervillain, real or imaginary. This will be important tomorrow.

"Enjoy dessert while you fill out the ballots. Since you're all billionaires, feel free to look over each other's shoulders, discuss your choices, make deals, or negotiate bribes. You've all bought elections before. You have thirty minutes to feed your ballot into the box and take your seats. Your security officers' ballots are secret. You can buy that information at the kiosk out front or pay the standard fee to change their votes."

☑ ☑ ☑

"Who is ready for results? We're certainly curious. The chefs are not telling us what meal choice you've made, so we'll find out when the menus appear. We're miffed about that, to be honest.

"For best presentation of costume: there were a lot of abstentions. You obviously don't follow superheroes. When we call your number—found on the table in front of your chair—please stand up. Starting with Batman and going counterclockwise: seven, four, six, two—alas, he's dead, and two. You will all see a bonus when you view the telescreens later. Your officers will receive bonuses as well, but not sufficient to put their names on the telescreens. You may sit down.

"For worst presentation: four, eight, one, two again, and six. Will you gentlemen please move to the empty sixth table, please.

"Regarding the issues. All forms of research extraction combined, of course, to claim number one. Those of you representing Batman can expect a bonus because of his generous use of resources to create his lair and gadgets. Well done.

"Keeping labor costs low was number two by a moderate margin. The Flash probably wouldn't like it, but we'll give this bonus to his table. He's notoriously fast.

"And finally, third place was space exploration. We're giving this bonus to the Superman table because, well, he's an alien, he can fly, and some of his compatriots did a bang-up job at subjugating galaxies.

"Undersea research came in lowest on the scale, which disappointed us, but environmental and animal protection was a no-brainer for the bottom of the list with almost no votes. Both land under the purview of Aquaman, so would everyone at that table please join table six?

"As we look upon you thirteen, we consider that thirteen is often an unlucky number. Some cultures won't build a thirteenth floor into their buildings— silly really since no one skips it when they count. But appearance and presentation are integral to a global leader. When seen, we want to be above reproach. We want recognition of our power, influence, and adeptness. While doing what we must to ensure that supremacy, we require invisibility. All of you would do well to remember that in the days that come.

"But, today, as arbitrary as results often are, you thirteen are the losers in this contest. Do any of the rest of you feel compelled to trade places with these men? No. We did not think you would. Please enter the door to the room behind you, turn on the light, and take a seat. You will negotiate your exodus from the campaign shortly.

"Now then, the rest of you, please keep your seats and watch. The gas they have engaged will work quickly. Their assets will transfer to the rest of us before you return to your quarters. Their security officers will receive a severance bonus and become available for hire. Those not hired by the end of Round One must leave.

"Most of you look on this turn of events with gratitude for the sudden increase in assets. Please realize, that for the winners of The Election, today's advancements are but a drop in the bucket. Most of you will start over with nothing more than your names, but most of you will rebuild.

"Your costumes for tomorrow will be on your beds when you return to your quarters. You can choose whether your security officers will dress the part or not. Gentlemen, until tomorrow. We'll meet again on the green."

☑ ☑ ☑

"Good morning, gentlemen. Another fine day for a round. The course, alas, is still a paltry one. Be wary of stray bullets from across the fence. You are likely aware that a full dozen of you decided to start over from scratch rather than to remain in the game. They will awaken on their respective flights mere hours after negotiating rather paltry settlements with The Plutocracy. Not a total loss for them, really, but what can you do efficiently with a mere couple million United States Dollars to your name? Nine of their security officers have decided to stay, meaning the sixteen of you have opportunity to add twenty-three prospective employees to your payroll. Two of them have escaped armed militia already. The newest nine officially still work at the same pay for the companies they did on arrival. You can decide if you want to find out what they'll do for us or what their knowledge may be worth to you. Select acquired holdings are available for purchase. A business office is open this morning only.

"Someone managing a significant amount of cyber-theft overnight remains undiscovered which affected twelve contestants in three campaigns. Well done. Bonuses will be visible in the telescreens, plus what you've stolen.

"Please, put on your costumes and we'll see you tonight at the elections."

☑ ☑ ☑

"Good evening, and welcome to tonight's election. It was an exciting day in the compound. Some of you may not know one another, so we'll give you some time to introduce yourselves before we begin in earnest. We anticipated one more day of campaigns, but the severity of today's changes render tonight the final election before round two. The office pool has left us divided on what we think is going to happen tonight, but tomorrow will be a free day while the other campaigns catch up.

"Six of your running mates have been murdered while six others dropped out of the race. One remains lost within the jihadist campaign to the west. His security Officer holds his key—please stand—so we do not expect he will make it back to this campaign, as only one group has clearance to attempt influence over your election. They have not visibly opted to try thus far, but many emails have been deleted.

"Five security officers have advanced to contender status, all working for the three remaining original candidates, or they did before entering this room tonight. Sixteen others are dead, and the rest all work for one or more of the eight of you. We love a good double agent.

"There are two races on your ballot cards. You must select three names to move on to Round Two, and one name of whom will be gassed. The other four will leave this table with nothing, so make any deals you wish before you enter your ballots and return to your rooms. Seven of you will learn the results in the morning."

WHERE SHE SLEEPS

CODY LARSON

She winced as the blade sliced her finger. Glaring at the safety scissors in her left hand, she popped her finger into her mouth. The taste of pennies touched her tongue, and she closed her eyes. *I'm not going to cry*, she thought. *I'm a big girl.* A shiver went down her spine and she opened her eyes to inspect her finger. *See? Not bad. Nothing to cry about. Just a little cut.*

She grinned to herself, but then noticed the droplet of blood on the paper crown she had been making. "Well, shit," she muttered. She shot a quick glance behind her to make sure nobody was around. Seeing no one, she giggled and whispered it again.

She wouldn't get in trouble for saying bad words if no one heard her say them.

After saying it a few more times, grinning wider each time, she grabbed a red crayon and started coloring the piece of paper. She stuck her tongue out of the side of her mouth just a little as she focused on making sure each section was colored just as she wanted it. Red changed to blue, blue transformed to yellow, and soon the paper crown looked as majestic as any she had ever seen in her favorite storybooks. She lifted it up, the sunlight from her bedroom window cutting through the dust in the air to touch her perfect little crown with excited fingers. Beaming as bright as the fingers of the sun, she jumped up, spun around once on her toes, waved the paper crown in the air, and rushed out of her room. Her small gray cat meowed at her as she ran down the hall, forcing her to stop in her tracks so she could scratch under the cat's chin.

"I'm busy, Buttons," she said, the cat purring. "Gotta go to a big meeting!"

The cat meowed again, as if responding, then proceeded to begin cleaning herself.

The girl wrinkled her nose, thinking of the inevitable hairball that would be her very own gift later.

"Just don't put it in my shoe, okay?"

The cat stared at her for a moment, then went back to her own important business.

Sighing, she patted her on the head and turned the corner into the kitchen.

Her father was slumped over the kitchen table, two hands around a giant coffee mug. He was staring off into the distance, dark circles hanging under his eyes.

She took another step closer, the corners of her mouth dropping.

He blinked, lifting the mug to his lips when his eyes caught hers. "Oh, oh hi, honey," he said. He rubbed his eyes with the back of his hand and painted on what he thought was a warm smile.

She tried to return the smile, the excitement she had felt just a few seconds ago beginning to evaporate.

He placed the mug back down, the air growing heavy. He blinked again and patted the chair next to him. "It's okay, honey. Come on and sit. I'm sorry."

Her lips curled up a little more as she hopped up into the chair. They stared at each other, him hovering over his coffee, her clutching her paper crown. The excitement, like bees in her chest, began buzzing again.

"Are you okay, Daddy?"

"Yes, yes, dear I'm okay. Just ... just tired is all." His smile grew warmer, but she could still see the small cracks underneath. He looked down at what she was holding in her hand. His eyes grew a bit wider as he nodded at her crown.

She put it on the table so he could see it. "It's my king's crown!" she said, unable to hide the buzzing of the bees. "It's for me! I know I'm a girl, but I don't care. I wanna be a king, so I made one that looks like all those ones from the stories you tell me!"

This time, his smile was far more genuine. He sipped his coffee and picked up the paper crown, turning it over in his hand. He nodded his approval and placed it back down in front of her. "Very nice, kiddo. And you can absolutely be a king if you want to."

There was a thump at the front door.

They both swung their heads at the same time.

"Who—" he began.

The little girl jumped up, grabbing her crown. "It's Katie and her brothers!" she said, the bees almost making her whole body vibrate. "Remember, Daddy? You said they could come over!"

He stared at the front door for what seemed to her like forever, then slowly nodded. "Right. That's right. I did." He glanced back at the crown in her hand. "So, that is what you made that for? Are you going to play fairytale stories?"

She laughed. The brightness in the sound chased the dark that had been looming over the room. "Not this time! Much more important!" She turned on her heel and ran toward the door.

"Tess! Shoes!" her father said, the chair scraping on the floor as he stood up.

She made a beeline for the pile of shoes next to the door and slipped into her sandals.

He followed her to the door and opened it for her.

On the front step stood a short, freckled girl with blazing red hair and buck teeth. Behind her two taller boys were wrestling on the lawn. The freckled girl's eyes widened, and she made a very loud, obvious throat clearing noise. The two boys looked up, their eyes also growing wide, and began climbing off of each other.

"Hi Tess's dad!" Katie said. She tried to sound cheery but there was strange lilt to her voice.

Her brothers mumbled greetings as well but neither could look him in the eye. They shoved their hands in their pockets and kicked at the grass.

"Hello there, Katie." Tess's father smiled. "Hello there, Ben! Jake!"

Again, they mumbled.

Tess shoved past her father and hopped down the steps. He opened his mouth but before he could speak, she spun around and looked at him. "We won't leave the yard!" she said, waving away his unspoken demand. She smiled and lifted the crown up. "We got a big meeting!"

He smiled back and nodded, then closed the door as she turned to her friends.

The thinner of the two brothers, Ben, looked at the house, then looked at Tess. "Is he okay?"

Tess stared at him, her expression grave.

He winced a little.

"Would you be?"

Ben lowered his eyes again.

Jake pointed at the crown in her hand. "Who's that for?"

Katie followed her brothers gaze, and Tess's eyes lit up again as she waved her paper crown in the air. "For me! I am the king of this group!"

"But ... you're a girl."

Tess shot another withering glare at Ben.

"But ... that's cool," he muttered, shuffling his feet.

Katie rolled her eyes at her brother, then turned to give the crown a closer inspection.

"I like it!" she squealed, her voice raising in pitch.

Jake started laughing.

Katie shot out a little fist and caught him on the shoulder.

His laugh cut short as he grunted and rubbed his arm.

This time, Tess rolled her eyes. She folded her crown and sat it up high on her mess of blond curls. "Then I now call this meeting to order!" she announced, her voice rising in volume and authority. "To the tree!"

They all marched behind King Tess to the lone giant tree stump nestled in a wedge of sunlight between two bushes in the front yard.

She spun around, waved her hands as if she were actually a king shooing away unsavory peasants, then perched on top of the stump.

The siblings formed a line in front of her, sitting cross-legged on the grass.

Jake snorted and mumbled something, then flinched when Katie lifted her little ball of knuckles at him.

Ben began pulling bits of grass out of the ground and ripped each one into tinier pieces.

"So!" Tess began, clearing her throat. She locked eyes with each of them in turn. "We are here to decide one very big thing!" She paused.

The siblings just stared at her.

"Who is the best mommy of all!"

This time, Ben snorted in laughter.

Tess fixed her glare on him.

He stopped laughing but shook his head. "But we can't be mommies; we're not girls."

Tess frowned and smacked her forehead. "Stop being a dummy, you dummy!" she said, shaking her head. "I mean ... who *has* the best mommy!"

Katie's eyes lit up. "Oh, oh I get it! It's like a ... like a..." She scrunched up her face in concentration.

"Vote," Jake finished.

Katie pointed at him and bounced her head, the sunlight sparking the fire in her hair.

Ben raised one eyebrow. "But how can we have a vote if—"

This time, both girls sent daggers from their eyes, and he slouched down to inspect his small mound of torn up grass, his unfinished sentence hanging in the air.

Tess jumped up and stood tall on the stump, flapping her arms as if she were batting the words away. Her crown began sliding off her head, and she cocked her head to one side and readjusted it. "Okay. First ..."

"Wait, can we have more than one vote?" Jake interrupted.

Tess frowned at him, looked down, furrowed her brow in thought, then lifted her eyes back to his and nodded. "Yes, sure. Anyway ... first, who is nom ... nomi ..."

"Nominated."

Tess rolled her eyes at Jake's interruption but kept talking. "Nominated. I say, my mom!" she said, raising her hands up.

"And our mom!" Katie yelped, jumping up.

"How about Mrs. Sarah?" Ben chimed in.

Everyone sent him confused gazes.

He tore up another piece of grass. "She's always nice to me," he mumbled.

"Okay, sure, Mrs. Sarah too!" Tess agreed.

Ben glanced up and smiled.

"Let's start with our mom!" Katie squealed. "All in favor?"

The three siblings raised their hands.

Tess nodded and pretended to write something on her hand. "Okay, three for Mrs. Thomas. Next, Mrs. Sarah!"

Ben's hand shot up.

Katie smirked but said nothing.

Jake shook his head.

Ben's hand went down as fast as it had gone up.

"One for Mrs. Sarah. Last, my mom!"

A sudden heavy silence fell.

Tess's hand shot up, and she started hopping up and down on the stump.

The three siblings sent each other sideways glances and each in turn raised their own hands.

Tess's face lit up in a smile so bright it could send the sun itself into a spiral of self-doubt. "Four! And with four votes, the winner is ..." She drummed the air with two tiny fists. "MY MOM!" She leaped off the stump and grabbed Katie up in a hug tighter than her little frame should allow.

Katie grunted but hugged her back.

The two brothers stood and brushed their jeans off, a solemn look clouding their faces.

Tess spun around and almost hugged Jake but stopped herself short. *He might have cooties*, she thought. Instead, she stuck out her hand.

He grabbed her hand with his own sweaty one.

She grimaced and wiped her hand on her pants. Turning to Ben, she just gave him a curt nod and small smile.

"So … um …" Katie began. She hesitated as Tess swung her head around to look at her. She ran her hand through the flame perched on her head.

Jake turned to Ben and began poking him, which caused Ben to poke him back. Soon they were once again wrestling in the grass, Ben's torn up pile finding its way into both of their mops of hair.

"I … well …" Katie stammered.

Tess raised her eyebrow and held out both hands palms up.

Katie blinked and shook her head. "My mom wanted to know how your dad was …" she mumbled.

Tess's face became dull and stony. "He is sleepy a lot," she said, her eyes dropping to her own still open hands. "He likes to drink coffee." She lifted her hands and plucked the crown off her own head. The sun-bright smile returned to her face as quickly as it had left. "But this will make him less sleepy I know!"

She shoved her hand into the pocket of her jeans and pulled out a single green crayon. With one movement, she turned and laid the paper crown out flat on the stump. With a steady, sure hand, she began scribbling something onto the crown.

Katie peered over her shoulder and began to smile.

Ben and Jake, now covered in dirt and grass stains and out of breath, stood and looked over to see what Tess was writing. Then they both smiled and nodded.

Tess, once again, waved the crown in the air, her smile infectious. "You guys stay right here!" Without another word, Tess ran to the front steps, jumped up them, and swung open the door. She could hear a clang in the kitchen as her dad came around the corner, a look of worry on his face.

"Tess? Are you okay? What happened?"

Her beaming face evaporated his fears as she bounded up to him and threw her arms around him.

"What's this for? You seem in a good mood," he said, a hint of confusion at the edges of his words.

She let him go and waved the paper crown in his face. "She won! She won!"

He took the offered paper from his daughter, an uncertain smile curling his lips. He glanced at it, then back to her. "Your crown? Who won? Did someone win your crown?"

"Turn it over, silly!" she said, laughing and pointing at the crown.

He looked down at the crown and flipped it over. The smile on his face faltered a bit, and he let out a small gasp. He stood silent for what seemed to her like forever yet again, then she noticed a single tear escape the corner of his eye and slide down his cheek. His eyes met hers again, but in that moment, they felt heavier.

She blinked, an edge of uncertainty touching her own smile, when he gently laid a hand on her shoulder.

"Oh, honey ..." he began, voice wavering. He squeezed his eyes shut and cleared his throat.

"Dad? I thought ... I thought you'd like it ... for Mom ..."

His eyes opened again, now wet with tears. He pulled her into a hug and kissed her on the top of her head. "I do. I do, sweetie. And ..." His voice cracked. "I'm sure she would too. It's just ... you know ... she's not here anymore."

He released her from his embrace, and they met each other's eyes. A wave of darkness crashed into them and threatened to engulf them, were it not for the shine in her smile. The smile that reached through that darkness, grabbed a hold of his heart, and staved off the very waves threatening to drown it. The very same smile that had touched his heart so long ago, but not from her.

"I know, Daddy," she said, grabbing his hand and squeezing it.

He couldn't help it. Her smile could always bring him back. He looked at the paper crown again. At the crooked yet perfect words written in bold green crayon: *World's Best Mom!*

"We could take it to her," she said.

He looked into her eyes again.

"You know ... where she sleeps."

THE TWELFTH STEP
WILLIAM THATCH

Sam Kinloch's fingers drummed on the edge of the cream-colored table. There was no rhythm or beat, his fingers were simply possessed by subconscious anxiety bubbling to the surface.

"Nervous?" asked Alice, sitting across the table. Her soft, knowing smile tipped her hand that the question was rhetorical.

"What makes you say that?" the deep, gravelly-voiced Sam replied.

"Years of experience. That, or you've had too much coffee."

That's when Sam noticed his fingers tapping away. He hesitated for a moment, tamping down on his hand in his lap before choosing instead to wrap both hands around the warm mug of coffee and taking a sip.

"Seriously, Sam, it's okay," she said. "It's out of our hands. All we can do is sit back and wait. Whatever will be will be."

What was he thinking running for Sheriff of Fremont County, Wyoming?

He had been content in his reclusiveness. He could let the name Samuel Elliott Kinloch fade from the minds and history of Fremont County, Wyoming until one day an obituary appeared in the Fremont Chronicle and a slab of stone bore his name. That was fine. He'd lived enough life for one man. He'd earned his retirement.

But then there had been a message waiting for him on his answering machine when he got back in from the garden that day.

He had never met Alice Stratton before then. He thought he remembered reading her name in the papers before, but he wasn't certain of it. She introduced herself as a journalist who'd heard about his story and wanted to interview him. His immediate response was that he wasn't interested. He didn't want to go digging through the past, bringing up bad memories and feelings. He still found himself struggling with the sudden onset of guilt and shame; the briefest flashes of things he regretted.

Yet he did not delete the message. Instead, he carried on about his day. Every day he would pass the machine and think on it, and every day he would decide he wasn't interested. It was about a week after she had left the message that Sam decided to call her back. With the help of Brian Morris, he figured if he truly weren't interested, he would have deleted it and left it at that. But something about the idea; the idea of laying himself bare to the community, had spoken to him.

Sam glanced out the window of Doris's Diner, a veritable landmark of Fremont County since the 1940s. Beyond the picnic tables—which had been set up for the crowd that had gathered to have barbeque and support Sam as they all awaited the results of the election—a truck had pulled up. He recognized the truck immediately. It belonged to Joseph Rhodes, a business mogul in the county. With the exception of some national chains which sold to the county's markets, Joe was the sole source of beef in the region.

Sam met Joe's eyes with the briefest of glances, but it was enough to tell Sam that Joe was there for him.

"'Scuse me a moment," Sam said as he scooted off the red booth seat before finishing the last of his coffee.

"Sure," Alice replied.

Sam strode toward the exit, knowing that Alice had looked to see what caused him to get up. Sure enough, as the bell above the door jingled to announce his exit from the diner, Alice had pulled a notepad out and was jotting down notes.

There was a small cheer from the crowd outside, accompanied by several hand waves and people saying "Hi, Sam!" His smile was concealed by the mustache covering his upper lip, but he was sure they knew what the reaction he got meant to him.

Sam made his way around the corner of the diner. He wanted to meet Joe on his own terms, or as close as he could get. Ideally, he wouldn't meet with the man at all, but at least he might be able to do it out of earshot of everyone else.

He had no sooner turned the corner than he saw Joe step out of his truck, cradling a bottle of whiskey in his arms and a smile on his clean-shaven face.

"Ah, Sam," Joe said, approaching with an outstretched arm. "Good to see you."

One of the most interesting things about Alice's article on him was learning things about himself that perhaps he knew subconsciously, but he had never thought enough to apply them to himself. "Sam isn't interested in beating around the bush," Alive had written, "Inviting me to sit down before telling me to ask him a question."

Sam smiled politely and answered Joe as honestly and directly as he knew how. "Why?"

"Well, I know it's a big night for you. I've not been shy about my supporting Wilbur for sheriff, but I wanted to offer you this—" Joe held out the whiskey. "Just a little something to say no hard feelings."

Sam stared at the bottle of whiskey. God, he could really go for a drink.

"Oh... I forgot," Joe said, pulling his arm back. "You don't drink anymore."

Sam smiled a little wider. The insincerity of it matched only by Joe's own words.

"No, you didn't," Sam said as he accepted the bottle.

Sam's long-standing affair with the drink was by no means a secret. If by some strange chance, residents of Fremont County hadn't heard when he was arrested and imprisoned for drunk driving in '87—or sought to make amends in '88 when he was released—surely Wilbur Townsend made sure everyone knew of Sam's past with constant reminders, in his campaign, that Sam was a recovering alcoholic.

Joe's eyes flashed to the bottle. No doubt he took it as a sign that, despite his protests, Sam would consume it.

"You know, Sam, I was thinking about last year when you were going around asking folks for forgiveness," Joe said. "I don't recall you making amends with me."

Sam had, in fact, gone to the Rhodes Family Ranch last year while making his rounds. To call it 'asking for forgiveness' wasn't wrong, but it wasn't wholly accurate either. When Sam was in prison, he had been given a lot of time to think and reflect, and to sober up. Sam was one of the prisoners who accepted Pastor Brian Morris's invitation to join the Alcoholics Anonymous program. Sam had worked hard to admit his weakness and give himself over to God. Joe was referring to the ninth step of the twelve-step program—making amends to those he had wronged.

"As I recall, you didn't want to hear it," Sam replied.

"No, I suppose I wasn't ready at the time," Joe said.

"I take it you're ready now?"

"Yes. These amends are supposed to be relevant to the pain caused, yes?"

Sam nodded to Joe.

"Well, you were a mean, bitter drunk, Sam. You cost me a lot of money at a time I couldn't afford it. I nearly lost the house, the business. The family ate, but even little Thomas was worried at the time."

Sam guessed Thomas was the name of Joe's son. If he had ever met the boy, he couldn't recall it. Although, to be honest, there were long stretches of time wherein details were fuzzy at best.

"Is that it, Joe?" Sam asked. "You want some money?"

The corner of Joe's mouth curved up in a brief sneer. The mere accusation that he, Joseph Rhodes, needed money was so repulsive that he could not stifle the expression of it.

"No," Joe said stiffly. "I don't need your money, Sam. We recovered from your neglect years ago. But I find most people don't understand the sacrifices and burden of running a business; the kind of hurt this county would be in if its top beef provider were ever hurting."

Joe paused, taking a moment to straighten the cuffs of his jacket. Sam got the impression he was buying time, either to consider how to phrase his next words, or for Sam to ask something. It was just like Joe to try to control a conversation like that, to force the other person to make a move when they weren't aware of what move to make, or even that they were supposed to at all.

"Thing is, Sam, I employ a lot of people," Joe continued. "I have a responsibility to those people and their families. Sheriff Stapp understood that. Wilbur understands it, too. I worry, however, that maybe you don't."

"Joe, it's been a long day," Sam said. "And I ain't never been any good at understanding people being coy. So, if you could get to it."

"How's the family, Sam?" Joe said, stripping away the veneer of politeness.

Although he had, in effect, asked for the bluntness. Sam was unprepared for it. It felt as if he had lurched forward, as if on a moving platform which came to a sudden stop.

"I think you know very well how they are," Sam said.

"Well, I know how Cheryl is."

Sam paused again. This time there was no denying why. It was more powerful to let the facts go unsaid. The fact was Cheryl had died in a car wreck back in '78. Although Alice's articles had been covered that, they had tastefully skipped over much of their marital struggles. They had gone over Sam's self-medication upon returning from the war in '73, and the deep hole he wallowed in with the drink for that time. What they hadn't discussed was that the demons he was trying to drown away had spread to Cheryl, causing her to try to drown out her own personal demon in Sam Kinloch.

Sam had, with no shortage of encouragement from Cheryl's parents, blamed himself for her death. Guided by Brian, he started trying to guide other recovering alcoholics through their struggle as a way to make amends to her. That was what had put him on Alice's radar in the first place.

"The question is," Joe continued, "How is...what was your daughter's name again?"

Sam stared Joe down for a moment. He was being coy again.

"Stacy," Sam answered.

"Yes, of course. How is Stacy? I haven't seen her in years. Do you even know where she is?"

Sam fought to maintain eye contact. It was a battle of wills as the truest, coldest nature of Joseph Rhodes revealed itself. Joe already knew the answer. No one knew where Stacy had gone. Following Cheryl's death, Sam tried sobriety for a few months before deciding, in a way, sobriety wasn't for him. He wasn't sure if it was months or weeks later, maybe even days, that Stacy had gone missing. In his stupor and self-pity, Sam had not gone looking for her.

Try as he might, Sam lost this battle as he had lost so many before, and he lowered his eyes.

"What do you want from me, Joe?" Sam asked after a pause.

"I want to know you're serious about making those amends. I want to know that when there's sides to take, you'll remember who you owe in this town."

"I'll keep it in mind."

"See that you do."

Joe tipped his cap before turning around, climbing back into his truck and leaving.

Sam, meanwhile, stood there for a moment, watching where the truck had once sat. He didn't have an impression that the community had forgotten Cheryl or Stacy. He often wondered, whenever he turned the corner in the supermarket and someone fell silent, if they had been talking about it. No one had ever said anything to him about his wife's death or his daughter's disappearance. It was always the elephant in the room.

Sam felt Fremont County had always been filled with good, forgiving people. There was a reason Alice's article resonated with people here. He exemplified redemption and overcoming. He was, in the eyes of the community, a war hero that fell victim to the drink and was now working with others so that they could overcome it as he had. Would they be so forgiving if they knew exactly what sort of monster he had been behind closed doors?

Subconsciously, Sam began twisting on the cap of the whiskey bottle, not noticing his attempt until his sweaty fingertips slipped and the ridges of the cap dug into his skin. There was a moment of hesitation; the call to wade back into the drink rising to the surface. Taking a deep breath, Sam turned around and walked back inside the diner.

As the bell jingled overhead, Sam saw his sponsor, Brian Morris, and his twenty-year-old wheelchair-bound daughter, Maggie, beside the table he had been sharing with Alice.

"Take this," Sam said with urgency in his voice as he pushed it into Brian's chest before collapsing into the booth.

"And where did you get this, Sam?" Brian asked, examining the bottle to see if he'd opened it.

"Joe Rhodes stopped by."

"And he gave you whiskey?" Brian asked rhetorically over the sound of Alice grunting her displeasure. "Well, good for you on the restraint, Sam."

Sam nodded his acceptance of the praise, but he said nothing. The confrontation with Joe had been taxing for multiple reasons. The man had never run for office himself, but he was well equipped to if he ever had the interest.

"And what did he want?" Alice asked.

"...to wish me luck," Sam replied.

Alice's brow furrowed. Sam hoped she was concerning herself about why Joe would do that and not suspecting that Sam was lying.

"How are you fairing with the wait? Brian asked, a low groan escaping as he sat himself beside Sam in the booth. He placed his simple, black walking cane beside his leg.

"I'm all right," Sam said.

"He's nervous," Alice said.

"What makes you say that?" Sam asked, before catching himself drumming on the edge of the table again.

Sam began rubbing the side of his index fingers against the pad of his thumbs as he waited for the coffee Brian had requested from Maggie. Turning, he watched as Doris's granddaughter deposited the mug on the counter. Maggie lifted it and, Sam assumed, tried to determine how bad it would burn if it spilled while she rolled over.

A woman at the counter noticed Maggie's hesitation and offered to carry it. Maggie reluctantly agreed. The woman who Sam recognized as Kim Appleton, took the mug of coffee from Maggie, and followed her over to the table.

As they walked, it struck Sam the ease in which he, and anyone in Fremont, could recognize any other resident. It was a perk of the small-town living, a sense of the familiar wherever you went. Sam remembered the uncomfortable feeling he had for the first couple of weeks in the military where he didn't know anybody.

"Oh, hey Sam," Kim said as she set the mug down. The two shook hands quickly.

"Hey. Thanks," he said, giving a nod to both Kim and Maggie respectively.

"I'm pulling for you tonight, Sam. I don't know if I can keep working there if Wilbur gets elected. Seriously. I've got my resignation typed up and ready."

That had been another of the articles Alice had published recently; an exposé on some of the seedier aspects of the current sheriff's office. Kim, who worked as the dispatcher, had spoken with Alice about misconducts in the office ranging from inappropriate jokes—which Sam had seen firsthand when he went to make amends to Wilbur for his belligerence the night he was arrested—and getting handsy at times. Both had suffered undue aggression from the sheriff's office since then.

"I appreciate it," Sam said with a smile, gesturing for Kim to join them.

Around him, the others delved into conversation discussing his chances, his supporters, and the detractors. But all Sam could focus on was Joe Rhodes.

It had been a long road to recovery. One that, as he understood it, would never end. As an addict, he would always crave the drink. He had put a lot of time and effort into making amends, contributing to those suffering the same addictions. It was unfair that Joe was holding the ruins of his family over his head, threatening to undo his progress and standing in the community that he had worked to amend if he didn't assist Joe in...whatever he was asking.

What was he asking? Sam wasn't sure, but Alice's article had focused a lot on the last sheriff and there wasn't much that would surprise him about Sheriff Stapp's conduct. If it were something honest, there wouldn't have been the need for the veiled threats. Losing the support of the community would be heartbreaking after everything he had done. Was he willing to sully himself in favor of not letting the full extent of his past get out?

"Everybody shut up!" shouted Doris, straightening herself as much as possible as gravity pulled her head and neck low. She was a no-nonsense sort of woman. She was, perhaps, the only person in the county that could get away with telling everyone to shut up.

Silence fell over the diner as Doris turned the volume up.

"—all tallies are in," said the radio.

Maybe I'll lose, Sam thought. Then it wouldn't matter.

"Congratulations to our new sheriff—" The diner collectively held their breaths. It seemed to hold for an eternity before, "Sam Kinloch."

There was a roar of celebration both in and out of the diner. Brian took him by the shoulders and shook him.

Sam smiled. He had, if nothing else, earned their trust after years of being the county drunk. Inside, however, his gut twisted into a knot. What was he willing to do not to lose everything he had worked for?

He was about to find out.

NANCY ARNOLD IS DEAD

DAWN TAYLOR

Charles joined his wife Sharon on the lanai for morning coffee. His cheerful greeting dissipated into the ocean breeze as she focused on the obituary displayed on her laptop screen.

Sharon's grin preceded her announcement. "I can't believe it! Nancy Arnold is dead."

"I'm not sure who she was, but your giddiness seems to be in poor taste."

"You don't understand. I hated her in high school. She's the only reason I lost the senior class president election, even though I was the valedictorian. Good ole Nancy. Gone."

Charles rolled his eyes. "Sharon, you're thirty-eight. You graduated twenty years ago and still harbor a grudge against a woman you haven't seen since then?"

"Her funeral is Friday. I'll see her then."

"Don't even tell me you plan to fly to Minnesota to attend a funeral? A service for someone you despised?"

Sharon nodded. "Yes. I'll book my flight after I call Mary and make plans to stay with her. She'll invite the girls to meet before the wake. It'll be fun."

Charles Thurgood III stared at his trophy wife and wondered how her beauty had blinded him to the poison flowing through her veins. He politely excused himself to enjoy his newspaper in the den.

Sharon secured her plans and excitedly packed her luggage. After she removed price tags from designer dresses, she coordinated leather shoes with handbags. She reconsidered stowing her jewelry, but just as quickly tucked it into the suitcase liner. Since her former classmates knew she had married a wealthy investment banker, she had an image to uphold. Sharon would not disappoint their expectations and anticipated dodging the envious daggers from those stuck in their dreary Midwestern existence.

☑   ☑   ☑

When Mary greeted her at the Minneapolis-St. Paul airport, Sharon scrutinized her friend's wardrobe choice of jeans and a plain tee-shirt—selections Sharon had not worn in decades. Mary's department-store-brand perfume mingled with Sharon's Maison Francis Kurkdjian, which she had purchased in France. Sharon tilted her head during their embrace to avoid crushing her coiffed hair, while Mary's ponytail freely swayed.

Mary filled the two-hour drive to her home with anecdotes about her family's country life. Her idyllic existence of raising four children on a dairy farm bored Sharon and she interrupted her host with tales of her luxurious lifestyle she shared with her third husband in a high-rise condo on Maui.

The long drive ended as Mary parked on a gravel driveway at a farmhouse with grayed wood siding and a sagging roof. An aroma of cattle manure wafted from a nearby barn and provoked Sharon to cough. She held her breath as she followed Mary into the foyer and was appalled by the clusters of children's dirty sneakers and muddy boots haphazardly tossed into a mound.

"Let's get you settled in the guest room. The girls will arrive shortly, and I've planned a cocktail party. It'll be fun having the gang together again."

"Except Nancy."

"I still can't believe she's gone. Such a shame to linger with a chronic illness knowing there's no cure. No hope."

Sharon cleared her throat. "Shameful, yes. Which way to the guest room?"

☑ ☑ ☑

The farmhouse's porch accommodated the four women, and Mary served a pitcher of margaritas. Each friend eagerly accepted a glass, except Sharon. "Do you have gin? I prefer a martini, three olives."

Sharon's request induced eye rolls from the group.

"Sorry. I have some of Bud's Miller Lite if you prefer a beer."

"Perhaps water. I drink Aqua Deco garnished with a lemon slice at my home in Hawaii. Don't suppose you have bottled water of any kind?"

Mary shook her head. "I have the best well water in the state. Could fetch you a glass with lemon if you'd like."

"Unfiltered water would not agree with me. I'll pass. Thank you."

Linda could not resist a jab. "Sharon, when did you become so cultured? Between your second and third marriage?"

"I'll make no apologies for my affluent lifestyle. I'm sure for those who have never abandoned their Midwestern roots, it's difficult to understand an entire world exists beyond corn fields."

"Well, la-de-da! It's good to know you haven't changed a bit since high school."

Nervous laughter followed Linda's comment.

Mary refilled glasses and settled for a tedious afternoon moderating misguided and on-target barbs.

"I was class valediction. Shouldn't be a surprise I've lived a better life than—"

"Than who?" Janet asked. "Better than us and Nancy?"

"Nancy was a miserable wretch. Have you all forgotten how she sabotaged my chance at winning the senior class president position?"

"Enlighten us," Linda said. "We would love to hear your version. I'm sure you've stewed over it for twenty years while you've traveled around the world and purchased objets d' art."

Mary hid her grin behind her hand.

Despite the insults, Sharon's defiance did not waiver. "You all know what Nancy did to me at our sleepover the weekend before the election. Still don't understand how mousey Nancy managed to wedge into our circle. Why was she invited? Did you pity her, Linda?"

Janet intercepted. "Did it ever occur to you, Miss High-and-Mighty, it was you who we pitied?"

"Me? Never!"

"Tell us what you remember, Sharon," Mary said. "I'm afraid I've forgotten the details."

Sharon blew away her disgust. "The sleepover at Linda's was supposed to be fun. Staying up all night, drinking forbidden alcohol, playing those immature truth-or-dare games." She tugged at her collar. "Then it got out of control."

Linda leaned forward. "I remember freezing Janet's bra into a block of ice. Then dipping your fingers, Mary, into warm water to trigger you to piss your sleeping bag."

Mary playfully slapped Linda's shoulder. "Didn't work though."

"Doesn't matter. It was still funny. Pour me another drink, please. We're getting to the good part."

"By good part, you mean when Nancy cut off my hair while I slept?" Sharon asked.

Janet and Linda exchanged grins before they burst into laughter.

Mary stifled her giggle but surrendered to the hilarity, much to Sharon's disdain. "It was twenty years ago. Surely, you can laugh about it now."

"She not only snipped off my beautiful long hair, she shaved one side of my head! I couldn't even leave the house. I missed the election and lost my votes, which was her intention. You think her malicious act hasn't affected me all these years? I was valedictorian, and I deserved the class president title!"

Mary responded to calm Sharon. "I recall Jeff Adams won. Everyone liked him."

Sharon pointed to her chest. "Everyone liked me."

Janet shook her head. "No, they didn't. C'mon. Get real."

"Everyone except precious dead Nancy."

Linda posed a question. "Why do you blame Nancy? What proof do you have she cut your hair? I mean, if you were sleeping, how do you know?"

"Because she didn't belong in our circle, as I have stated. Who invited her? Why would we have wanted to associate with white trash like her anyway?"

Linda scoffed. "White trash? Because her mother died when she was four, and her father did his best to raise her and five other kids? Maybe she didn't wear fancy clothes or live in the best house on the block, but she was a kind, loving friend. Won't let you tarnish her memory over a trivial matter. I was at her bedside when she died. You know what she talked about? The good memories she had shared with friends who loved her. People who helped her. She didn't waste her dying breath lamenting about a stupid high school election. Doubt she even remembered it."

Sharon leapt from her chair. "She cut off my damn hair to humiliate me."

Linda replied. "No. She didn't"

"And how do you know?"

"Your head was shaved not to humiliate you, but to humble you. I did it."

Sharon pointed an accusing finger. "You? You were the nasty instigator who violated me? You purposely disrupted the election and caused me to hate Nancy all these years over your vile act? How dare you claim to be her close friend?"

"Your reasoning is skewed, my friend. Nobody forced you to hate Nancy. You arrived at that conclusion on your own. Time to jump off your high horse, Sharon. You're no better than the rest of us."

Sharon folded her arms. "I live in Hawaii and I—"

"Oh, please!" Janet held up her palm. "I vacationed in Hawaii during my honeymoon, and I've been married to my husband for fifteen years. We farm like Mary and Bud, and our lifestyles are no better or worse than yours."

Mary nodded. "That's right. I love that my children have learned hard work, and they can play outside without the threats that plague big cities. We're just plain folks living our lives until the Lord calls us home. We don't need fancy homes, cars, or safes jammed with money to enjoy life." Mary paused. "Maybe our view of a good life is different than yours, Sharon."

"So, even you've resented me since high school. Don't know why I accepted your invitation to visit if that's the case."

"I didn't invite you. You invited yourself. Not to mean you're not welcomed at my home, because you are. It's time to let bygones be bygones and enjoy the time we have now. If nothing else, Nancy's death should be celebrated as a tribute to long-lasting friendships. That's the reason we've gathered here."

Linda glanced from Mary to Sharon. "I'm sorry, alright? I didn't know you would carry this burden with you all these years. You were always bragging about your straight-A report cards. I just wanted to bring you down to earth a bit. We're nearly forty now. High school years are over. Let's not hold grudges. Again, I'm sorry."

"Nancy played no part in it?"

"No. Actually, she was the only one among us who admired your smarts. She always said you were a born genius. That's exactly what she called you—a born genius."

"You're lying now. Did she really say that?"

Janet piped in. "All the time, yes. She was thrilled to be invited to our sleepover to spend time with you."

"I never knew that."

"If you had taken the time to know her, you would have," Mary said. "And, for twenty years you thought she was your enemy."

Sharon pondered the revelations. "Mary, I'd like a margarita, please."

"You sure?"

"Yes. When you get a moment, could you provide me with a florist's telephone number? I think I owe Nancy a final apology."

When Mary returned with a fresh glass and refilled the guests' drinks, she proposed a toast. "To Nancy."

Glasses clinked acknowledging the friend's passing.

"And to lasting friendships!" Sharon added.

☑   ☑   ☑

Charles greeted Sharon at the airport. "How was your flight? Your visit?"

"Honey, it was the saddest funeral I've ever attended. Beautiful bouquets, melancholy music, a huge crowd packed the church."

Charles arched an eyebrow. "You seem genuinely sad. Seems like you may have had a change of heart. I'd like to think so."

"So many years … So many years wasted harboring a grudge against her. She had nothing to do with sabotaging the high school election, just the opposite. I discovered through friends Nancy had admired me. Respected me as class valedictorian."

"This matter is now laid to rest?"

"Yes. Laid to rest with Nancy."

"Good to hear. I'll mix martinis when we arrive home. Celebrate your homecoming."

Sharon reflected on her weekend trip. "Charles, I'd prefer a margarita."

If you enjoyed this Of Words anthology,
check out the other volumes.

A Matter of Words
A Journey of Words
A Haunting of Words
A Contract of Words
A Flash of Words
A Bond of Words
A Game of Words
An Election of Words

Get your copy today at
www.scoutmediabooksmusic.com/of-words-series
or at your favorite book store/retailer.